KIMBERLY KAYE
TERRY

Make it Last

ELLORA'S CAVE
ROMANTICA PUBLISHING

An Ellora's Cave Romantica Publication

www.ellorascave.com

Make it Last

ISBN 9781419956379
ALL RIGHTS RESERVED.
Design of a Lifetime Copyright © 2006 Kimberly Kaye Terry
Pull My Hair Copyright © 2006 Kimberly Kaye Terry
Cover art by Syneca & Willo.

This book printed in the U.S.A. by Jasmine-Jade Enterprises, LLC

Trade paperback Publication June 2007

Content Advisory:

S – ENSUOUS
E – ROTIC
X – TREME

Ellora's Cave Publishing offers three levels of Romantica™ reading entertainment: S (S-ensuous), E (E-rotic), and X (X-treme).

The following material contains graphic sexual content meant for mature readers. This story has been rated E–rotic.

S-*ensuous* love scenes are explicit and leave nothing to the imagination.

E-*rotic* love scenes are explicit, leave nothing to the imagination, and are high in volume per the overall word count. E-rated titles might contain material that some readers find objectionable—in other words, almost anything goes, sexually. E-rated titles are the most graphic titles we carry in terms of both sexual language and descriptiveness in these works of literature.

X-*treme* titles differ from E-rated titles only in plot premise and storyline execution. Stories designated with the letter X tend to contain difficult or controversial subject matter not for the faint of heart.

About the Author

෨

Kimberly is a multi-published author who offers her fresh take on multicultural romance with a unique, sexy blend of romance, love, and true eroticism. Kimberly lives with her husband of 12 years, along with their child. Her husband is currently a Lieutenant Colonel in the U.S. Army.

Kimberly has a bachelor's degree in social work and a masters degree in human relations. She is also a life-long member of Zeta Phi Beta Sorority, Inc. Please visit her at her website. She also has a blog where she mostly waxes poetic. Drop by at www.kimberlykayeterrys.blogspot.com.

Kimberly welcomes comments from readers. You can find her website and email address on her author bio page at www.ellorascave.com.

Tell Us What You Think

We appreciate hearing reader opinions about our books. You can email us at Comments@EllorasCave.com.

MAKE IT LAST

ℰℴ

DESIGN OF A LIFETIME
~11~

&

PULL MY HAIR
~95~

DESIGN OF A LIFETIME

&

Trademarks Acknowledgement

☙

The author acknowledges the trademarked status and trademark owners of the following wordmarks mentioned in this work of fiction:

Godiva Chocolates: Godiva Brands, Inc.

Honda: Honda Motor Company

Little Debbie: McKee Foods Corporation and Affiliates

Macy's: Federated Department Stores, Inc.

Wonder Bread: Interstate Bakeries Corporation

Chapter One

ဆာ

"Girl, I ain't had any in a minute, darn it! My coochie is dry as the Sahara desert, and I am so feeling this drought!" Karina bemoaned to her best friend as they both sat at Liza's kitchen table drinking herbal tea and watching Judge Matthis.

Judge Matthis was two hot seconds away from lowering the boom on the defendant. For a moment, both women got caught up in the drama and humor as the defendant whipped off her wig and slammed it on the podium in front of her, as she seriously told her ex-roommate slash ex-girlfriend off. "Bitch, I caught you red-handed with that tramp..." the defendant screeched.

"Are you even listening to me?" Karina felt both stressed and pissed at the same time as she tried to draw her friend's attention away from the angry woman on the show.

"Yes I am. You 'ain't had any in a minute'," Liza spit back her words, her eyes trained on the small screen.

Karina knew the heifer was distracted, but couldn't she at least *pretend* to act like she was paying attention? To feign concern?

"I guess it's not really a big deal to you. I mean you get sexed up on a regular basis, so what do you care?" Karina asked, and knew the ugly jealousy she felt for her friend's love life was shining through like a beacon on a lighthouse.

"Okay," Liza sighed, as she moved to turn off the television. "Sorry. So what's the problem?"

Karina was slightly mollified.

"Same ole, same ole. Where are all the brothers?" she wailed and crossed her arms over her ample breasts as she leaned back in the chair and stared moodily at the ceiling. To gaze with ugly envy at Liza's beautiful ceiling with its customized tile.

Liza stared at her friend in exasperation. Karina was pretty and smart as hell. But sometimes she could be dumb as a doorknob. This was an ongoing discussion for them and although Liza loved her friend to death, she was sick and tired of her moaning.

Particularly because it was all Karina's fault. How in the world would she ever find all these "brothers" she was in search of, much less any man, if she stayed cooped up behind that computer of hers all day long?

"Karina, have you ever thought about maybe broadening your horizons a little?" Liza asked, and ducked her head as though dodging a blow.

"With a white guy? Girl, you know that is not my flavor. No offense to you and yours…"

"None taken," Liza said, holding back a smile.

"But honestly, I wouldn't know how to start."

"Start what?"

"How do you even attract one?" she asked.

Karina's pretty face was twisted up. Her thick winged eyebrows were lowered and her full lips were pooched out, making her look seriously confused. Behind her small wire-rim glasses, Karina's large, light brown eyes squinted as though she was trying to figure out a complicated math equation.

And although one part of Liza wanted to laugh, the other part knew her friend was deadly serious. As shy as Karina was, she was still liable to curse her out if she did, so she wisely held her laughter in check. She loved her friend, and didn't want her to think she wasn't taking her problem seriously. Karina looked so small and forlorn as she sat gloomily at her kitchen table.

"Karina, what do you think they are? Brahma bulls?" she asked, and this time couldn't keep her giggles in check.

"Girl, I don't know. I mean, how do you meet them?"

"Number one, you're asking me this as though white men are some alien life form, and secondly as though I am the premier authority on how to find and catch the alien wild beast! You meet them just like you meet any other man. And for you that means getting away from that darn computer of yours," she gently admonished her friend.

"I know, I know. But right now I have so much work in front of me I don't know when that will be. Which reminds me, I have *got* to go," Karina said, glancing down at her watch and hastily climbed to her feet.

"I have a new client who's supposed to contact me today about a redesign. It's really cool. I've already outlined the entire site. I plan to add an online catalogue and redo the whole thing in XML so it's easier to update. A Flash menu would be awesome…" Karina's voice trailed off at the glazed expression on Liza's face.

"When you talk that computer lingo, I don't understand a word you're saying. You know how they say when you talk to your dog all they hear is 'blah blah blah, ROVER, blah blah blah'—I swear that's what it's like for me!" Both women laughed over Liza's familiar complaint.

Karina knew her best friend thought she was a nerd. And that was okay with her. She loved her computer and her nerdiness. Embraced both, in fact. But lately, she wanted to embrace something other than her nerdiness or her computer. She needed a man to embrace. Oh hell, who was she kidding? She needed a man to get buck wild with.

"I know, I know," she laughed as she shrugged on her bulky pea coat, and picked up her oversized bag near her chair. "I'd better go. I need this job."

Karina turned and briefly hugged her friend as they stood inside the arch of Liza's impressive front entry. She barely suppressed a sigh of longing as she took a quick visual of her friend's beautiful home.

One day, she thought on a mental sigh.

"Look, I have to go. Smooches!" she said in an upbeat tone she truly didn't feel on the inside. She jogged the short distance to her beat-up Honda, and with a final wave, climbed behind the wheel of the car. Her gloved hands gripped the cold steering wheel and without waiting for the car to warm, she reversed out of the circular driveway.

Chapter Two

ॐ

As Karina carefully drove along the icy streets, the old car finally began to warm up, and her thoughts raced back over her afternoon chat with Liza.

She and Liza had been best friends from early childhood and Karina loved her like the sister she didn't have. But sometimes she really didn't like Liza very much. It wasn't because of anything Liza had done, she just admitted to herself that she was the smallest bit jealous.

Liza had it all. She was tall, thin as a damn rail, drop-dead gorgeous and living in Regency Hill, the wealthy section of town, with her fine as hell, rich as Midas husband. She didn't have to work, and spent her days doing whatever she wanted, while Karina struggled to keep her small web design business afloat. In fact, as soon as she checked her email for communication from her new client, she was headed toward her temp job at Macy's, wrapping Founder's Day gifts. The City of Stanton celebrated Founder's Day as though it were Valentine's Day, and Karina wasn't looking forward to wrapping scores of gifts for nameless, faceless, women.

She finally made it to her apartment on the other side of town. After she cut the engine and slammed out of the car, she raced up the stairs to her second-floor apartment. The short sprint had her gasping for breath as she unlocked the door.

She swore to herself she was giving up her late night addiction to Little Debbie Oatmeal Crème Pies. She didn't know how Debbie stayed so doggone little eating that addictive, creamy crack, but Karina knew *she* obviously didn't have the same metabolism, as she glanced down at her ample hips.

15

With a short sigh, she kicked off her snow boots and tossed her bag on the forest green couch as she shed her coat. She made her way through her cozy apartment toward the second bedroom she'd converted to her office and looked around in appreciation.

She loved her apartment, and although she might not live in Regency Hill, the wealthy section of town as Liza, she was comfortable and happy with what she had.

She loved color, and each wall of the small apartment was painted a different color, each room with its own scheme. The living room was done in various shades of green, warm and inviting to her guests. Her office was painted vibrant red, with bold geometrical prints adorning the walls, to help spark her imagination.

Her bedroom was her favorite room in the apartment. She'd painted it in deep shades of gold and orange, and the large four-poster bed was covered in the brightly patterned quilt her grandmother, Big Momma, had given her, the day she'd moved in. As she walked past the room on her way to her office, she stopped and turned on the light to peek inside. She had to laugh at herself.

It wasn't like she was hiding a man in there. The closest she came to having something warm and cozy to cuddle up to these days was her overstuffed Winnie the Pooh, who was currently taking up residence on the slick black silk of her bedspread.

Well, that and her vibrator.

But she kept Big Willy hidden away, buried beneath her old, raggedy period panties, which lay underneath her ratty nightgowns, which lay underneath her pantyhose, in the middle bottom drawer of her bureau.

Old habits died hard.

Here she was, a grown woman of thirty-one years, and she still felt the need to hide her toys. As a teenager, she'd discovered the joys of taking care of her own needs, and knew if her mother ever found out what lay hidden in her drawer there would be hell to pay. So she hid them. More than ten years later, and she still was. She turned off the light, more than disgusted with herself.

After she walked into her office, she went directly to her phone to check her messages. There were no messages from the client. She sat behind her desk and eagerly logged on to the Internet as she reached down to rub her achy feet. It had been a long day, and it wasn't over yet.

She pushed her glasses further up her nose as she waited. As soon as her home page came onscreen, she quickly logged into her business email account. Maybe the woman had emailed her the information she requested and was waiting for her reply.

She quickly scanned her emails, but saw no emails from the referred client and wanted to cry. She really needed this job, damn it!!

"Maybe she left an email and it went to bulk," she mumbled. She scanned the addresses and subject tags, and her shoulders hunched in disappointment. Unless the woman was sending her a message about improving her stamina, she hadn't emailed. She glanced at the time in the corner of her computer screen.

Marissa Greene was supposed to email the information about her small bookstore-coffee shop hours ago. The new client had been a referral, and Karina was excited about redesigning the site, and the money would help her purchase the new programs she wanted to buy. The new software would allow her to step up her game and add more services for her existing clients, as well as attract new business. She reached over and picked up the phone to call the woman.

After several rings, a chirpy voice finally answered. "Hello, you've reached the Mocha Reader. Please leave a message, and we'll get back with you!" After the longest beep in recorded history, Karina opened her mouth to leave a reply and the machine cut her off mid-sentence.

She hung up the phone and typed a quick email to the client, asking if she was still interested in employing the services of Design of a Lifetime.

She perused her other emails, answering those she'd put off and sending out feelers for potential clients. As she took care of business, she kept hoping to hear from the client. As she was in the process of logging off, her email alert flashed on the screen. She clicked on the envelope and a feeling of dread pooled in her belly when she saw the return address.

It was from the client, and she had a foretelling that was confirmed after she read the brief email. The woman had decided to go with another web designer.

Damn.

Karina finished and logged off the net, and laid her head down over her crossed arms on the desk. She was counting on that money to fund the latest available graphic design program that recently hit the market.

Oh well. She shoved the sharp pang of disappointment to the back of her mind. There wasn't anything she could do about it. She'd just have to put off buying the program until her money wasn't so funny.

She glanced at the time and was surprised to see how late it was. She barely had time to grab something to eat before she'd have to go to her night job at Macy's.

After she ate her warmed-up leftover dinner from the previous night, Karina sped through the house like a possessed demon, changing out of her baggy sweat suit and into jeans and sweater, before heading off to work.

As she carefully maneuvered through the slick streets, she asked herself why she stayed in the Midwest. She hated cold weather and finding a good man was like finding hen's teeth.

Damn near impossible unless you found one freaky looking hen.

And Liza had it all wrong. True, she tended to work a lot on her computer, but she *tried* to get out once in a while. She started her web design business less than a year ago, and was struggling to make ends meet. In what free time she did have, she visited all the places they said to hunt down...uh, meet...a nice guy. Church, museums, bookstores, cultural events. She'd tried them all.

Nothing. Nada. Zip.

It didn't help that she was somewhat of an introvert, and had never approached a man on her own. If the guy didn't initiate the conversation, it wasn't going to happen. She wished she had a tenth of Liza's outgoing, "go with the flow" personality.

She once read in a women's magazine that the local carwash was *the* place to meet single men. And while her ten-year-old vehicle never looked so shiny and new, it was a total waste of time and she'd canceled her subscription to the magazine that had given the advice.

The only men she saw hanging out were a bunch of young, wannabe players. And Karina realized she was too old to play games. She wanted a man. A real man. Not a boy trying to be one.

She gave serious thought to Liza's question of why she wouldn't, as her friend put it, "broaden her horizons". She hadn't given it serious consideration before. She barely felt confident enough to approach a black man, much less a white one.

What would she say? What would their expectations be? Would it be the same? She laughed out loud thinking of Liza's reaction to her question. A Brahma bull? Hmmm. That brought up tantalizing images.

She pulled her car into the mall's secured, underground parking, and felt seriously harassed when she couldn't find a space to park on the lower level. She'd have to catch the slow-moving elevator to reach the basement level where the small gift-wrapping department was located.

Karina rushed out of her car and ran through the parking garage on her way to the back elevator. The elevator doors were fast closing as she approached. If she missed it she'd be late, and she couldn't afford to be late anymore. Her supervisor already warned her that she was temporary help.

"Hold the door, please!" she cried as she saw the doors slowly coming together. A hand reached out from the inside in the nick of time to prevent the doors from closing. Karina made a mad dash the short distance, and eased inside.

"Thank you so much, I really appreciate…it…" Her voice came to a halt as her gaze slid up and over the one responsible for holding the door open for her.

Woo, he was fine.

Although Karina was only a few inches over five feet, she'd always appreciated a tall man. Especially one built like a Mack truck, like the one in front of her.

Her gaze took in the man in front of her, from the tip of his black boots, to the top of his dark blond, slightly curly hair. Along the way, she didn't miss the way his loose jeans fit a lot more snugly in certain places. Or the way the surrounding area was seriously worn.

She was only thirty-one, but suddenly felt as though she was being slammed straight into menopause with the sudden flash of heat that flooded her.

When her eyes met his deep-set blue ones, and she noticed the shit-eating grin on his face, which emphasized the cute little dimples in his cheeks, she knew she must have stared too long. But honestly, the man was hot. So hot, she felt her traitorous kitty kat do a little jump for joy as though the end of her drought season could possibly be at hand.

The strong lines of his jaw were emphasized by his square chin, that—oh Lord, why did he have a dimple there too—was lightly covered with stubble. Karina wasn't normally the type to go for facial hair, it tended to be…scratchy on contact. But he had just enough to look sexy, and make her long to feel that scratchy contact. She felt weak in the knees at the thought.

She didn't know the last time she'd had such a strong reaction to a man. She quickly looked away, silently chastised her kat by clenching her legs tightly together, and fumbled with the buttons on her coat, her ears hot with embarrassment.

"Umm. Thanks. I don't want to be late again. I think I'm on my last warning with my supervisor. And I need this job," she blurted the confession. When she was nervous she had an ugly tendency to babble.

"No problem. Anything I can do to help a pretty lady in need, I'm the man to call," he told her in the sexiest, deepest baritone she'd ever heard.

Good Lord, did he have to have a voice like that and be fine? Gees! She didn't even want to think too deeply about him calling her pretty, or volunteering to help her out in need. Her kat was already acting up, no need to give her more ammunition.

"Thanks," she mumbled and studiously watched the doors of the elevator as it slowly made its way down to the basement. She breathed a sigh of relief when the elevator came to a halt.

"This is my floor. I guess it's yours too. There's no where else to go, but up." If she said one more inane comment, she'd slap her own self silly!

"I have some things to get wrapped," he said, holding the elevator door open as she stepped through. It was then she noticed the bundle of packages near his feet.

"You're headed my way. I work in the gift-wrap department," she told him as he followed her out of the elevator.

Chapter Three

ഔ

As Cooper walked behind the pretty woman, he was hard pressed not to stare at her shapely round butt, cupped so nicely in the faded jeans. She'd taken off the ugly, bulky coat and slung it over her arm as she briskly walked, obviously in a rush to clock in. He loved the way her hips rolled with each hasty step she took.

When she'd walked into the elevator and looked up at him with those big, pretty, brown eyes of hers, he'd felt a curious clench in his gut. She looked so adorable staring at him behind the foggy glasses, looking like a lost little girl. It was all he could do not to push the glasses up the bridge of her short nose.

She wore a small wool cap that covered her hair. He thought her hair was braided at first, but upon closer inspection, he realized she wore her hair in dreads. He wanted to touch them to see if they felt as soft as they looked. But he didn't want her to think he was a weirdo and pull the emergency cord in the elevator, so he'd kept his hands to himself.

At the same time, he'd noticed her reaction to him. She looked as though she liked what she saw as her eyes had stolen over him. Cooper grinned to himself, as he followed the pretty woman to the gift-wrap department.

He'd bought several gifts for Founder's day for his mother and all five sisters. His father had passed away long ago, and Cooper had always taken care of his mother and sisters like he'd promised his father that he would.

So that meant Founder's Day was Christmas for his ladies. It was hell on his wallet, but he didn't mind spoiling them. He could afford it, and besides that, he didn't have anyone else special in his life to spoil.

"Is this a busy time of the year?" he asked, as he took two long steps to catch up, and walk along side her.

"Actually I wouldn't know. I only recently started working here," she said, and glanced up at him from the corner of her eyes before looking away. He got the feeling she was shy, but something about her pulled at him.

"Do you like working here?" He couldn't think of much else to say to prolong the conversation, and she wasn't giving him any encouragement. They'd arrived at the closed-door entry into the gift-wrapping department, and Cooper gallantly opened them, and inclined his head, for her to precede him into the room.

"It's okay, I guess," she said. She gave a small wave to the clerk at the counter before stopping short to stand directly in front of him. "Umm…did you want to have those wrapped?" She nodded her head in the direction of the packages in his hands. "If so, Susan can wrap them for you. I've got to go clock in," she said and turned around to walk away.

She'd only taken a few steps when she turned back around. "Thanks for holding the elevator door for me," she said and smiled, and the deep dimple appeared near the corner of her mouth, and just as quickly as it appeared, it disappeared.

"No problem." He smiled back at her and saw the tips of her light brown ears turn a very cute shade of red, before she turned around and nearly tripped over the laces on her snow boots in her haste. Cooper's eyes stayed trained on her butt as she hustled away.

"Hey, what's your name?" he asked, but she'd already closed the door behind her and no doubt didn't hear him. He glanced toward the clerk the woman had said would help, and felt his own face heat at the knowing look on the older woman's face.

* * * * *

"He waited around for a while," Susan said to her as soon as she'd returned from clocking in.

Karina had fussed with her hair in the small bathroom in the back, straightened her clothes, examined her teeth, and did a few deep knee bends for light exercise.

Okay okay, she'd admitted to herself, she was stalling. She was nervous as hell with the man from the elevator and didn't want to chance him being out there when she came to the counter.

She needed therapy. Deep, intense, one-on-one therapy. No at-home reaffirming rituals were going to help her. Nope, not this time. She needed a professional.

"Who?" she asked as though she had no idea to whom Susan was referring. She studiously ignored Susan's humorous eyes as she stashed her purse under the counter.

"He also asked what yours was," Susan paused before adding, "and...he wanted to know what time you got off work," she finished the sentence, as though Karina hadn't even asked who she'd been referring to.

"What? Did you tell him?" Karina bumped her head on the edge of the counter in her haste to look Susan in the eyes to see if she was lying.

She rubbed the top of her head and grimaced as she stared at her coworker. She really liked Susan, with her sunny laugh and weird sense of humor. But sometimes she didn't know if Susan was serious or messing with her. She hoped she was messing with her this time.

"Thought you didn't know who I was talking about," Susan asked slyly, and had the nerve to laugh. She turned away and smiled her cheery grin as a customer approached.

The two women worked nonstop wrapping gifts for the next hour, and Karina was nearly ready to explode with nervousness by the time the stream of customers ended. There was one customer left in the store at the end of the day, and Karina was helping the picky woman choose the gift-wrap, when Susan glanced down at her watch.

"He left his packages to be wrapped," Susan told her, as though Karina would follow her conversation and know what she was talking about. Which she did.

Susan reached under the counter for her sweater and purse. "It's time for me to go. I'll see you later Karina!" She laughed and walked from around the small counter.

"Wait Susan! You can't just go like that. What about the, um… the customer? When is he coming back for his gifts?" She asked, trying to play off her interest.

"He said he'd return before we closed," she said, and waved goodbye. Two seconds later she bobbed her gray head back in the door. "Oh, and his name is Cooper. And he thinks you're cute," she laughed and left.

Karina felt the familiar burn on the tips of her ears when the customer looked at her curiously after her exchange with Susan.

In half the time it took Karina to help the fussy customer pick the perfect wrapping for her miniature poodle, "Puddin's" new sweater (whose picture the woman insisted on showing her), Karina had the gift wrapped and the happy woman out the door.

After she'd helped a few more straggler customers, a few minutes after nine o'clock, closing hour, the man from the elevator breezed into the room. Karina tried feigning nonchalance when he walked inside, thankful he couldn't see the way her heart was leaping inside her chest.

He'd drifted in and out of her thoughts with irritating and nerve-racking regularity throughout her shift. Irritating, because she'd had to wrap more packages than she'd ever had before. Nerve-racking, because she was a pure mass of jitters as she waited for him to show up to pick up his packages.

She didn't know why she was so excited anyway. The man must have a harem with the amount of gifts he'd left to be wrapped. Bottles of expensive perfume, cashmere sweaters, pretty nightgowns, it was unreal!

But all that flew out of her mind the minute her eyes came into contact with his, her admiring glance encompassing him in one quick stroke.

Chapter Four

ɾᴑ

Cooper rushed through his errands in time to make it back to the gift-wrapping department and the pretty woman, before closing time.

Karina Woodson. That's what the older clerk said her name was. The clerk had also volunteered the information that little Miss Karina was single and shy, after Cooper had asked what time she got off work.

As he'd done his errands, thoughts of the woman had taken up residence in his brain. He'd been attracted to her in the elevator, and that helped him make the decision to leave and come back for the gifts. Especially when the other clerk said Karina would be the only one left working.

He was glad there were no customers left in the small department.

He smiled a secret grin when he noticed the tips of her ears turn red after she'd given him the once-over when he walked into the department. Good. She was interested too.

"Great, looks like I made it in time," he told her with a relieved grin.

It was then that she glanced at the clock. "I hadn't realized what time it is. Actually, we're closed," she laughed.

"Wow, you did a beautiful job," he complimented, as he walked to the counter, his glance taking in the small mound of gifts on the counter. "I think my sisters will like the packaging better than the gifts," he laughed, and picked up one of the small boxes. He missed the look of relief that flashed across her face.

"Thank you," she said. "You have beautiful taste, I'm sure they'll love the gifts you picked out. How many sisters do you have?" she asked, as she opened a large bag and deposited them inside.

"Five. Three older and a set of younger twin sisters," he told her, his eyes glued on the fullness of her bottom lip as he spoke. He'd always loved a woman with nice full lips, and hers were red and lush. He adjusted his jeans as he thought about what it'd be like to have those pretty full lips on his.

Karina looked up from placing the packages in the bag, to see Cooper's eyes trained straight on her lips.

Oh Lord.

Please don't let me do something stupid, please don't let me do something stupid, please don't let me do something stupid, she chanted over and over in her head. But it'd been sooo long. And he looked sooo good.

And he's looking at me like I'm a big bowl of gravy and he wants to sop me up with a biscuit, she thought. She almost laughed out loud at her own silliness, despite the ache in her heart.

She was tired of being alone. And she was going to do something totally unlike anything she'd ever done in her life.

She took a deep breath, and leaned across the counter. Standing on tiptoes, she pulled Cooper's face down to level with hers, and kissed him with everything she had inside her lonely heart.

After a shocked moment of disbelief, he hauled her across the counter and covered her lips with his. He grabbed both sides of her head as he kissed and kissed her, taking her full lips betweens his and licking inside the rim, before raking his tongue across in a full sensuous lick.

He lifted his head, his breathing heavy. He nudged her thighs apart and centered himself between her jean-clad legs. "Oh my God. You taste better than I imagined you would," he said huskily, before he grabbed the back of her head with one hand, and the other went to her butt and pulled her to the edge of the counter, grinding her softly against the hard, thick ridge behind his zipper.

He leaned down to kiss her again, when they both heard the loud knock on the door.

"Oh Lord! That's probably the night security," Karina cried, glancing at the wall clock.

She nearly fell to the floor as she pushed herself away from the counter, and Cooper's arms. When he tried to help steady her, she brushed his hands to the side, swayed a little on her feet, and went to answer the door.

"Hi Walt!" She said, tottering on her feet, feeling a bit drunk, and crazy as hell.

"Hey Karina. Just doing rounds, and wanted to make sure everything was okay. The door was locked, and I didn't know if you all had finished for the night," the guard told her, looking at her as though she'd grown horns. She must look as crazy as she felt.

"Oh yeah, well, I...um...have some work to do in the backroom and didn't want the door left unlocked in case someone wandered in. We're closed," she rambled. She hated when she did that. She felt all of ten years old when she did.

"That's fine Karina. Well, if you need anything, you know how to contact me," he said, while doing everything in his power to see what was behind her as she blocked the doorway.

"I will Walt, I mean, I do," she said, and gently closed the door and relocked it. She took a second to compose herself before she turned around to face Cooper.

"Everything okay? Are you all right?" He asked in his deep, sexy, "let me take you there", voice.

He leaned against the counter. Concern was etched into his deep-set, blue eyes. Karina had the feeling that, despite his obvious...excitement, witnessed from the larger than life hard-on pressing against the heavy material of his jeans, Cooper had put his own needs secondary to her comfort.

For some unknown reason, this made her want to cry. As she thought about everything going on in her life, the tears started to flow. The minute she started crying, he was there, wrapping his arms around her and soothing her.

This man who didn't know her from a can of paint was putting her needs first. As he hugged her, she reached up and wrapped her arms around his neck and held on for dear life. He was simply extending emotional support, one human being to another without having to know what had made her cry.

This was something she hadn't experienced in a while, this selflessness from a man. It propelled her to make an instant, "probably wake up in the morning and feel like a ho, but what the hell", decision. She was going to sex him up as though her life depended on it.

Chapter Five

ဢ

Cooper resigned himself to not getting any. Damn. He didn't know the last time he was so hard. It had been a while since he'd had sex. His cock was so hard, he felt like he could slay dragons with the damn thing. He didn't want to slay a fucking dragon. He wanted to fuck the damsel.

But then his eyes met Karina's. She was so sweet. And this was obviously something she didn't do. While one part of him really wanted to have sex with her, the other part knew she was special. He didn't know why, had never felt it before. But she was special. When she looked up at him, tears glistening in her big brown eyes, he felt as if he'd been punched.

He quickly adjusted his pants and walked to her, gathering her body close to his. "Its okay, Karina. We don't have to do anything baby. Everything will be okay," he said, rubbing his hands over her thick sable locs, loving the soft coarse texture against his hands.

He tilted her head up, and looked into her eyes. "Listen, I got a little carried away. We can take this slow, okay? We don't have to do anything you don't want to do." He couldn't resist the temptation of her pretty full lips. He leaned down and captured the tear that had fallen, and rested just at the corner of her mouth.

He snaked out his tongue to lick the tear away, before he opened his mouth the slightest bit, and pulled her lips into his.

She tightened her arms around him even more, as she totally gave in to his kiss. He slanted her head for a better angle, pulled her tight against his body, and sucked and pulled at her lips. He deepened the kiss, his tongue plunging inside her mouth, looking for hers. She tasted so good.

He licked and sucked her plump bottom lip, the lushness corresponding with her full round ass that he was caressing and pushing closer to his cock.

When her hands tangled in the short hairs at the back of his neck, he lifted her and turned to walk with his small bundle, the short distance to the counter. She looked up at him with those soulful eyes of hers, her look questioning, but trusting, as she gripped his arms for support.

Her hair was wild and all over her head from his hands, and his cock grew harder, as he took in the picture she presented to him, all messed up and ready.

"Do you want me, Karina?" he asked.

He'd been fully prepared to leave her alone, not try anything further. But the way she'd looked at him, and the way she'd given herself to his kisses made all chivalrous thoughts fly out the window.

There was no way he was walking away from this. He spread her legs farther apart as he stationed himself between her jean-covered thighs. But as hard as he was, and as badly as he wanted to just *do* her, he waited for her response.

"Yes," she breathed. Her breasts rose and fell heavily behind her sweater. His cock twitched in response.

Without waiting further, Cooper reached out and lifted her sweater over her head, and tossed it on the floor. Beneath the sweater, she was wearing a silky, little red thing, he was afraid he'd tear.

Damn, she looked good.

His hungry gaze traveled over her. Her breasts were larger than he thought, the tops cresting over the sexy top of the camisole. He reached out with a shaky hand, and lightly caressed the exposed skin of her breasts. She was soft and silky to his touch, and he had to close his eyes from the excitement coursing through him.

* * * * *

"Can we take these off?" he asked her, his big hands resting at the top band of her jeans. Karina was so tongue-tied she could only nod her head. She couldn't believe what she was doing. She'd never felt so bold before. And she had never felt so free.

After she nodded her head, she lifted her bottom from the counter to help him as he eased her jeans down her thighs. When they reached her ankles, she stopped and looked down at her feet. Her white furry snow boots had impeded progress.

"Momentary bump in the road," he said with a small husky laugh. His light comment put her at ease.

He then unzipped the side of her boots and took them off her feet and tossed them to the side. After pulling off the boots, she waited for him to return. But instead, he lifted her foot, and took off her socks, and tossed them to the side also.

With a groan, Karina wished to heaven she'd worn a nice pair of trouser socks, instead of the thick gray ones she'd chosen. But granny socks were a lot more effective keeping little toes warm. All thoughts of granny socks vanished when his strong fingers lightly massaged her feet.

"Umm," she moaned. "That feels good." She glanced down to see the dimple appear in his cheek and seconds later, he'd taken her big toe into his mouth, and she damn near came on the spot.

"Oh my God, that feels good," she panted. She'd never had her toes sucked. He took each one into his mouth and carefully licked and laved them, making sounds in his throat as though he was eating Godiva chocolate.

Damn. Hell. Shit.

She almost cried out loud when he gave her pinky toe a final lick, and eased up her body. "If your toes taste that good, I can't wait to taste the rest of you," he said with a wicked gleam in his deep blue eyes.

The way his intense look of lust mixed with something she couldn't name traveled over her exposed body, forced Karina to close her eyes. She was barely able to contain her excitement.

He spread her legs further apart and gently placed them over his shoulders before he leaned down to the juncture of her thighs. He moved her soft silky panties to the side and lightly brushed his fingertips over her mound. She didn't even try to stifle her moan.

Without warning, she felt his tongue stroke her aching pussy with a slow heated lick. She arched her back in automatic response, and covered her mouth with the pad of her hand to stop her scream. With a toothy grin, he licked her from the back of her kat to the tip of her clit, and Karina reached down and grabbed both sides of his head.

Not to pull him up, but to keep him right where he was.

He took the small nub of her clit and softly worked it with his tongue and lips. Little, pointed, stabbing flickers made her body strum as she accepted his tongue loving. Long, luscious glides of his tongue over her clit had her moaning and whimpering, her head tossing back and forth in sensual agony. When he placed two fingers alongside her seam, spreading her wide, and placed his mouth over her entire pussy and sucked, she lost her mind.

"Stop, please Cooper. I can't take it," she choked the words out.

"Baby, we've just begun. You can take it. You can take all of it," he promised before he leaned back in, and went to work.

This time, he worked two fingers into her sopping, wet entrance at the same time that he placed her nub into his mouth and pulled. She came. And came. And came. And came.

She screamed and yelled until she was hoarse, the release pulling every ounce of energy from her body. She came so hard and for so long, that by the time she finished, her body was weak, and she slumped forward unable to keep her body erect.

Cooper lifted her from the countertop, and she automatically wrapped her legs around his waist as he carried her behind the swinging doors that led to the back. He leaned down to kiss her, and she could taste her essence on his lips.

"Do you have an employee lounge or something?" he mumbled the words around her mouth.

"Yeah, but it's pretty small."

"That's fine. We'll make room," he said, and she pointed the way to the small employees lounge.

* * * * *

Cooper was so excited, it was a wonder he didn't come when she orgasmed. As soon they reached the small lounge, he closed the door, and immediately turned her around, with her back braced against the wood.

"Hold me tight for a minute," he said, and placed her legs higher up his waist, and with just enough room to ease his hands between them, he unzipped his jeans, and freed himself.

With a groan, he grabbed her panties and yanked. "I'll replace them," he said, moments before he lowered her carefully onto his aching cock.

"Oh damn. Are you on the pill?" he asked, realization dawning for a brief moment, wrenching him out of his sensual haze.

"Yes," she panted, with her eyes shut tight.

He was so hard, he was afraid he would hurt her, so after he adjusted her sweet, snug little pussy, he waited, allowing her to set the pace.

"Wait a minute," she panted. "You're big, and it's been way too long." If possible his cock grew even bigger from her husky words alone.

"It's okay baby. I can wait. Just breathe and take your time. It's no rush. I love the way you feel just resting on me," he told her.

He'd said sexy words to women before in the heat of the moment, but he felt different saying them to Karina. He meant what he said. As crazy as that sounded, having just met her. And as hard as he was, and as bad as he wanted to just bang the fuck out of her, he waited. He didn't want a simple bang with her.

He wanted more.

He could feel her twitch and the lips of her vagina grabbed his cock with such feminine ferociousness that he had to clench his teeth not to go to town on her. Finally, her walls opened, and he felt it the minute she eased, and the cream from her pussy eased over the length of his erection as he lay buried deep inside her.

But still, he waited.

She slowly began to ride. As she rode him with an earnestness that made him question how long he could last, he looked into her face, and loved the way she'd closed her eyes, taking him with a sensual cast to her face, that stole his breath.

He gripped her hips, and surged up deep as he could go, but not nearly deep enough. He pulled her tight, and worked her body until she cried out, coming long and hard as he continued his sensual assault.

"I need to be deeper." She heard him cry out when he pulled out of her scorching hot pussy, before turning around and laying her on the carpeted floor of the lounge, in front of him. He snatched his jeans the rest of the way off his legs, and pulled her close.

Her cry died out on her lips when he lifted her hips, and surged into her from the back. Cooper paused after he'd carefully eased himself back inside. He was so deep, he felt her womb.

* * * * *

Karina glanced over her shoulder at Cooper as his hard body blanketed her back. She loved the classic beauty of his face. She'd never realized how appealing symmetrical lines and classically chiseled features could be.

Damn. He was so thick and hard. And impossibly long. She hadn't thought she'd be able to take all of him in. But as soon as he'd rocked all the way into her, once she was seated to the hilt, crammed full, she'd nearly wept. And when he moved. Hell, when he moved, it was over. She couldn't get enough of him.

The utter beauty of his face, along with his total focus as he plunged and retreated, his hands on either side of her hips, forced her to lose her concentration. His eyes were half closed as he put his back into it, loving her the way she'd wanted to be loved for a long time. Doing her in a way she'd never been sexed before.

Caught up in the sheer pleasure of his hard strokes as he went deeper and deeper with each, she felt like she was going to burn up from the pleasure. On and on he stroked, moving her body in ways it wasn't meant to go, raising her thigh up, and placing it over his leg for a better angle to dig into her.

Shit that felt good. At that angle, she felt every long hard inch of his cock. Every long hard inch of heaven.

She could feel the fire gather, pooling right below her belly. When he reached a hand, nudging aside the soft folds of her kat, and played with her clit, she lost it.

"Now baby. Come for me now," he whispered behind her back, his hot breath scorching her ear.

She came. And came. And came.

Depleted, her body spasmed until she was left weak and dizzy with pleasure. Her body mindlessly accepted his final thrusts of sensual punishment until she heard him cry out his release in a hoarse voice of triumph.

Chapter Six

ဢ

After Cooper lay behind her and caught his breath, he was overwhelmed with what happened.

Damn. He was in trouble.

When the thought crossed his mind about having sex with her, he had no idea it would be like this. He knew she was sexy as hell with all those round plump curves of hers. But he had no idea the sex would be like that. He felt strange even thinking of it as sex. But to call it anything else scared the shit out of him.

He toyed with one of her small locs of hair, near her ear. He loved the way it felt. He then noticed the contrast of their skin color. He wasn't pale by any stretch, but her light, creamy, brown skin seemed to be highlighted in the dim light of the small lounge. He found himself aroused again, and felt his cock twitch against her soft bottom in response.

He was attracted to this woman. He thought it would be one a one-time thing. He thought he'd have sex with her, ease his curiosity, and ease on down the road. But a crazy thing happened. He didn't feel as though they'd had sex. It felt like more. He wanted it to be more. She was shy, and he knew, without being told, that this wasn't something she normally did.

He also felt the tension in her as she lay in front of his chest. He felt it invade her body moments ago. But that was okay. He wasn't about to let her run away. He had every intention of learning everything he could about little Miss Karina Woodson. He wasn't going anywhere, and neither was she.

She lay quiet and still in front of him as he played with one of her locs. He wondered what she was thinking.

* * * * *

Karina had never felt so alive in her life. And scared.

What had she done? Made love…no scratch that…had sex with a complete stranger! A man she'd known for only a few hours. But damn if it hadn't been the best sex she'd ever had in her friggin' life. And damn if he hadn't made her pussy sing like Leontyne Price.

She felt him play with one of her locs near her ear, and was suddenly self-conscious. She wore her hair loc'd. Some called them dreadlocks. But there was nothing dreadful about her natural coiled hair. She simply allowed her hair to do what nature wanted it to.

No chemicals to straighten out her kinky coils, no color to add flair. Just natural. And loc'd.

She'd never given thought to what it must look like, much less feel like to a white guy. Half the black men she'd met or dated had made negative comments about her natural look. What must Cooper think?

She suppressed a sigh. She was who she was. She couldn't or wouldn't change that for anyone. She stretched her spine, in a subtle attempt to move away when she felt his once soft penis, twitch against her ass.

No way.

He'd worked her so hard she didn't think she'd be able to walk normally for a week as it was. No way could she go another round. She eased her body up and away from him, as she sat up and searched for her clothes.

"Thank you Karina, that was amazing," he said. His deep voice had a huskier timbre to it as he leaned on one arm to stare at her with brooding eyes.

"You're welcome."

She felt lame after she said it, but they were the only words that came to mind. She felt her ears warm. She stood and searched for her clothes, but after putting on her camisole and panties, didn't see the rest of her clothing in the room.

"Where are my clothes? I can't find my clothes!" she cried, and felt tears prickle her eyes, blinding her as she looked around for her jeans and sweater.

When the tears fell, she frantically looked around the small room for her clothes, shame and feelings of remorse clawing their way through her gut, making the act of dressing unbearable and disgraceful to her over heightened senses.

"Sweetheart, I think they're out in the other room, I'll go and get them for you," Cooper said, coming to his feet to approach her.

"Don't," she said. Karina knew if he came any closer she'd come unglued. "I'll go and get them myself."

"Okay. I'll get dressed too," he told her softly.

She had to get away for a minute to compose herself. She ran out of the room and closed the door behind her. Before she'd closed the door, she looked at Cooper, and saw the look of concern, and something more etched on his handsome face as he put on his jeans.

She had time to calm down as she dressed, and do a quick reality check. Check one. She met a man who was finer than fine and he seemed interested. Check two. She then let said fine man *do* her. Check three. Fine man did her like it she'd never been done before. Check four. She was a grown-assed woman of thirty-one years, and although she'd had a one-night stand, she refused to allow herself to feel ashamed, disgusted or remorseful about what she'd done.

She felt slightly better. Sex could do that for you. Especially incredible, *I can't believe I had it*, sex, she thought with a little giggle.

Her friend Liza told her to broaden her horizons. Well…she had. She had no idea at the time Liza had suggested she broaden herself, that she'd do it so soon.

Damn. Life was crazy sometimes. She wondered what Liza would think when she told her. And tell her she would, Karina thought and giggled again. She wiped her eyes with the corner of her sweater as she bent down to put her granny socks back on and tug her snow boots back on her feet.

"Hi sweetie, are you okay?"

She glanced up from zipping her boots and felt the grin threaten to split her face. Cooper was framed in the doorway, looking at her with all that emotion on his handsome face. Emotion that he probably didn't even know was showing.

But Karina saw it. And it helped her straighten her spine, and boost her confidence.

"Yes. I'm fine," she croaked out the answer. "I think I'd better clean up and we should probably leave before Walter comes back." She slowly rose. When he rushed to her side, she allowed him to help pull her to her feet. "Thank you…" he took hold of her lips.

* * * * *

With one hand on the back of her head, and the other resting at the curve of her hip, Cooper kissed her. He didn't just kiss her. He *sucked* her. He pulled and tugged on the lush rim of her bottom lid.

Damn if her lips were addicting. They were so pretty and plump, and tasted like sweet chocolate and vanilla… and sexy as hell.

He pulled her close, before he lifted his head. "We'd better stop," he said, forcing himself away from the temptation of her mouth. "If we don't, I'm hauling you back to the lounge to finish what we started." He could barely get the words out.

Karina looked at him with a look of astonishment mixed with curiosity and a little bit of lust, which made his cock thump a happy encouragement against the tight restriction of his jeans. Her pretty face had a distinct flush across her cheeks, and the tips of her ears had the same reddish hue.

"Umm. I'm not sure if that would be such a good idea Cooper," she mumbled and tried to squirm out of his arms. His hold didn't budge.

"What?" she asked, looking up at him with those big brown eyes of hers.

She'd put the little glasses back on her face, and he nudged them up her nose. Their kiss had fogged up the lenses, and he grinned slightly at the image she presented.

Her hair was wild, locs streaming in her face, and down her back. Her face and the part of her neck that was visible above the scoop neck of her sweater remained red from their lovemaking. Her doe-shaped eyes still had a sleepy look of satisfaction in their deep, brown depths.

"Nothing," he said, his voice hoarse. He had to clear his throat before he spoke again. "Why don't I help you clean this up and I'll follow you home."

"What do you mean, you'll follow me home?" she asked, desperately trying to dislodge herself from his arms.

"It's late Karina, its dark, and the streets are icy. I want to make sure you make it home safely, that's all."

She looked at him and he felt her indecision. It was palpable. She was having some kind of mind fight with herself, he could tell. As she stared at him, she worked her bottom lip with her top teeth over and over. He was scared she'd break the skin she was working it so hard, so he allowed her to ease away from his arms, and watched as she sprang away.

She went to the counter and began to pick up stray wrapping paper and bows. He leaned against the doorframe and waited for her to speak.

* * * * *

Damn it. What the hell was wrong with her? One minute she was on cloud nine, the next she was scared shitless. Ready to take on new challenges and broaden her horizons? Yeah right.

Her emotions were all over the place.

She took a deep breath and turned around to face Cooper. "I appreciate the offer, but I'm fine. I've done this before," she said, and at his raised brows, hastily amended her statement. "I mean, I've closed the department by myself, not, um, well you know…"

She was so embarrassed, she felt like kicking her own ass if she could reach it. As many Little Debbie Oatmeal Crème Pies that she'd *inhaled* over the last few weeks, it shouldn't be that hard a task. Worry and stress were her number one reason for turning to her Debbie pusher.

Well that, and they were so damn good. That creamy middle *had* to have a patented secret! It just had to. She'd tried to recreate the recipe on numerous occasions, sadly to no avail. The last time she'd tried using a combination of confectioner's sugar and…

"Karina?"

She glanced at him and saw the worried look flash across his face. Oh shit. Here she was daydreaming over the potential recipe for a friggin' Little Debbie pie and there stood the living embodiment of what she *should* be daydreaming about.

Yep. She was going straight to the phone book to look up a good therapist bright and early in the morning.

"Umm. Yes?" It was entirely possible that she'd missed something of importance.

"I said that I don't want you to drive home alone. I would like to follow you. To make sure you're safe. You do trust me, don't you?" His face a study of nonchalance but his eyes…

"It's not that I don't trust you. Well. Actually, I don't think I *should* trust you, I don't know you, and I know that probably sounds dumb considering what we just did. But I don't normally do that. I was in a lonely place, and…" She stopped.

Tears threatened again, and she hurriedly put everything in its place so she could get the hell away from the store, and even further away from this man. This man who she didn't know from Adam. This man whom she wanted desperately to take home and let sex her up all over again. To lay it on her. Put his damn leg in it. Take her to the moon and back. To rock her kat.

To. Pull. Her. Fuckin'. Locs.

Shit.

The words floating in her head were coarse, crude, nasty…and tantalizing. She took a long, steady breath and released it.

If she trusted him enough to lay down with him, then she decided she'd trust him enough to let him follow her home.

"Okay," she said simply. "You can follow me."

An unhurried, "I've got plans for you" smile, spread across his sensual mouth. "Let's go."

Chapter Seven

෩

"So that's when you decided to start Design of a Lifetime?" Cooper asked, drinking the herbal tea she'd prepared minutes ago. He never drank herbal tea. When she asked him what type he wanted, rosemary or chamomile, he'd opted for chamomile. He'd heard of that one.

He couldn't believe she'd allowed him to follow her home. He'd played it cool on the outside as he waited for her answer, as to whether she trusted him. On the inside, that was a different matter. He wanted, no needed, for her to trust him enough to allow him to follow her home. He needed to make sure she understood that this wasn't a passing thing. That he hadn't just fucked her for the purpose of a quick lay.

As he'd followed her home, he made up in his mind that he wasn't leaving her alone tonight. He was staking a claim. As crazy as it sounded, this woman was his. He knew it the minute he laid eyes on her.

Now, they sat at her small kitchenette and he tried not to stare too hard at her as she animatedly talked about her business. She was so damn pretty and sexy, and was totally unaware of her unique appeal.

"Yes, I enjoyed the company I worked for. I started with them right out of college."

"What made you leave?"

"I wanted to see if I could do it on my own. I didn't want to always work for someone else. What about you? What line of work are you in?" she asked, as she placed the cup on the table.

She casually flipped several of her locs behind her shoulder, and smiled at him as she asked the question. His eyes followed the motion of her hair as it landed softly on her back.

"What?" she asked.

"Um, nothing," he said slowly. He loved her hair. He'd never known a woman to wear her hair in dreadlocks.

"Why are you looking at me like that?" she asked, and he could see the hesitancy cross her face, the doubt. He reached across the table to finger one of the small long coiled pieces of hair.

"I like your dreads," he said simply.

"My hair isn't dreadful, Cooper."

"What?"

"I'm sure you didn't mean anything by that. Most people call them dreadlocks, or dreads. But I don't like that term. I prefer to call them locs," she answered simply.

* * * * *

"I'm sorry, I didn't know," he told her. "They're beautiful," he said with sincerity.

When he reached a hand out to touch another one, she neatly avoided the contact. He dropped his hand, and tilted his head to the side and stared. The look in his eyes was curious, the smile that played around the edges of his sensual mouth, made her heart thump heavily against her chest.

Damn.

"Do you want any more tea?" she asked and heard the small catch in her own voice. She stood unsteadily on her feet, and gathered the small dishes and walked the short distance to the kitchen sink.

"No. I don't want any more tea. I want you," he said starkly. No hesitating. No beating around the bush. Just said it like it was no big deal.

"It's getting late. I think maybe…" her voice trembled.

"Maybe…what?" He whispered. He walked over to stand behind her, as she placed the dishes in the sink.

He took the small cup from her hand and set it aside, before he turned her around. As he boxed her in, his large body gave her no way out. He bent his head low, near the hollow of her shoulder, lifted her locs and just…inhaled.

What was he doing to her? She allowed her head drop to his chest, moments before she pushed him away.

"It's getting late. I think it's time for you to go, Cooper." She didn't know how much longer she could stand it. He had some type of hold on her she didn't know how to break. Or that she even wanted to try.

"Is that what you want Karina? For me to leave? Because if that's what you want, I'll go. But is that really what you want, baby?" his nostrils flared as he asked the words, his eyes piercing as they bore into hers.

She hesitated, and her eyes widened.

* * * * *

She looked like a butterfly caught in a spider's web. Helpless. Scared. Waiting to be devoured.

And he wanted to devour every luscious inch of her. He took the decision out of her hands and lifted her into his arms, his mouth descending on hers. "Where's your bedroom?" he mumbled around her lips.

"Mmthat mway," she mumbled back, pointing her finger in the direction of the room without opening her eyes.

Cooper walked through the apartment with haste, his small bundle nestled close in his arms as he found the bedroom. Shouldering the door open, he walked inside, and deposited her on the comforter. He followed her down to the bed, and covered her body with his. He never lost contact with her lips during the walk from the kitchen to the bedroom. As he drank in the nirvana of her lips, Cooper felt drunk with the pleasure from simply kissing her.

He lifted his head. His breath was labored when he demanded. "Take off your clothes."

He saw her brief hesitation and gentled his demand. "Please baby. I want *you* to do this. On your own." He didn't know why it was important that she be the one to initiate it. But it was.

The moon, streaking through the window, was the only light in the dark bedroom. But he could see her as she worked her bottom lip into a frenzy. He leaned down and captured the reddened rim between his, and licked and soothed her self-inflicted small injury.

"Please," he asked again. "But do it real slow. Take your time."

Lord have mercy, he wanted her to strip.

She opened her mouth to voice an instant protest, but swallowed the automatic refusal before it could spring forth from her mouth. She was so afraid, she was trembling.

"I'm scared," she admitted in a low voice.

"Don't be."

"I can't do this," she barely croaked out.

"There are only the two of us in this room Karina. No one else. Do it for me, baby."

Why'd he have to ask her that question in his sexy "do me baby" voice? The voice that promised he'd do things to her body that would send her to confession for a solid month. He lifted a loc and absently played with it.

And his eyes.

His eyes, that even in the moonlit room, she could see were half closed and...waiting.

"What do you want me to do?" Her voice was barely audible in the still of the room.

"I want you to be comfortable with me. I want you to lower your inhibitions. To free yourself. Can you do that?" He whispered in a dark voice.

"I barely know you," she said. His face was mere inches away from hers, and played havoc with her ability to think straight.

He didn't say a word. Just looked at her, and continued to toy with her hair.

The small smile that played around his mouth, the way he played with her hair, and the utter seriousness in his eyes raised goose bumps down her arms. She didn't know what it was about him. He made her weak. His look dared her to believe. Damn.

She was hooked.

She eased away from him on the bed. He laid his body fully stretched out, elbow propped on the bed, his hand resting on his face as he watched her.

Karina turned on the small clock radio on her bedside table and soft sounds filtered into the quiet of the room. When she turned to glance back at Cooper, she saw the grin spread across his face and laughed.

"Oh God," she laughed self-consciously. "I've never done this before," she told him.

"That's okay. That's what makes it special. Do it for me, baby," he urged her.

With a deep breath, she threw back her shoulders and smiled at him. "Are you sure you're ready for this, big boy?" She asked and batted her eyelashes at him, trying to make light of what she was contemplating.

His startled laugh eased her nervousness and she found herself excited with the tantalizing thought of taking her clothes off and playing the stripper role for him.

She felt just the tiniest bit nasty.

A grin spread across her full lips when her oldies but goodies radio station announced that one of her favorite songs, one she secretly named her *do me* song, was up next. Oh shit.

This was her *jam*. This man was in trouble, she thought with an evil grin, as she moved away from the bed, and closed her eyes, her body beginning to sway with the sensual beat of the song.

Chapter Eight

ဢ

Oh shit. He was in trouble.

Cooper raised himself when Karina moved away from the foot of the bed and closed her eyes as the song started to play on the radio. He watched her, mesmerized.

She eased her hands down her thighs in time to the beat of the song.

She rolled her hips and spun around in a slow circle, as her hands glided up to take the hem of her sweater in both hands and pull it over her head. She gyrated her body, moving her ass back and forth in time to the music. Her eyes remained closed as she danced.

His cock was so hard he could choke a horse with it.

When she slowly unzipped her jeans and began to ease them down her legs in time to the slow, seductive music, she turned around, and bent over to ease them over her feet. He was so turned on he thought he was going to lose his damn mind.

She spun around and lifted her arms up and crossed them over her head. Her breasts were pushed out and proud, the smooth brown globes resembled two big melons. All ripe and ready, her nipples long and stiff.

No way in hell she'd never done this shit before. No way. She was too damn good at it. He watched her roll and thrust, gyrating and moving that plump ass of hers.

She toyed with the waistband of her panties, and eased her hand inside…

He leaped from the bed.

"What!" she yelled when he touched her. She had been so into her little dance, she'd obviously tuned him out.

"Striptease over," he growled, and picked her up and tossed her gently on the bed, before he ripped the clothes from his body.

She had the audacity to giggle.

"Oh, you think it's funny, do you?" he asked and covered her body with his.

"Yep, funny as hell." There was a definite squeak in her voice when she answered.

She pushed against his unyielding chest, and glanced into his eyes, for a moment the predatory gleam in his deep blue depths gave her pause. The more she struggled, the deeper the gleam.

She was filled with nervous excitement.

He took both of her arms in one of his and stretched them high above her head, forcing her breasts to slap against each other. Her nipples were hard and stiff, begging for his touch.

He kept his eyes on her, as though she'd try and escape and gave one of her beaded nipples a long swipe with his tongue. When she groaned, he laughed.

"Not so funny now, is it Karina?" he asked and took the nipple fully into his mouth, swirling and nursing her until she felt the cream from her pussy ease down her leg.

She kept her mouth shut this time. He released her arms, and cupped her breasts in his hands. "You sure do have pretty breasts. Has anyone ever told you that before, Karina?"

When she refused to answer him, he chuckled low. "Well you sure do. They're the prettiest things I've ever seen. Do you know what I'd like to do with these big beautiful mounds of yours?" He stroked his tongue between her cleavage and she bucked against him with the sensation and his low talk.

"I'd love to see how my cock would look nested between them. I'd love to ease it up and down, and fuck your breasts like I'm about to fuck you. Would you like me to do that, Karina?"

She gasped at the visual image that played in her mind at his suggestive words. She'd never had a man talk dirty to her before. She herself had never felt comfortable uttering the words that played in her mind out loud before. She desperately wanted to fully engage in his dirty talk, but held back. Afraid.

"It's okay baby. You don't have to say a word. I know what you want. Do you want me to give you what you want, Karina?" he asked, and made his way down her body, licking and stroking every part of her along the way.

"Yes," she breathed.

"Do you trust me, Karina?" The look in his eyes was hot and fierce. If she had any damn sense she'd be, at this very moment, running and screaming from the bedroom instead of nodding her head in silent acquiescence to whatever he had in mind.

"Don't worry baby. I won't hurt you. You'll like it, nothing too kinky," he promised.

He lifted her thighs and braced her feet against his shoulders and lifted her butt high in the air. She expected him to eat her pussy. She felt herself grow embarrassingly wet as she closed her eyes and waited for his tongue to caress her kat.

What she felt instead was his hot stabbing tongue in her ass.

He swirled and played with the small opening, carefully pushing his tongue deep inside, while he gently rubbed the rough pad of his thumb around the outside of her anus. While his tongue and fingers were busy with one opening, he used the other hand to play with her clit. The combination drove her straight over the edge.

Her butt was sacred territory, she never let a man near it during sex.

Damn. She'd had no idea what she'd been missing.

She cried and moaned, as she moved her head back and forth mindlessly on her silk-covered pillow, as the hard spasms of her orgasm ripped through her body. He worked both ends of her until she thought she'd die, her body bucked and writhed against his talented fingers and tongue.

The orgasm totally took her by surprise. When she released, she screamed. And screamed and screamed, and screamed until she was hoarse and depleted.

When she came to herself, Cooper was lying next to her, caressing her locs.

* * * * *

"Was that too much for you, Karina?" he asked in the quiet of the room.

"No. A little at first. But it was good," her soft voice was barely discernible in the dark, and he was afraid he'd scared her with the way he'd made love to her. When she cuddled closer to him, he felt a small bit of relief.

"I've never done that," she admitted. He heard the catch in her voice.

"Did you like it?" He held her tight against his body as he crossed his arms in front of her. He liked that he was the first man she'd allowed to do that to her.

He lightly toyed with the gentle curve of her belly. She was so soft. He was fascinated with the perfection of her creamy skin. It looked the color of coffee with just a little cream. Carmel colored and smooth.

"Couldn't you tell? All that hollering and yelling I did could have awakened the dead," she laughed, and he chuckled in relief. If she could joke about it, she probably wasn't too freaked out.

"But what about you? You didn't get much out of that," she turned her face, and glanced at him from the corner of her almond-shaped eyes.

Cooper took his hand and ran it down the length of her cheek. "I wanted to do that for you, but we have all night, don't we? Who says we're done?" he asked, and she felt a quiver in her belly with his low words.

"Do you have any family, Karina?" he asked after she'd settled back against his chest.

"No. I was an only child. My grandmother and my mom raised me. I never knew my dad. I called my mother Mom, and my grandmother Big Momma. Everybody called her that. Big Momma was special. She died a couple of years ago."

"I'm sorry," he said. He heard the pain in her voice.

"It's okay. We're from New Orleans. Our heritage is that we celebrate death. It's only a transition from this plane of life to the next. Only a bridge." He felt her fingertips as they tickled the back of his hands.

He thought about his own family as they lay content in the dark—sharing. "I have five sisters. My father passed my senior year in college, and it wasn't easy. Financially we were okay, but emotionally, it took a toll on my mother. She relied on me to fill the gap."

"That must have been hard."

He didn't want to talk about his father. He'd died over ten years ago and Cooper still had a hard time, emotionally, when he thought of him. "It was. It still is. He had cancer, so it wasn't unexpected. But that didn't make it any easier."

"Is that why you spoil your sisters?" she asked, her voice light. The upbeat tone of her voice and the gentle way she was caressing his hands, helped eased the sudden constriction in his heart.

"Yeah, I do spoil them. I always have. I think they expect it now. I've been so busy in my career, I haven't had much time to find that someone special, so my ladies get it all," he laughed.

The thought that came to his mind instantly was that he wouldn't mind spoiling Karina. That the idea of her being one of his ladies was overwhelming in its appeal. He wasn't ready to say that to her.

"I love your locs," he said instead, as he ran a hand through her hair.

"Really?"

"What? You don't believe me?" he asked, detecting the doubt in her voice. When she didn't answer he spoke again. "I like the way they feel on my bare skin as we make love." He leaned down and kissed the hollow of her shoulder. One hand lay against her breast and he felt her heart leap with his words.

"You like the way they feel, Cooper?" she asked, and turned around in his embrace, and pushed his willing body down on the mattress. As soon as his body landed she fell on top of his chest, and immediately snaked her way slowly down his body.

"Ummm. Yeah. They feel really good baby," he said, allowing her hair to feather against his body as she did. He inhaled sharply. It felt like a thousand fingers caressing his skin. He closed his eyes and let his head fall back, reveling in the sensation.

When she reached the tops of his thighs she paused, and he felt her locs against the inner skin of his thighs as she hesitated. It was his turn to feel his own heart thud against his chest, wondering what she would do next.

* * * * *

He liked the way her locs felt against his body.

No one ever said that to her before. It gave her the confidence she'd needed to do something she'd always wanted to do to a man, but lacked the courage.

She felt a purr escape from deep within, as she closed her eyes and inhaled. He smelled sooo good. His scent was genuine, unlike anything manufactured from a lab. He smelled like sandalwood and soap. Clean and heady.

As she inhaled, she leaned closer and allowed her hair to cover his groin as she rubbed her head back and forth on his thigh, pausing to kiss the soft hair on his leg. Ummm. He tasted good too. His heartfelt groan brought her out of her own little world.

"That feels incredible, what are you doing?" he asked on a shaky laugh.

His obvious enjoyment was evident in the rigid length of his penis. Moments earlier it lay soft and curved against his thigh, now it stood thick and erect, curved against his belly.

"Just wait," she said, and gently took his hard length into her hand and stroked. His body completely jerked off the bed.

She used her fingers at first. Softly feathering them up and down his length. With each gentle caress, he forced himself not to grab her by her hair and pull her closer to his cock.

Then he felt her tight little hands grip him tight, as she softly rubbed his entire length against her cheek.

"Damn Karina, do you know what the hell you're doing to me?" he groaned as her soft cheek nudged his shaft.

She glanced up at him from her position between his legs, and smiled a small sexy grin. "Ummm. I sure do," she said huskily, before she engulfed the entire length of his erection in her mouth.

She slowly worked him into her mouth. He was big, so it took several sucks and pulls, nibbles and caresses before she worked him into her mouth and down her throat. She slowly eased him back out and swirled her tongue around the bulbous end of his cock, before she swallowed him again.

"Deeper, go deeper," he moaned harsh and long.

She pulled away and lapped his cock from stem to tip and smiled.

That was it. Once again, he had to call a halt to her playtime antics.

"Come here, damn it," he growled and hauled her up his body. Without warning, he lifted her by the shoulders and raised her body high, before slowly lowering her onto his waiting, throbbing shaft.

It was her turn to cry out as he eased into her tightly swollen, cream-slicked lips. Slowly, mercilessly, he stroked deep. He lifted her high with every stroke, and her head and upper body jostled and bobbed, while her hands reached out to grab the tangled bed sheets in an attempt to steady the wild ride.

"Oh Lord, Cooper, you're so deep I can feel you in my damn womb," she cried out, as he pumped her with deep, steady strokes.

"Yeah, well it's not deep enough," he grunted and lifted her off his cock despite her wrenching cry of protest.

He easily flipped her over, and reached his arm underneath her waist. He positioned her ass in the air, and after steadying his shaky hands at her waist, speared her tight, soaking wet entrance with a deep satisfying moan.

"Cooper! You're too big…I can't take it!" She keened.

"You can take it baby. You can take it and more," he promised with a low harsh laugh.

He plunged and stroked, moving her body in directions that suited him, ways designed to pleasure them both. As he stroked long and deep, he could feel the orgasm well up from his balls.

With mindless abandon, he gripped her hips and cried and roared his release as she simultaneously cried out hers. He came long and hard, hauling her close, ramming himself as far as he could into her tight opening, as he released and spilled himself into her.

As the last of his spasms racked his body, Cooper felt himself return to normal. He was stunned. Stunned and dazed. He pulled out of her and, with unsteady hands, laid her down and settled her body in front of his. He drew her close and laid his head on top of her head, and closed his eyes, slowly drifting off to sleep.

Chapter Nine

෨

Bzzzzz. Bzzzzz.

The jarring sound of her alarm clock jolted Karina out of her pleasant dreams.

"Grrrr. What time is it?" She groaned, and reached over and patted the table until her hand made contact with the loud buzzer. She slammed it off and re-tucked her arm inside the blankets, cozying down into the warmth of her covers.

"Come and lie a little closer. I'm cold," a sleepy masculine voice asked, from close behind her.

"Aahh!" Karina yelped and shot straight up in bed, her locs flying as she grabbed the blanket to cover her naked body. She felt as though her heart was leaping right out of her chest.

"Baby, what's wrong?" The alien, deep scratchy voice asked.

"Oh my Lord. It wasn't a dream," she frantically half whispered to herself as the memories of the previous night crashed down on her.

She turned desperate eyes toward the man who lay sprawled on her bed, one sexy, hairy leg on top of the blanket, the other was buried beneath the covers. As her glance stole over him, she felt the tops of her ears burn when she saw his penis lying thick and curved on the inside of his thigh.

And hard. Thick, curved and hard. She couldn't overlook the hard part. She felt sweat break out on her forehead.

"Come back and lie down with me Kari," he asked huskily, the sleep in his voice making it scratchy sounding. He opened his arms for her to come to him, and Karina had to exercise serious willpower to resist the lure of those arms. He had the sexiest arms.

She never realized a man's arms could be so sexy. His skin was smooth. And although they were in the middle of winter, his tone was light olive, with a light dusting of smooth hair on his forearms.

Not too much to scare her with images of Bigfoot. Just enough to turn her on. That same sprinkling of hair was on his inner thigh. It lay so smooth and pretty on his thick thighs...

"Karina, are you okay?" he asked. He sat up in the bed, and leaned his big body against the etched wood of her headboard.

"Um...yes," she barely got out. She cleared her throat. This was ridiculous. "Yes, I'm fine, Cooper. I better get up, it's already six," she said, gathering the blankets more closely around her body.

"Are you shy now, Kari?" he asked, and before she knew it, he'd reached for her, and laid her against his chest.

She started to protest but...this close to him, and it was over. Why fight it?

"Maybe a little," she admitted. It was so easy for her to talk to him. She felt as though she'd known him forever.

"Why?" The question rumbled in his chest, and tickled the side of her face.

"I wonder," she laughed dryly.

He thought about what he'd just said, and laughed with her. "I guess you're entitled to be a *little* shy," he dragged out the word little.

"You think?" she glanced over her shoulder at him, laughing again. He could feel some of the tension ease away from her body.

"What are your plans for the day?" he asked. It was Saturday, and if he were home, he would be poring over the financial section of the morning paper in his office at home.

He felt her snuggle closer to him before she answered. "I'm going into Macy's today. With Founder's Day coming up, I can get as many hours as I want," she said.

"You work there a lot?" he smoothed his hands over her hair as he spoke.

"No. Susan is the only full-time clerk in the department. But whenever a holiday comes up, they hire a few extra temps to help out. This is my first time. I can use the money to help build my business."

"How long have you had your design business?" He enjoyed hearing her speak, and used the opportunity to learn more about her.

"It's been a little over a year now," she sighed. "It's going okay. A little rocky. Yesterday I was darn near suicidal. I had a client decide to go with another designer. I really needed the job too." He heard the despondent tone in her voice and was surprised at the clinch he felt in his heart.

He had it bad.

"It's going to work out baby. Don't worry," he whispered and then laid his head lightly on top of her hers.

"I know. It always does. One way or another," she whispered back, and uttered a small laugh.

"Do we have time to grab something to eat before you have to go to work? Is there a little café around here that you like?" he asked, his hands lightly smoothing down her body.

He loved how soft and feminine she felt. She was round in all the right places. He liked a woman to feel like a woman. Nothing wrong with a woman who worked out, kept her body tight and honed. But he'd take softness to chiseled and cut muscles any day. His hands eased down her breasts slowly as he spoke, cupping the full round mounds in his hands. They were too large for him to contain, so the overflow of plump tit lay on his forearm.

"Karina? Would you like to go and eat somewhere?" he asked again when she didn't answer.

"Umm hmmm," she murmured.

She was turned on.

That was the other thing he loved about her. She was so damn sexy and sensual, and totally unaware of it herself. He could look at her, touch her, feel her up a little, and she was turned on. He knew without touching her pretty little pussy that it was wet and creamy. And ready.

He was on his way to find out just how wet she was when her phone rang.

With a groan, she turned around. He saw the regret in her eyes when she said, "I'd better get this."

He tried to hide his disappointment when she picked up the phone. He parted her locs and buried his face in them, and took a deep breath. He loved the way her hair smelled. Like warm vanilla and peppermint. Sweet and spicy, just like Karina.

"Hello," her voice was still husky from lack of use. "Oh. Hi Liza, nothing much. What are you doing?" She pulled slightly away from him and he noticed the rigidity that invaded her once loose limbs.

"I'm going to take a shower. I'll give you some privacy. We can decide on where to eat after you get off the phone," he told her quietly, and reached over and kissed her.

He reluctantly released her and rose from the bed. Without bothering to put on his jeans, he went into the bathroom and closed the door.

* * * * *

Karina watched him go and felt a pang in her heart. Damn. When he buried his face in her hair, she almost wet herself. How the hell did he do that? Why was it that when he *smelled* her it turned her on so much? He accepted and seemed to like everything about her. From her loc'd head to her thick thighs. And everything in between, she thought with longing.

He hadn't bothered to put on clothes when he left the bathroom. He had the nicest ass she'd ever seen. So tight and muscled. Plump too. No flat cheeks on that man.

That was a total overgeneralization. People came in different shapes and sizes no matter what race they were. And men came in all sizes and lengths, she'd found out over the last twelve hours to her utter delight. If Liza's husband was *anything* like Cooper in…proportions…it was no wonder her friend was always so damn happy.

"Karina!" Liza nearly gave her a heart attack as she yelled into the phone.

"Girl you don't have to shout, I'm right here," Karina told Liza, hoping she hadn't missed something vital in the conversation as she'd gone off into la-la land, thinking of Cooper and his proportions!

"*What* is going on with you?"

"What do you mean?" she asked, trying to buy time.

"Karina, don't mess with me! I could have sworn I heard a very masculine voice say he was off to take a shower!"

"Yeah…um…that's a long story."

There was a heartbeat of silence on the other end.

"I've got time. Spill," Liza demanded.

Karina gave a mental shrug. She might as well get it over with. When she heard the noise from the pipes, she knew Cooper was taking a shower, so she rose from the bed. She cupped the phone, and allowed it to nestle between her ear and the top of her shoulder as she shut the door.

"I met a man at Macy's, he spent the night with me, and I had the best sex of my life, and he's taking a shower, and then we're going to…"

"What!" Liza yelled into the phone. Karina made a mental note to make an appointment with an audiologist Monday morning.

Maybe she shouldn't have thrown the news at her best friend like that. But, she'd always gone by the belief that it was best just to lay it all out. Put all the cards on the table. A giggle escaped before she could clamp her hand over her mouth.

She'd never giggled so much in her life.

"No, she does *not* have the nerve to giggle after dropping that bomb!"

Karina found it funny how Liza would speak to some unknown third party whenever she was irked. She was *really* irked now.

"Start the hell over, Karina! What do you mean you met a man and spent the night with him?" Liza had taken a deep breath, obviously trying to calm herself down. Liza had asthma. Karina didn't want her to have to take a hit off her inhaler, so she forced her nervous giggles away.

"Remember our talk about broadening my horizons?"

"Yeees," Liza drew the word out with caution.

"I was in a weird spot Liza, you know that."

"You mean about not having sex?"

"It is…was…more than that. You know that girl."

"More than your 'coochie being dryer than the Sahara?'"

"Much more."

Both women were quiet for a minute.

"Okay give me details, and don't leave anything out," Liza demanded.

Karina sat back and leaned her head against the headboard and closed her eyes. Starting at the beginning, she told her friend everything. "I was running late as usual…"

Chapter Ten

ഇ

Cooper gave Karina the space she needed. When he'd awakened, and felt her warm body next to his, he'd lain there, content in a way that was foreign to him. He'd been busy lately, and his love life had suffered because of it. Like Karina, he worked for himself.

After completing his MBA, he'd worked for a few upper end brokerage firms, building a reputation for his ability to turn high profit that yielded maximum returns for his wealthy clients.

He'd invested his own money in many of the stocks he recommended, and had made his first million by the time he was thirty years old. This was the same time he opened his own firm. That was five years ago, and his business had grown, and he was ready to expand into foreign markets.

Because of his dedication to building his business, his focus on his love life was all but nonexistent. He'd only dated occasionally lately, and his lovers were few. For his last social engagement, he'd had to go to one of his sisters to act as his companion. That had cost him!

He loved his sisters, but they either mothered him, or pestered him no end with their endless questions about his life. They had an inordinate interest in his personal life.

Cooper knew his mother was disappointed in his lack of determination in securing a wife, or at least a woman he was serious about. She'd thrown a few hints around about getting older, and having no grandchildren from him. Although one of his sister's had already given her several, she wanted a grandchild from Coooper. When she started talking like that, Cooper felt himself break out in hives. He had no desire to either get married, or have children. At least no time soon. He had goals and aspirations. A family of his own at this time in his life didn't figure into his plans.

He hummed as he lathered himself. He took a deep sniff of the soap. Damn, it smelled good. Vanilla and peppermint. Just like Karina.

As soon as he thought of her name, he felt the smile grace his face. He'd had plans for that morning, before her phone call put an end to his amorous intent. He turned off the shower, and stepped out the stall. After swiping the towel through his short hair, he quickly dried the rest of his body before leaving the shower.

Karina should be off the phone with her friend by now. He walked back to the bedroom and was in the process of opening the door, when he heard the sounds of tears, and his heart leapt from his chest. He quickly opened the door and rushed inside.

"Karina? Baby, what's wrong?" He felt each pounding beat of his heart as he took in the sight of Karina, looking dejected, sad, and if the tips of her ears were any indication…embarrassed.

* * * * *

"All right, Karina. Let me get this straight. And if I miss something along the way, let me know, okay?" Liza asked. Karina already felt the queasy feeling of dread pool in her gut. The kind she used to get when Big Momma would call her by her full name.

Karina Marie Woodson…you'd better explain yourself young lady! Karina could hear the echo of Big Momma's voice in the recesses of her mind.

"Go ahead, Liza."

"You're late for work and a man holds the elevator door open for you, thus helping you not be late for work. Then you and this man have a five-minute conversation before you clock in. You go and put your things away, and he's left a mountainous amount of gifts to be wrapped when you return. These gifts range from perfume, sweaters, lingerie...am I on point so far?"

Karina didn't say a word.

"Where was I?" Liza asked before plunging on. "Oh yes. This man comes back, you've wrapped his gifts, and he tells you they're for his mama and sisters. Something about him gets to you and you kiss him. You two are going at it like a couple of horny teenagers, when you're interrupted. Instead of seeing this as a sign from the good Lord to stop, your grown ass sees it as a sign to go full out and you let him screw you in the employee lounge."

Liza's voice was so shrill at this point that Karina had to move the phone away from her ear to prevent permanent damage to her eardrums. She knew the audiologist visit was definitely going to be needed by the time she hung up the phone.

"Then you let this man, who you don't know from Adam, take you home? And sleep with him again. And again. Damn Kari. What in the world were you thinking?"

Karina nearly cried with the disappointment she heard in Liza's voice. "Listen, I don't need to hear all this right now. I don't need to hear you beat up on me either, Liza. I thought you were best friend," Karina couldn't stop the tears that flowed and neither did she try and check her anger.

"Karina, I don't really give a damn what you want to hear," Liza all but yelled in her ear. "I love you and I don't want to see you hurt. Not mentally or physically. I heard what you said. You think this is some kind of love at first sight, don't you?"

"I don't know, Liza. He's special. That's all I know," Karina whispered into the phone.

"Honey, I'm not trying to burst your bubble, but you have to think. And while you're doing this thinking...what about protection Kari? All this time you've been telling me how good it was, how this man is the best since Wonder Bread, and *not one darn time* do I hear the words, 'we used a condom' come out of your mouth. So Karina Marie Woodson, please tell me you weren't so caught up in the rapture that you neglected to protect yourself, girlfriend. Please tell me you were more responsible than that."

There was a long pause of pure, unadulterated silence.

"I've got to go, Liza. I'll call you later…" Karina removed the phone from her ear, and as she replaced it on the receiver she could hear Liza yelling at her to pick the phone back up. "Karina don't you hang up this pho…" *Click.*

After she hung up the phone, she turned the ringer off, and put her face in her hands and cried. She cried and cried as she called herself every foul, *what the hell is wrong with me, I must be smoking crack*, name she could come up with.

Was she that desperate?

Liza's words came crashing down on her head like a tsunami, devastating and complete. What *had* she been thinking? As her tears fell, she was so absorbed in her own little world that she was unaware that Cooper had entered the room until she felt his arms around her, and without thinking she returned his embrace.

"What in the world have we done? I'm on the pill, but it's a low estrogen pill because I get sick with the more powerful one, and you didn't use a damn condom!" She cried and buried her face in the crook of his neck.

She withdrew from him. The look of horror that crossed his handsome face had her wanting to scratch his damn eyes out. The bastard. Karina promptly burst into frustrated tears.

"Okay. Okay, calm down Karina, everything's going to be fine baby, let's just think this out," Cooper tried to reassure her, when he himself felt as though he'd gotten punched in the gut. What the hell had he been thinking? He'd had the one moment of clarity, *after* he'd entered her, when he'd asked if she was on protection, and truth be told he would have probably kept on even if she'd said no. He'd *never* forgotten to use a condom, no matter if the woman was on the pill or not.

Not one damn time.

He rubbed the top of her head, trying to reassure her, and saw the way his hand slightly shook. The ramifications of what they'd done weren't lost on him. Not only had they risked pregnancy, they didn't know each other and she probably thought he did this kind of thing all the time. That he was some kind of irresponsible player. There was no way in hell she'd easily believe otherwise.

"And don't call me baby. I'm not your baby," she raised her head from where it was nestled on his chest to utter the retort, and laid her head back down.

He knew she was upset so he resisted the urge to say that wasn't what she was saying last night. In fact, if memory served right, baby wasn't the only thing she cried out.

"And don't even think about reminding me what names we called each other last night." This time she didn't even bother to lift her head.

"I don't know if this will reassure you or not, but this isn't something I do either, Karina. I haven't been sexually involved with a woman for a while, and I'm not indiscriminate in my sexual partners. And I always use protection. Without fail."

"You expect me to believe I'm your first…one-night stand?" The embarrassment in her voice slammed him head on.

"I believe I'm your first," he said, after the pause.

Karina lifted her head and drew slightly away. "How do you know that?" she asked.

"I can't answer that Karina. I just know this isn't something you do."

She said nothing in the quiet, just allowed him to rub a caressing hand through her locs.

"I'll go to my doctor on Monday and get a health certificate and bring it to you. Would that help ease some of your worries, sweetheart?" he asked and felt her nod her head.

"Do you want me to go to the doctor with you when it's time to find out, if…"

"If I'm pregnant?" she finished the thought.

"Yes."

He felt her take a deep, shaky breath against his chest. "And if I am? What then?"

What then? There was no going back in time, even if he wanted to. The fact that he didn't regret what happened scared him more than the fact that he'd engaged in risky unprotected sex. "We'll take it as it comes. I won't desert you," he reassured her.

Chapter Eleven

ॐ

"Do you want any more tea, sweetie?" Liza asked, swinging the kettle in front of her, back and forth. When she didn't get the instant response that she wanted, she turned off the television.

"What did you do that for? Judge Matthis was just about..."

"To lower the boom. Yeah. I know. We need to talk. And not about Judge Matthis. And you *know* how much I love Matthis," her comment drew a reluctant chuckle from Karina.

Karina sighed. It had been a few days since she'd seen Cooper, and with each passing day, she'd felt more and more depressed. She'd called her doctor to set an appointment for a physical, and on the same day, she'd gotten her period. She'd called Cooper and told him he didn't have anything to worry about, she wasn't pregnant.

For some crazy reason, getting her period hadn't given her the feeling of exaltation that she'd thought it would. She knew the chances that her irresponsible behavior would result in pregnancy were scarce because of the timing of her cycle.

So why didn't this make her happy?

"Because you're in love," Liza said on a deep inhalation and flopped her long frame in the chair next to Karina.

"Huh?" Karina was totally lost as to what her friend was saying.

"You probably were kind of wishing you were pregnant, weren't you, Kari? Be honest."

"What are you talking about?" Karina could feel the tips of her betraying ears heat up.

"You said you didn't know why you weren't happy about getting your period and you didn't know why. It's because you've gone and fallen in love with him, that's why."

"Oh hell, did I say that out loud?" A reluctant laugh escaped from her gloomy lips.

"You sure did, girlfriend."

Both women looked at each other and doubled over laughing. Liza laughed until she started losing her breath, and Karina felt like she needed a hit off her friend's inhaler too, as her chest started to hurt, she laughed so hard.

Laughter always seemed to lighten the mood and put everything in perspective.

"So what in the world do I do now, Liza?"

"About what?"

"Don't be obtuse." Karina rolled her eyes as hard as she could at her friend.

"Well. What do you expect from this relationship, Karina? You have to be honest with yourself. What do you want?"

Karina thought about what Liza was asking. She and Cooper had spoken every night since they met, and he said sweet things to her, told her he wanted to see her, but was in the process of starting a new project, and time was tight for him. He'd planned on coming by Macy's earlier in the week to take her to eat, when a call from one of his sisters had put a wrinkle in his plans.

This time it was Angela, one of the twins. She was starting a new business and wanted Cooper to help finance her venture. When he'd called to cancel, she'd had to bite her own tongue in protest. She'd been hoping to see him. She needed to see him, if nothing else than to see if that magical time they shared was a once-in-a-lifetime moment. She'd tried telling him that, but had gotten tongue-tied…

* * * * *

"I'd hoped to see you, Cooper," Karina took a chance and verbalized what she felt. She felt a keen sense of disappointment when he told her he wouldn't be able to come by and pick her up after her shift was over at Macy's.

"Me too, Karina. You believe that, don't you?" he asked.

Karina wasn't sure what to believe. When she'd told him about her period coming, he'd sounded way too damn relieved. Okay maybe that wasn't fair of her to think, but who cared about being fair? Now he had some emergency to take care of and was backing out of coming to see her. Whatever.

"Karina, are you there?"

"I'm here. I have to admit, I feel like…"

"Like what?" he prompted when she stopped talking.

"As though you don't really want to see me. No one's forcing you to do anything, Cooper. If you'd rather back out, that's cool. I'm not pregnant, so you don't have anything to worry about, and we can go our separate ways. It's not like we have a relationship or anything. It was only a one-night lay."

"Is that how you feel? That's how you see it?"

"Don't you?"

"If I did, I wouldn't be talking to you now. Is that how *you* feel? Don't play games with me. It's a two-way street, you know." The tone in his voice had deepened, and sounded funny to her. Karina didn't know him well enough to say, but she *knew* he was pissed off.

Good. That made two of them.

"I'm not playing games. I wouldn't be talking to you either buddy if I weren't interested." She fought hard against the crazy tears she felt welling up.

"Good. Now that we've established that neither one of us is playing games, where do we go from here? What do you want from this relationship?"

* * * * *

74

"I can't really answer that question, I guess Liza," Karina admitted on a choked cry, her last conversation with Cooper reverberating in her ears.

"Is it too hard to believe that I could find a man like that? Someone who would fall for me as hard as I obviously fell for him? To believe in the whole notion of love at first sight? Don't I deserve the fantasy?"

Liza didn't say a word, but the look in her eyes filled Karina with shame and she turned her face away. She felt Liza reach out for her, and she turned her body into her embrace and hugged her hard. Kari buried her face in her friend's chest and cried.

"You deserve that and more, baby girl. And one day you'll get everything you deserve," Liza promised softly.

* * * * *

"Hello."

"Hello, is Design of a Lifetime?" The woman on the other end asked.

"Yes it is, I'm sorry. I was expecting a call from someone else on this line. This is Karina with Design of a lifetime, I'm sorry!"

"If it's a bad time, I can call you back another time. I was interested in having my site redesigned," the woman on the other end said.

"No, no. This is a perfect time. I'm sorry. I haven't really been myself today. Let's start over, okay?" Karina asked on a forced laugh, "Design of a Lifetime, this is Karina Woodson, may I help you?"

"Yes! My name is Angela Tolson. Six months ago, I started a web-based boutique and recently I've had a boom in business and I'd like my website redesigned!" Her enthusiasm was warm and contagious, and Karina found herself liking the young woman instantly.

"Great, Angela. That's my specialty, small business designs and redesigns and we'll make your presence known on the web! What type of business do you have? And could you give me the website URL?" Karina fell in line instantly with the young woman's enthusiasm, and went straight into business mode.

"Sure, its www.*TheWorldTraveler.com* and I sell one of a kind jewelry and accessories from around the world. I have some really beautiful pieces, and my prices are reasonable. I think that's why business is going so well. I sell my pieces for less than some of the more expensive boutiques do and I try and give my customers one-on-one attention, even though our interaction is via the internet," Angela told her on one long breath.

As she'd been speaking, Karina had quickly logged onto the net and typed in the web address. Within seconds the site loaded and Karina was pleased with what the young woman had created on her own. "Okay! Let's go check it out," Karina laughed.

Sometimes Karina got scared at some of the homemade creations she came across. She knew the client meant well, and had done the best they could with limited HTML skills, but like her Big Momma used to say, some of the sites were a *hot mess*. She hated to be mean, even in her own thoughts, but it was true.

"Your site looks wonderful Angela," she complimented the girl. "But I can definitely help you jazz it up a bit! Why don't I shoot some ideas your way, and we can go from there?"

"Sounds great. What do you have in mind?"

"The good news is that I'll only have to put in a lot of work initially but after that, maintenance is easy. Looking at your site, we can easily rewrite the web pages with searching capabilities. So for instance, if one of your customers wants to view all purses you sell for under forty dollars, they can see a page with only these products."

"Wow. You can do that?"

"It wouldn't work with the way it's currently set up, but with a little HTML magic, your pages will be personalized just the way you want!" Karina promised on a laugh.

"Sign me up!" Angela said, and both women went to work plotting the redesign of the site.

* * * * *

After Karina hung up the phone with Angel Tolson, a big smile remained on her face. So what if she still felt a little ache in her heart, it probably was the tofu lasagna she'd eaten earlier that refused to digest.

It had *nothing* to do with Cooper.

The smile slipped a little, but with determination, Karina turned her thoughts away from the man who'd captured her heart, and on to the more rewarding task of redesigning the site.

The smile fell off her face when she realized her new client had the same last name as the man she'd fallen in love with.

Chapter Twelve

❧

"Well?"

"Well what?"

"Don't play games with me, Angel. Did you call her?"

Angela Tolson looked at her big brother and considered continuing her teasing. But the look in his eyes suggested she not, so for once, she listened to her inner cautionary voice, and decided not to yank his chain.

"Yes I did," was all she said. She couldn't resist a *tiny* bit of teasing. She retrieved the pot from the overhead cabinet in the large airy kitchen.

They were in their mother's home, where Angela and her twin sister continued to live. Cooper had come home earlier in the day to ask her if she would be interested in his financing the redesign of her website. She'd looked at him like he'd grown horns…

"What? Are you serious? Of course!" She'd whooped and jumped up and grabbed him around the neck and hugged hard. She leaned back in the embrace to ask, "Why the change of heart?"

Cooper had been the one to give her the upfront money she'd needed to start the business and had been adamant about her doing the rest. The fact that he *volunteered* more financial aide gave her pause.

"What? You don't want the help Angel girl?" he'd teased and ruffled her hair like she was ten years old as she jumped out of his arms.

Cooper had a tendency to treat her and the rest of her sisters as though he were their father. When their father had died, Angela and her sister had been young, and Cooper had taken over as head of the house. He'd only been a young man himself, but he took his duty seriously, and did his best to make sure they were all taken care of.

But he could be a total scrooge with doling out the cash. So when he offered to give it up freely, she'd jumped at the chance. He'd even given her the web designer to contact. Said he'd come across the name from an associate.

Angela had really liked the woman. She had a contagious enthusiasm that came across without benefit of a face-to-face meeting, and they'd had a great time shooting ideas back and forth. After she ended her conversation with Karina, Angel was more excited than ever about her web-based business.

As her glance stole over her brother, his nonchalance wasn't fooling her for a minute. She stopped her search for the pan and glanced at her brother. She tilted her head to the side, and really *looked* at him.

"Who is this woman to you, Coop?" she demanded with dawning realization.

* * * * *

Cooper stared at his sister. He felt his cheeks warm at the way she was staring at him. Like he had grown horns.

He'd been busting his butt at work, assigning projects to his small staff, and working on his client's portfolios so that he could take time off. He'd not seen Karina in over a week. And it was killing him.

After she'd called to say she'd gotten her period, he'd felt a sharp pang of disappointment, which should have scared him shitless. But it didn't. It only confirmed what he thought was impossible. He'd fallen in love with her.

He, who'd thought the concept of love at first sight a ridiculous notion invented by romance writers.

How in the world could you meet someone and know in that very instant they were yours? How could you look in a woman's sad brown eyes and know without being told she was your soul mate? That her funny, sometimes distracted, warm, loving personality would draw you in and completely wrap itself around your heart?

In little over a week.

Damn.

Cooper laughed out loud. Well, if someone had told him that a week ago, he would have thought they were crazy. He scratched his head and looked at his sister as she sat there waiting for his answer.

"Nothing gets by you does it Angel girl?" he laughed.

"Oooh. This is going to be good, isn't it? Okay spill..." His sister laughed with him and pulled up a stool to sit. She cupped her face with her hands, and propped her elbows on the counter.

"Karina's a wonderful designer, and I want to help her business. So I'm willing to pay for her to redesign your site."

"That's it? Come on, Coop! Give. There's got to be more to it than you trying to get some! Is that what this is all about? Are you trying to impress some chick to get laid?" His irreverent sister asked. "Well, if it helps me take my business to the next level and helps my brother...um...get some, I'm all game!"

"I don't need your help in *getting some* you brat. And it's no game. You'll do well to remember that when you meet your new sister-in-law," Cooper told her straight-faced, and openly laughed when Angela's jaw literally dropped.

Chapter Thirteen

෨

"I think that's it, Karina! I can't believe it's over." Susan laughed as she arched her back and rotated her head. It had been a long day and the two women had each wrapped the last gift for the night, as the department was closing early on Founder's Day.

"Lord have mercy! If I never see another perfume bottle, cashmere sweater, or pair of pearl earrings with a cute little bow at the top, it will be too soon!" Karina said, as she too arched her back. The strain of standing on her feet for eight hours was murder on her sore lower back muscles.

"I hear you," Susan seconded, as she began the task of cleaning up ribbon, wrapping paper, and tape.

The two women worked harmoniously cleaning the department, until Susan asked, "Do you have any plans for the evening?"

Karina's pseudo attempt at lightheartedness crashed and burned at her feet.

Doggone it.

Just when she'd pushed his smiling, handsome, lying face to the back of her consciousness, one small question catapults him right back where he'd been from the moment she met him.

"No, not really. Probably work on a few clients' sites," she mumbled and put away the psychedelic pink wrapping paper she'd used to wrap the last customer's gift.

"Today? No hot date?" The older woman asked and laughed. She turned and looked at Karina, and her misery must have shown on her face because Susan's jovial expression was instantly dropped.

"Oh sweetie, I'm sorry. I wasn't thinking. I'm sure it will all work out," she said, and patted Karina's shoulder.

The day that Karina had returned to work, she'd given Susan the abridged version of her "date" with Cooper. She'd told her how he'd come back for his gifts, and with a bit of imaginative editing, told Susan that she and Cooper had spent time together.

Okay, so she out-and-out lied. But there was no way she'd tell the woman the truth—that she and Cooper had screwed like rabbits. After the reaction she'd gotten from Liza, she had no intention of going through a similar grill with a woman who was a casual friend.

But as the days had passed and she and Cooper had only spoken over the phone, her doubts and insecurities had reared their ugly collective heads and she'd broken down and told Susan *some* of the truth. She needed someone to talk to and Susan reminded her of her grandmother.

After she'd told the woman what happened, she'd mentally prepared herself to be flogged. Instead of fussing at her, the older woman hugged her, and said it would all work itself out. It always did, she said.

After she released her, the two women went back to work and Karina didn't mention Cooper to her again. But the simple words had calmed her spirit. She knew Susan was right. In the end, all things worked to the good, as Big Momma used to say.

"Don't worry about it, Susan. You're right, it'll all work out. So what about you? What plans do you and Harvey have?" she asked, infusing enthusiasm in her voice as she neatly changed the subject.

"I think I'll let him surprise me and take me to Carrabelle's," Susan laughed, allowing the change of topic. She and Harvey had been married over thirty years, and for every anniversary, birthday and special occasion, Harvey took her to the same restaurant where they first met. As a surprise.

As Karina giggled with her over Harvey's predictable behavior, the bell above the door jingled. Both women let out a groan because they'd forgotten to lock the door. Karina's groan turned into a small cry when Cooper waltzed into the room with a cheesy grin on his face.

* * * * *

Cooper rushed to make it to the department before closing. He knew they were closing early because Karina made it a point to tell him when they spoke on the phone the day before. He knew she wanted to see him. He longed to see her too. But he had to clear up his schedule, so that he could do this right.

A man only got one chance to do it right, and he wanted everything to be perfect. He'd secured reservations at the exclusive restaurant she'd told him was her favorite, the limo was waiting with champagne and flowers, and he didn't want to blow it.

Everything had to be perfect. They started their relationship full speed ahead. He wanted to do right by her this time. He wanted it to be something she'd never forget.

He was relieved when the door opened, and he rushed inside. Karina and Susan both looked at him with varying expressions crossing their face. At first glance, both women's faces showed disappointment at his entrance. Upon recognition of him, Susan's face split in an ear-to-ear grin, and Karina's…well hers defied description. Happy, sad, mad, pissed off, nonchalance.

In that order.

Oh hell. Things probably weren't going to go as smoothly as he thought…

* * * * *

No the hell he didn't!

No the hell he didn't think he could waltz in with that big shit-eating grin on his face, one hand held behind his back, probably holding some pretty, "let me see before I burst gift", that if she didn't see she'd burst... and *then* expect her to fall out crying, "Lord Jesus, my man is back, my man is back!" and turn flips, dips and cartwheels as she ran buck naked through Macy's...

"Karina?" he stopped her mental tirade in its tracks.

"I believe I'll leave you to lock up. Happy Founder's Day. I'll see you next week sweetie," Susan said, patting her on the shoulder.

"Oh. Yes. You too, Susan. I'll see you next week," she mumbled, her eyes trained straight on Cooper. She heard Susan laugh as she said goodbye and left the two of them alone.

Cooper slowly walked toward her. He didn't say a word, just kept smiling that small half-smile. The one that made her heart flip and jitters settle in her tummy with just one look. The one that made her want to attempt a Serena Williams move and try and leap across the counter that separated them and fling herself into his arms.

Instead, she attempted to be smooth. She wasn't about to show him how much he affected her. Let him work at it. Let him explain himself. No way was she going to show her emotions. She was cool. She was calm. She was in control...

"Where the hell have you been?" she cried out and did her version of Serena by hopping on the counter. That was as far as she could take it.

When he rushed to the counter and pulled her the rest of the way across, she grabbed him, and mentally calling herself a shameless hussy, kissed him with every bit of pent-up frustration, anger, and love she had in her heart.

"Baby, I'm sorry. I know. I know. You have every right to be upset with me. I wanted to see you, but I needed to clear my schedule, so that I could spend time with you. I tried to tell you that when we spoke on the phone. Didn't you believe me?" Cooper asked around her kisses, one hand stroking the length of her locs.

"Yes, but I didn't know what to think. I thought you didn't want me, that it was just a one-night stand, that you…" The rest of her rant was smothered by his kiss. He lifted her from the counter, and with her legs wrapped around his waist, he walked backwards to the door, and turned the lock.

"No interruptions from Walter this time," he said, and lifted her butt higher on his hips and strode purposely in the direction of the employee lounge.

"Where are we going?" she asked, as though she had *no* idea where they were headed. "Turn off the light just in case Walter does come by," she said, and felt the tips of her ears burn when he lifted his head from kissing her neck to give her a *look*.

"No use in getting busted for no reason," she said, and moved her neck, giving him the signal to nuzzle her again.

"No. What I have planned for you is illegal in a few states I think," he said and laughed when her eyes grew large in alarm.

"Oh Lord," was her only response.

* * * * *

Damn, he missed seeing her. It had only been a week, but it sure felt a lot longer. As he carried her through to the employees lounge, he couldn't stop kissing her.

After shouldering his way into the room, he slowed down and allowed her body to ease down the length of his. When he broke their kiss, he took her round face between his hands.

"Karina, I'm sorry. I didn't mean to hurt your feelings or make you wonder what was going on. I have a tendency to charge ahead and I get tunnel vision sometimes. It's something we'll work on."

Karina looked at him, and he saw the doubt flash in her eyes before they cleared. "It's as much my fault as yours. This is new, and I tend to wallow in self-doubt. I could have just as easily expressed how I was feeling instead of hiding my feelings. Pretending that I was cool with everything, including you having your sister hire me to redesign her site."

Cooper wondered when she'd figure that one out.

"How'd you know it was my sister? Do a little cyber hunting?" he ventured a guess.

"It wasn't that hard Cooper. Any amateur could have found out the connection between you and Angela. Why'd you do it? And notice I'm not flogging you about sending business my way. 'By any means necessary' is my personal motto. Send me as much business as you want!" she told him and shrugged, a half-smile on her pretty lips.

He laughed out loud. He'd worried how she'd react when she figured out it was his sister. He hadn't wanted her to think he was buying her off, and had even thought about asking his sister to use a different last name, but knew if he did, he would never hear the end of it.

"When we first met, you were depressed about losing a client to a competitor. I knew my sister wanted to expand her business and needed someone to help her with her site."

"That's it. That's your entire explanation?"

Cooper laughed. "What else do you want me to say, baby? Two women I love needed me. It's a no-brainer as far as I'm concerned."

"What? What two women you love?" she asked, and pushed away from the luring temptation of his lips.

"I know what I said, Karina." He pulled her closer and leisurely kissed her. He caressed her lips with a smooth glide of his tongue. "Ummm. You taste so good. Have I told you how good you taste and how much I missed you?"

It took everything she had inside, but she pulled away from his sexy mouth, and stared dumb founded at him. "No way. You can't just say something like that and start kissing on me like that."

"Why not? Don't you love me?"

"Cooper, let's stop for a minute. I can't think. We just met, no way are you in love with me. I mean, I have a lot of things to work on, I promised I'd start dieting, my business is just getting off the ground, then there's my addiction to Little Debbie Oatmeal Creme Pies, and…"

"Karina. Do you love me?"

She stopped. Here she was babbling about Little Debbie, once again, and he's proclaiming his love for her, asking her if she loved him in return. What in the world was wrong with her?

"Yes. I love you," she said. "But I think it's too soon, I don't know you as well as I should, we probably should take it slower…Liza says we should get to know each other…"

He swallowed the rest of her diatribe with a tongue-scorching kiss.

Cooper picked her up and carried her the short distance to the table in the middle of the room and planted her on top.

"To hell with the rest, Karina. This is about you and me. Not anyone else. I don't give a damn what Liza says or thinks. This is personal," he said as he lifted her ass to pull her jeans down her legs. With impatience bordering on savageness, he ripped her favorite pink panties in half.

"Damn it, Cooper, those were my favorite panties! You owe…ohhhhh!" she finished on a long sigh.

Right in the middle of her rant, he spread her legs, separated her vaginal lips, and licked her with a long, slick stroke. Karina spread her legs further apart, one leg dangling, the other hooked over his shoulder as he ate, licked, and rubbed his face in her pussy. She felt greedy. She wanted everything he had to offer.

He gave her what she wanted. With her legs spread so far apart, she was wide open, and he took full advantage of her. One of his big hands went beneath her sweater in search of one her breasts and the other toyed and played with her pussy as he laved the hard nub of her clit relentlessly.

He worked two fingers into her the tight opening as he continued to lick and eat her out. She was on the brink of orgasm, and he worked her over in earnest. Within moments, she screamed and came so hard her entire body bucked off the table. Cooper kept his mouth over her entire pussy the whole time she was coming, relentless in his desire to give her what she needed. What she craved.

When she finally slumped back on the table, the orgasm leaving her totally spent, he stood and all she heard was the rasp of his zipper. The next thing she felt were her thighs grasped and spread apart before she felt his hard cock impale her.

"Cooper!" she cried.

She felt stuffed. She'd forgotten how big he was. How he filled her like she'd never been filled before. She felt every thick, hard inch of his massive cock. She had to bite the insides of her cheeks to prevent a scream.

He leaned down and covered her mouth with his. "Ready baby?" he asked against her mouth. She barely nodded her head before he went to work.

He withdrew slowly and she instantly cried a protest.

"Sshh, its okay baby. I won't leave you. You feel so damn good, that pussy is so nice and slick, I'd die before I leave this," he promised, his breath hot against her face.

Nice and slow, he rolled his hips, grinding the full length of his cock into her. Doing her the way she liked to be done. "Cooper, that feels so good. Don't stop, keep it right there," she begged shamelessly.

He laughed rough and low. "I'm not going anywhere." He tightened his hold on her butt and moved her body for a better angle as he dug into her. "Come for me baby, come for me. And let me hear you say my name when you come this time."

That was all the encouragement she needed. As he pumped into her, loving her harder and sweeter than he ever had, she screamed, "Coooooooper!" and came so hard she saw stars.

Her orgasm triggered his, and she held on for dear life, gripping his muscled butt as he gave one final push. The muscles in his neck corded in stark relief when he came.

"Karina!" he roared her name long and loud, and she felt the scorching splash of his hot cum splash deep inside the walls of her womb. For a long moment they both lay limp against each other, breathing harsh and loud in the quiet of the room.

"So you love me, huh?" he asked her with just the tiniest bit of smugness in his sexy *do me* voice. Of course she was all *done* out at that point. She decided to be nice and not smack him for his smug tone.

"You're all right, I guess." she giggled when he pinched her backside.

He'd made a small pallet from their discarded clothes on the carpeted floor of the lounge and Karina lay nestled in front of him.

"Would I be better if I gave you this?" he asked, and reached behind them to fumble in the pocket of his jeans. She stretched her neck in curiosity, wondering what he was searching for.

When he pulled out a small square box her heart almost leaped out of her chest. *No way, no way, no way, no way...*

"Karina, I don't want this to end. I don't want you to doubt my feelings for you. I knew from the minute I saw you that you belonged with me. It sounds crazy. People are probably going to talk about us like we've lost our minds. But I don't care. You once told me you wanted to expand your horizons, remember?" he asked, and brushed the solitary tear away from her cheek.

"Yes. I remember," she whispered.

"I'm asking that you take a chance and believe. That you give us a chance to expand our horizons with each other." Karina was completely overwhelmed with the tender emotion he allowed to freely show on his face.

She was stunned as she looked at the perfectly cut emerald that he held out in front for her.

She was speechless. She felt like turning cartwheels. She felt like jumping up and running buck naked through Macy's wearing nothing but the gorgeous ring Cooper held out for her.

Was he serious? As she glanced back up in his eyes, she answered her own silent question. He was serious as a stroke, as Big Momma used to say. She felt tears sting her eyes again as her gaze returned to the beautiful ring.

She'd been a slobbering fool every since he walked into the store over an hour ago. Now here she was crying again.

But damn, who wouldn't? She thought. Less than a week ago, she was sad, lonely, and broke. Scared to take a chance.

But she was tired of hiding, and damn tired of being scared. She was going to grab life by the lapels and hang on for the ride. She wanted to take a chance for once in her life and believe that what was meant for her was meant for her alone.

She refused to give in to fear. Fear was such a worthless emotion anyway.

She turned her body to fully look into his face. She saw the honesty and love in his eyes. She also saw a spark of doubt—fear. She took both sides of his face, and kissed him with all the emotion and love she felt for him.

"Yes," she said, and had to clear the frog from her throat. "Yes. I'll marry you." No sooner had the words left her mouth when Cooper grabbed her and hugged her hard.

Tears streamed down her face. This time they weren't tears of frustration. There was no way on God's green earth she was going to let him go. He was special. She could feel it deep inside, in that place that defied logic. That part that was now whispering to her to believe...

Nope. She wasn't running this time. She wanted to give them the chance to explore and broaden their horizons...together.

The End

PULL MY HAIR

໑

Dedication

ஒ

This is dedicated to my beautiful soul sister, Tina. Love you, girl.

Trademarks Acknowledgement

ஒ

The author acknowledges the trademarked status and trademark owners of the following wordmarks mentioned in this work of fiction:

BlackBerry: Research In Motion Limited

Bose: Bose Corporation

Little Debbie: McKee Foods Corporation

Louis Vuitton Mallatier: LVMH

Mercedes: DaimlerChrystler AG Corporation

Prada: Prefel S.A. Corporation

Yoplait Marques Internationales Corporation (France)

Chapter One

ဢ

"You don't pull it anymore, so why the hell did I need all that hair for anyway?" Liza yelled at the top of her lungs. Buck-naked she knelt on the bed beside her husband's lounging form.

After she yelled her response, she promptly broke into hysterical tears and plopped back down on the bed.

"Liza, what in the world are you talking about? Baby, you're not making any sense! And what does hair pulling have to do with us having sex?" He sat up swiftly and tried to pull her back down onto his chest.

"If you were still *pulling* it, you'd *know* what I was talking about!" she snatched her body away, refusing to allow him to pull her back in. "Oh just forget it, Greg! It's a lost cause anyway."

Liza sprang from the bed and her newly bobbed, freshly relaxed hair whipped around her face as she grabbed the black silk kimono sprawled on the foot of the bed. With precise, angry motion, she shoved her arms through the sleeves. After she tied the sash, she nearly ran to the bedroom door with her need to escape.

As she was opening the door to leave, her husband strode up behind her and slammed it shut. He turned her around to face him.

All six-foot-plus of gloriously naked, ticked off male glared down at her. She read it all in his deep, green eyes, there was anger, irritation, concern, and…horniness. Her glance ran over his angry face, noting the red flush of anger that ran alongside his squared jaw. She turned away from him and reopened the door. She refused to be drawn back in. And that's all it would take. All she'd have to do is take one look into his eyes and she was sprung.

Just like an addict.

"Don't run away from me!" His breathing was harsh as he made the demand.

He slammed the door shut. Again. This time he boxed her in, giving her no chance to escape him.

"Come on, baby. If you're happy about your hair then so am I. Let's just make love okay? It's been a few days, between working later hours on this case and your period...big daddy needs some lovin'." He laughed low and bent his dark head to nuzzle the side of her neck as he stood behind her.

Big daddy was right.

She could feel his long, thick penis nudge her butt as he pulled her close against his chest. She tried her *damnedest* to stay rigid against his hard, tightly muscled body. She *refused* to acknowledge to herself how good his rock-hard thighs felt resting against the back of her thighs or how good it felt to feel his cock push against her, looking to gain entry.

Hmmm. *She was so wet, she was afraid she'd start dripping all over her new, silk oriental rug.*

"You don't like my hair," she murmured softly.

No way was she going to let him off the hook. She didn't give a damn how good he felt rubbing against her. She'd cut her hair and she'd had to bring it to his attention.

She clenched her legs together to ward off any more treacherous, wayward cream making its way down her thighs.

"I *do* like your hair, baby. Just come back to bed," he whispered. He tucked a stand of her bobbed, bone-straight, relaxed hair behind her ear and trailed a line of kisses down her neck.

The real issue was not her hair. If he didn't know that, then they were in more trouble than she thought. It was as though he didn't notice anything about her anymore. As though he no longer *saw* her.

She moved her head to the side to give him better access.

"I love everything about you." His deep, hoarse voice sent shivers running down her spine. "From the top of your newly cut hair to the bottom of your pretty brown feet. *And* your stinky little toes."

The real issue was that they had lost...touch, with each other, not the fact that she'd cut her hair. The fact that he'd not noticed her new haircut was just the icing on the big old fat chocolate cake.

"We don't even have to go to the bed if you don't want," he continued his low-talking, sensual barrage. He lifted her arms out in front of her and placed them on the door.

After seven years of marriage, she felt disconnected from her husband.

His kisses trailed down her spine and she cried out in automatic response when he delivered a light nip to one of her butt cheeks. He laughed when she yelped and grabbed the flesh between his lips and suckled the small injury.

Damn. No matter what, he still knew what she liked when they made love.

His other hand trailed to the front of her body and he sank two big fingers deep inside her wet channel and she cried out from the exquisite feeling. With an expertise born from intimate knowledge of what turned her on, he stroked her deeply. He slowly lapped a leisurely tongue over her butt as his fingers pumped in rhythm inside her vagina.

He added his thumb to the mix and began to torture her clit. The rough pad of his thumb circled her tightly drawn nubbin. She felt like screaming the pleasure was so intense.

"Do you like that, baby? Does that feel good? Do you want to come, Li?" he asked in that dark voice that made her squirm even more around his talented fingers.

"Yessss," she whimpered on a long hiss. "Please, baby…let me come." Liza heard the desperation in her own voice but didn't give a damn. She was so close, her orgasm was just hovering right there…out of reach.

"What do you have to say in order to come? What do I like to hear?"

She knew what he wanted to hear, what he wanted her to say in order to bring her to release. "Please, big daddy, I want to come. Let me come. I need it so badly," she whispered, head hung low, strung out from the intensity of the feelings he'd created in her.

"That's what I like to hear," he said and laughed low in his throat the same time that he pinched her clit, not hard enough to hurt but hard enough that she felt the small sting.

She felt the orgasm as it rippled through her body right before she damn near exploded as she came. She cried out as she bucked against his fingers and had to hold the doorframe or she'd have fallen down straight on her face. Her heart beat so strongly from the intensity of her climax that she felt tears sting her eyes.

When he flipped her around and her back slammed against the door, she widened her stance in automatic response. It had been over a week since they'd made love and she was ready for anything he had in store for her.

Anything.

He teased her by brushing his hand back and forth over the springy curls covering her mound. He leaned down and took a deep breath. "Ummm. Your kitty always smells so good, baby," his breath was becoming more ragged the more turned on he became.

Liza loved when he called her vagina, her kitty. The lord only knew the man knew how to make it purr.

With bated breath, she waited to feel the heated stroke of his talented tongue on her crease. She allowed her eyes to drift closed in anticipation.

The sudden and very jarring ring of his cell phone caused Liza to jerk her eyes open and whip her head around to locate the offending sound. She looked down at her husband as he crouched down in front of her, face inches away from her aching clit...and wanted to *scream* when she saw the resigned look that crossed his handsome face.

"*Oh, hell no*! Greg, they'll call back. No way are you going to do this to me!" she wailed in disbelief. She felt like howling when he raised himself and quickly kissed her, frustration stamped on his face.

"Baby, I'm sorry. This isn't easy for me either, look at my damn cock!" he said and she *refused* to look down for fear she'd jump on it and do it and him some serious damage.

"You know, I'm waiting to hear from my client. I go to trial soon and I have to get the case ready. This will only take a minute, I promise. That's Renita; she wouldn't call unless it was important. We'll pick this up where we left off..."

His voice trailed off as he swiftly crossed their large bedroom to reach the phone before Renita could hang up. Renita was his paralegal assistant and he'd assigned a *special* ring tone when she called so he'd know it was her.

Greg gazed at her intently as he picked up the phone and mouthed an apology. He held out a consoling hand when she flipped him off.

Whatever.

His loss.

With a dejected sigh, she left the bedroom and walked down the long, curved mahogany stairwell and made her way through their beautifully decorated home.

Her bare toes sunk into the deep pile of the Persian rugs that covered her hardwood floors as she padded barefoot through the house, making her way to the kitchen. Maybe a cup of herbal tea was just what she needed. Her best friend Karina swore by the stuff.

As she walked through her house, her eyes slowly glanced around, admiring her home for what it was. A sign that she'd made it. She'd made it out of that life she'd grown up in, a life of food stamps and government housing.

And free cheese given out once a month at the local Catholic Church.

And a mother who couldn't wait until she was eighteen and "grown" before she left town with no forwarding address, but had no problem calling once or twice a year to hit her up for money.

She'd grown up in the north side of Stanton, the part of town where welfare and public assistance was a way of life for many of its inhabitants. A place she *refused* to revisit.

No matter what.

She reached the kitchen, searched for the small red kettle, and filled it with water from her porcelain sink before placing it on the stove to boil.

Liza loved her porcelain sink.

She leaned against the counter and smiled as she thought back to the day when she and Greg had gone shopping for the sink. It was the day before Thanksgiving and his parents were coming over to celebrate Thanksgiving Day with them.

She'd wanted the dinner to be perfect for her new in-laws. She admitted to herself that she was nervous. Not only was she preparing dinner for her in-laws, but she still felt as though she had to prove something to them; that their son had married the right woman.

There was a part of her that wondered at their easy acceptance of her, and not just because she was black. They'd not even questioned it when her only family to show up for their small wedding was a few friends from work, along with her best friend Karina and Karina's mother. At least not verbally.

But as nice as the Colburn's were, Liza had never made a connection with them. Greg's parents were nice enough, but she'd always felt as though she fell short in his mother's eyes. Whenever they would spend time with his parents, she often felt his mother's assessing scrutiny when she thought Liza wasn't aware of her close regard.

She remembered how badly she wanted everything to be *just right* for his parent's visit on that Thanksgiving holiday. Greg had *assured* her that he knew what he was doing and could install the new sink. She wasn't sure who she was more surprised, herself or her new husband, when the sink had sprung a leak. So close to Thanksgiving and there were no plumbers available on such short notice. Liza felt like screaming.

* * * * *

"Greg, what are we going to do? Your parents are coming over for dinner tomorrow and I don't have a sink! Oh lord, they're going to think I'm a raving loon!" Liza cried and fell on the floor in a dejected heap, covering her face in her hands.

"Baby, they are *not* going to think you're a loon, raving or not!" Greg plopped down next to her on the floor and lifted her into place on his lap, laughing as he rubbed his big hands over her hair.

"It's not funny," she cried and punched him before laying her head on his chest.

"Sweetheart, I'm not laughing at you. It's going to be all right. We'll find a plumber, I promise you," he told her and lifted her chin. "And if we don't, it's not that big of a deal. My parents will love you no matter what, turkey or no turkey. Okay?" He looked deep in her eyes with a smile on his handsome face and she melted.

Her eyes roamed over his face from his deep-set green eyes and darkly fringed eyelashes, down his proud aquiline nose, to the small cleft in his stubble-covered chin. All he ever had to do was look at her and smile and she was like hot butter on plastic wrap in his hands.

"And how about instead of worrying about the sink, we christen it instead?" he asked, as he nibbled the side of her neck.

"What do you mean *christen* it? How do you christen a sink?" She laughed through her tears. He'd taken her mind off the busted sink for a minute.

"Well..." The wicked gleam in his green eyes alone had her instantly wet and wanting.

Damn.

How did he do this to her? They'd been married for two weeks and she couldn't get enough of the man. Thank God he was as sprung on her as she was on him or she'd be in trouble.

It wasn't just how fine he was that did it for her. Although that never hurt. How could six-foot-plus of overwhelming male *not* do it for a woman? He wasn't over muscled like the *hulk*, but the man was packed with chiseled, defined muscles that turned her to hot butter whenever he glanced her way with that *look*.

She looked down at his arms wrapped loosely around her. She loved the contrast in their skin colors. Although Greg wasn't particularly pale, because of the deep brown color of her skin, the contrast in their complexion was heightened even more.

And sexy as hell to her.

He lifted her easily into his arms and placed her on the counter. That was the other thing she loved about him. How easily he picked her up and carried her around. As though she were his personal baby doll.

Although she was thin, she was tall and she loved the fact that she had to lift her arms in order to place them around his neck. She loved when he took control.

Her secret kink was her desire to be dominated.

"How 'bout I show you what it means to *christen* something, baby?" He laughed throatily, raised her butt high in the air and slipped her panties down her long legs. After flipping her underwear to the side, he lifted her pleated miniskirt and allowed it to fan around her thighs as he spread her legs.

"What are you doing, Greg?" she asked, out of breath with her heart racing because of what he was about to do to her in the middle of the day…on her brand-new kitchen counter.

Her suspicions were confirmed when she felt the long, hot sweep of his tongue against her aching mound. He separated the folds of her cleft with his fingers and drew her clit deeply into his mouth, swirling it around his tongue, working it until she thought she'd die from the pleasure.

She held on to the edge of the counter, helplessly accepting his sensuous torture. "Oh Lord, Greg…what if someone sees us?" she asked as she squirmed, bare-assed on the counter, moaning when he slowly eased two big fingers into her tight opening.

"Who gives a damn? You're my wife. We're legal now." He removed his face from her mound long enough to answer and laughed gruffly. With a slow smile and a wink he bent his head to go back to his feast.

He captured her clit gently between his lips and worked it carefully, swirling his tongue around the small nubbin. He licked and ate at her pussy like it was manna from Heaven, with his face buried so far between her legs she could only see the top of his head.

Damn, he knew how to eat pussy.

He'd been the first man she'd allowed to eat her out and it had taken *much* begging on his part for him to sample her goodies. That and a ring on her finger.

Had she known what she'd been missing, she may have given in a long time ago, with or without the ring.

She loved the way his dark, curly head looked between her spread thighs. He stroked and ate at her until she was weak and forced to lie back against the counter.

It was either lie down or fall down.

As he laved her relentlessly, Liza could feel her orgasm bubbling up, ready to break free. She bucked against him and rose from the counter to grab either side of his face and smash it into her pussy, grinding herself helplessly against him.

All previous shame and decorum flew out the window.

She felt the orgasm rip through her body and moments later she uttered a long keening sound of release, tears falling down her face from the intensity of her orgasm. When she finally relaxed her body, it was to see Greg smiling at her.

"You like the way I ate that tasty little pussy, didn't you, Li? I did too." His voice was low and his breathing ragged. "Are you nice and ready for something more, sweetheart?" he asked and rose from his kneeling position on the floor to stand big and tall above her on the counter.

She could barely talk and was afraid that if she tried, she'd embarrass herself so she simply nodded her head.

"Good. Because I'm ready to give it to you," he told her before lifting her ass high and away from the counter with one hand. With the other he unzipped and freed himself from the confines of his jeans just far enough to allow him to plunge his big, hard cock deep.

They exhaled simultaneously long and harsh, the mutual feel of the other giving them pause. He was so big and she was so tight, they both grimaced in sensual delight as their bodies adjusted to one another.

Greg smiled that smile she loved so much as he leaned down to gently kiss her on the corner of her mouth. She could smell the essence of herself on his breath.

"I love you *so* much, baby. No matter what happens, busted sink or anything else, we'll work it out together. Always have faith in me, okay?" he asked. And only after she nodded, tears on her lashes, did he begin to slowly grind into her…

* * * * *

The screech of the kettle brought her out of her memories. Her breathing was heavy, and surprised she glanced down to see her hands buried beneath the folds of her vagina, as she sought release from her own horniness, pent-up anger and frustration.

She quickly completed what she started, adding a second finger to speed along the orgasm she felt ready to release. As she worked her clit, trying hard to reach the pinnacle, she looked up and standing in the doorway was Greg, with his Vuitton briefcase in one hand, Blackberry in the other, staring at her with wide eyes, mouth slightly ajar and one dark eyebrow slightly raised.

Chapter Two

ဢ

Greg felt bad, but there was nothing he could do about it. Liza was going to have his balls on a platter.

He had to take the call from his assistant. His client needed him, the trial was coming up and he currently didn't have a damn thing to help his case, nothing that would get his client out of paying his cheating wife the multimillion dollar settlement that she was demanding.

Renita had called to tell him she needed him in the office, because she'd found some evidence that he'd been looking for that might help their case. He'd been so relieved, he'd lost track of time as they spoke, and when he looked around after he'd gotten off the phone, Liza was nowhere around.

His manhood was still hard, the excitement he'd had for his wife hadn't gone away after hearing the good news and he wanted to make love. He ran a quick hand over his cock and sighed.

"Too bad, boy. I don't think it's going to happen. I have to go to the office and meet Renita and I don't think Liza would take too well to me trying to get a quickie in before I have to go. It's what she's so pissed off about now."

He walked over to his side of the large walk-in closet and pulled a dark, blue suit from the hanger as he thought over the situation with his wife. He eyes stole over to her side of the immense closet and he smiled.

The woman had a serious shoe addiction. She kept them in individual small plastic containers with a picture of the shoe on the outside of the box. It was the strangest thing he'd ever seen. He'd asked her why she did that and she acted as though it was the most normal thing to do. She'd said if she didn't put a picture on the outside she'd have no idea which pair they were.

They'd just gotten married at the time and had been moving their things into their new home. He had no idea she needed the pictures until she started moving in her clothes and shoes. He knew he must have looked crazy staring but she had enough shoes to start her own department store.

But he liked providing for her. Liza had grown up very poor and had moved around a lot as a kid. She told him that she and a cousin once had to share a pair of shoes because her mother had been between jobs and couldn't buy her a new pair.

That explained, in part, her shoe addiction.

And besides that, the woman just loved shoes.

But in all their seven years of marriage, sometimes he felt as though he really didn't know his wife. He knew all her likes and dislikes. They discussed everything from politics to religion to her favorite ice cream flavor. They shared most of the same values and concerns about the world.

In the past, they'd spent long hours talking about what was going on in the world, but he'd always felt as though she kept a part of herself hidden away from him. That she closed a part of herself off, not only to him, but to the world at large. Maybe even to herself.

She rarely talked about her childhood and always said it was the past and was a place she never planned on revisiting.

Until last week, he'd always thought it was not worth discussing if it caused her such undue stress. If she didn't want to talk about her childhood, he respected her right not to do so. He didn't think it had any bearing or impact on their relationship.

He no longer felt that way.

He picked up his briefcase and pocketed his wallet as he walked out of the bedroom. He knew she was going to be pissed. He'd promised her they'd spend the day together with no work interference. They'd already started the morning off badly when he'd made the comment about her new haircut.

She'd cut off her hair and he'd innocently asked her why she did it. She still looked beautiful to him, long hair or short. It just came as a surprise. When he'd come home from work, she'd greeted him and he hadn't paid as much attention as he should have and properly complimented her.

It was late when he got home and he only wanted to take a shower and curl up with her in the bed.

They'd talked as he showered and done just that. He fell asleep listening to her talk about her day, in her low, husky, sexy voice.

God he loved her voice.

It was one of the things that had first attracted him to her. She had a scratchy low voice that captured his attention from the first time he heard her speak when he was in law school. He'd dropped by his favorite diner for a late night meal after studying for the bar exam.

He'd ordered from the menu without looking up and when the waitress had spoken, asking him if that was all, he'd glanced up and was startled when he heard her speak. Her voice was low and earthy sounding and caused an immediate reaction before he'd seen her. When he looked into her face, his fate had been sealed. She was beautiful. Tall and lean, she had the body of a long distance runner.

She wore her hair straight and long and pulled away from her face. Her face was angular and her skin was the color of coffee with just a hint of cream and just as smooth looking.

Her eyes were large and slightly tilted in the corner, giving her a kewpie doll look. Her small bow-shaped lips were an off shade of pink and the bottom lip was fractionally plumper than the top. Her lips were small but lush and he instantly got hard thinking how good they'd feel wrapped around him.

Greg remembered how he'd taken his time looking her over from the top of her head down the length of her body. She was thin but she had nice round hips and a nipped in waist that made his imagination run wild. He envisioned how he'd be able to rock her, holding on to those nice round curves the whole time.

His gaze had gone back to her mouth.

Damn.

He must have stared too long at her pretty lush mouth. She'd coughed lightly to get his attention and he glanced away from her mouth and noticed she had one hand on her on hip, with her head tilted to the side, staring at him.

He'd liked the sexy smile that flickered around her mouth. She *knew* he liked what he saw.

That had been the beginning of their whirlwind relationship. It had taken a few trips back to the café, but she finally agreed to go out with him on a date. They'd dated for a short time before they'd become intimate. He'd been the first man she'd been with sexually and that had turned him on.

He loved that he'd been the first man to introduce her to lovemaking as well as being the man to introduce her to the finer things in life.

She'd been in graduate school when they met and had been working at the café in order to pay her tuition. Within their short time of dating, Greg had known she was the woman for him and had asked her to move in with him. He'd been surprised when she declined his offer.

He thought she was playing hard to get until she continued to reject his offer. She would make love to him, let him do all types of freaky shit to her, but she drew the line at living with him. She said she wasn't going to live in sin and chance busting hell wide open for him.

He'd had no idea what she was talking about "busting hell wide open". She explained that if she lived with him without benefit of marriage, she'd go straight to hell in a handbasket.

Greg laughed out loud in memory. He knew then and there this woman was his. She was a nut.

His smile died as quickly as it erupted. He missed the "nut". They seemed to be strangers more than anything else lately and it was partially his fault. The other part...

As he walked through their home, he glanced around at the works of art on the walls, the Persian rugs and Waterford crystal in the mahogany, glassed-in curio cabinet. He'd bought it all for her. Nothing was too good for his Liza. She deserved the best.

He'd been working longer hours lately, taking on more clients and they seemed to be growing farther apart. His latest case had him in the office so late that he not only missed dinner with her, he missed going to bed with her, arriving at home when she was already sound asleep in bed. His shoulders slightly sagged when he thought how angry she would be when he told her that he wouldn't be able to spend the day with her. As he rounded the corner and walked into the kitchen, it took his mind a moment to catch up with the scene he was presented with.

"What the fuck...?"

* * * * *

Here she was, in the middle of the kitchen in broad daylight with all the blinds opened, friggin' masturbating.

And Greg busts her.

Liza was so mortified. She wanted a big hole to appear smack down in the middle of her newly tiled kitchen floor, swallow her up whole. And die.

Damn it. Simply die.

"Liza, what are you doing?" Greg's deep voice sounded puzzled. As though he couldn't *possible* understand what she'd been doing, leaning against the counter with her hands buried in her pussy.

What? Did he think she was hunting for buried treasure?

"What does it look like I'm doing, Greg? I had to do something. Obviously you have no intention of helping me out!" Instead of crying and running off embarrassed, she decided to hell with it. So what if he caught her playing with herself! She needed relief and from the looks of the briefcase in his hand...

"Where are you going? Renita called so now you have to go running off to the office? What about our plans, Greg?" She brazened it out. She *refused* to discuss what she'd been doing. It was his fault anyway for leaving her high and dry. She calmly turned the faucet on and washed her hands before drying them and turning back to the stove.

To hell with it...whatever.

* * * * *

Liza busied herself at the stove fussing with the kettle, looking at everything but Greg. She may play the role of sophisticate for her friends and the women at the country club, but he knew her well enough to know it was a partial front. Always perfectly coiffed and immaculate in her dress. Never a hair out of place or the wrong shoes on her perfectly matched ensemble.

He loved looking at his wife. She was so beautiful to him that after seven years of marriage, all he had to do was look at her and he was rock hard. Her smooth chocolate skin and deep, dark eyes turned him on like no other.

Her face was angular but not sharp and she had the sexiest lips he'd ever seen. He loved the way the bottom lip poked out a bit farther than the top. He loved pulling that bit of lushness into his mouth and nursing it.

And her smile.

She had a way of smiling that melted him like hot wax on a burning stove. She'd look at him from underneath those long eyelashes of hers and like a dog, he'd come panting and sniffing, begging for just a taste of her.

Until recently, Greg thought that he knew everything about his wife, from her slight embarrassment at public displays of affection to her secret love of being dominated in the bed. She'd shown more real emotion upstairs in the bedroom when he'd been unable to finish what he started with her than she had in a long time.

He felt like shit that she'd had to resort to finishing something he started in the bedroom. But it couldn't be helped. He had to take care of business or he wouldn't be able to give her all the things she deserved.

He walked over and turned her away from her tinkering with the kettle. "Sweetheart. Liza, look at me. Big Daddy's sorry. Do you forgive me?" He knew it would take more wheedling on his part but he tried to pull her into his arms.

"The Big Daddy shit stops at the bedroom. And I'm not too sure it's working there anymore, either *Big Daddy*," she bit back and snatched her body away from him and walked over to the chrome-colored, oversized refrigerator.

He was stung by her retort but refused to acknowledge it. She was just mad. He'd make it up to her.

"I'll try and get this finished ASAP, okay? Then we'll have the rest of our Sunday together, just like I said, baby. I promise."

"Whatever, Greg. Don't rush on my account. Maybe I'll call Karina and ask her if she'd like to go to lunch with me. Although the way she and Cooper have been going at it, I doubt if she'll have the time or the inclination to step away from the bed."

He heard the anger, frustration and jealousy in her voice when she mentioned her best friend who'd just recently gotten married.

"I'm sure she'd love to go out for lunch. Call her and I promise I'll be home soon, okay?"

When she simply nodded her head, he walked over and tugged at the back of her hair and raised her face to his as he kissed her on the mouth. He was startled when she moved her face out of reach.

"Just go! Don't try and pull it now! You made your decision, so get the hell out!" Liza wrenched her face away from him and shoved him away; the unexpectedness of the gesture threw him off balance.

"What the hell is wrong with you, Liza? And why do you keep telling me I'm 'not pulling your hair'? What's that supposed to mean?" He was angry and didn't get her at all, but she obviously didn't give a damn.

"What do you *think* is wrong? I can't believe I have to tell your ass what's wrong with me! How in the hell do you *not* know what's wrong with me, Greg? God! How could you be so damn obtuse?" she demanded in a voice gone shrill in its intensity.

"Finally, some real emotion," he muttered, stepping back out of reach.

"What the hell is that supposed to mean?" she demanded.

"Nothing, just forget it." He moved away from her.

"No, don't run away now. If you have something to say, just say it!" Her face was tinged with a distinct reddish hue as she grabbed his arm to get his attention.

"I don't feel like fighting with you right now, Liza. I don't have time for this. I'm late."

He knew they needed to talk but he didn't have time to fight with her and he knew that's what it would be.

A down and dirty fight.

She was mad as hell and wanted to let him know everything about him that was pissing her off. Her anger escalated his.

"Damn Greg, I used to come first…what happened?" She looked up at him with raw emotion on her angry face. "It used to be that you didn't put anything…or anyone before me," she said with dejection. The slump of her shoulders instantly brought his anger to a low simmer.

He turned her into his arms and hugged her close. "Sweetheart, you do come first. You always have, but…"

She eased out of his arms.

"Just go."

"Damn it! Everything I do is for you, Liza! Every damn thing and you don't appreciate a fucking thing!"

"Just what the hell is that supposed to mean?" she yelled back, her voice rising to octaves beyond anything she'd ever accomplished.

"It means just that! I work and try to give you the things you want, the things you obviously need to make you happy and it's never good enough. It makes me wonder why you married me in the first damn place."

"I can't believe you're saying something like that. All I've ever wanted was my husband. I never asked for the rest! You wanted them more than I did! All I've ever asked for was a husband who loved me."

"That, and a nice Mercedes," he shot back.

When she stared at him, tears gathering in her eyes, chest heaving, he reached out to pull her into his arms. She neatly avoided his arms and spun around and the look in her eyes gave him pause.

"If that's all you think I want, a fucking Mercedes, after seven years of marriage, than we're in more trouble than I thought."

Their harsh breathing was the only sound in the large, bright kitchen for long moments. He felt at a total loss. It felt as though something precious was slipping from his grasp.

He kissed the back of her head once again. "I'll be home soon, baby," he said and left her standing in the kitchen, head low, body turned away from him.

He loved her so much. But there wasn't anything he could do about their situation right now.

His heart ached to see her even the smallest bit sad. He'd make it up to her as soon as he could. Greg glanced down at his watch and hurried to the garage. He opened the door of his SUV and climbed inside before reversing out the circular driveway.

His thoughts turned to the case and the shitload of work he needed to complete in order to get back home to take care of his wife.

Chapter Three

✍

Liza felt the slight kiss to the back of her head and had wanted to turn around and straight smack his face.

How the hell did he do that? Act sweet and loving, sexy as hell and then leave her as though everything was cool? Like he hadn't just caught her completing *his* job and obviously didn't feel the least bit of guilt about it! And the heated words they'd exchanged…

Liza slammed the door to the refrigerator with her hip after grabbing a small container of light yogurt from the shelf. She picked up a spoon from the silver drawer, pulled back the silver aluminum foil cover and sunk the spoon in the middle of the yogurt.

There was nothing like a Yoplait peach blend smoothie to calm the savage beast. As she slowly licked the spoon she thought over what she could possibly do to get her husband to act the way he used to.

Back when she came first in his life.

This morning's fiasco starkly highlighted just how bad things were. There was a time when all she had to do was shake her ass a little, and horny dog that he was, he'd drop whatever he was working on and come panting and sniffing behind her, follow wherever she led.

Most times she barely was able to keep him calm enough to make it to the bedroom. She gave him a look and that was all it took.

Just one damn look.

She'd run from him to give it just that much more of a thrill.

The thrill of the chase always did it for the both of them. She'd race away only to get caught within a few yards of her start point. He allowed her that much.

He'd then flip her around and the look in his eyes had given her pause and she swore at the time her heart skipped a beat.

He looked so big and overwhelming as he towered over her. He'd tell her to drop down on all fours and with her heart beating loudly in her chest she'd do exactly what he demanded.

Dropped to the damn floor.

What happened after was her first journey into playing the subservient role with Greg. Letting him tell her what to do and when to do it with their sex play.

Shit.

It had been so long since she'd played the *game* that she felt like howling. This morning she'd had it all planned out, knew just what to do to get him ready, prepare him for what *she* wanted him to do to her.

She sighed.

No use in crying over what happened. Or better still, *what didn't* happen.

She licked the spoon after polishing off the last of her yogurt before she tapped the lever on the small chrome trashcan and one-hand dunked the empty container.

She shoots, she scores... she needs a damn life.

Liza turned on the small Bose radio that was mounted under one of the cabinets, determined to dance off the blues.

Music always did that for her.

No matter how sad, angry, disappointed or whatever she felt, she could always turn to music to force her out of her dour mood. She quickly found the station she needed.

That was the other thing she required.

She needed just the right music depending on the situation. *This* situation required hard beating rock or rap. And she found what she needed when one of her favorite female artist's hard pounding lyrics came belting out of the small powerful speakers.

Bet it tastes like candy...melts in my mouth just like...chocolate candy...

She danced around the kitchen, folding dishtowels, thinking how much she missed how good Greg tasted in her mouth. His cock was absolutely perfect. Long and thick, and perfectly curved.

I love the way you work that magic stick baby...working it and working it and working it.

Just thinking of the way he worked her pussy with his magic stick made her grow wet and wanting.

...The more I fall in love with you, the more I get scared...the way you work your magic stick baby, the more it gets scary...don't stop, please just keep on working it...just keep working me...

Liza dropped the dishcloth and sat down heavily in the chair, all temporary joy leaving her as she sat gloomily staring at her ceiling.

With its beautiful customized tile.

That symbolized everything she *thought* she wanted. Wealth, success...and no more damn welfare.

She sighed and picked up the phone to call her friend, Karina.

* * * * *

"Give me a break Liza, you're my best friend. That's what friends are for," Karina told her after taking a sip of her herbal tea.

Liza had called her friend and with hesitancy asked if she'd mind having lunch with her at her favorite café. Her treat.

"You just said the two magic words, girlfriend. The Trio café and your treat. Honey, I'll meet you there in twenty..." her friend's voice trailed off and the phone was muffled. Liza heard Karina's crazy giggling in the background, along with her new husband Cooper's deep voice. A minute later she came back on the phone. "...um how 'bout I meet you there say around noon?"

Liza laughed and agreed and now they sat in the lively café waiting for their salads to arrive. Liza felt bad about pulling Karina away from her husband on a Sunday, but she was desperate.

"Thanks for having lunch with meKari, I love you for spending a little time with me. At least you care."

"What in the world? That's a given Liza! What's wrong? Trouble with Greg?" Karina guessed and sat back as the waiter placed their salads in front of them.

Liza caught the way Karina glanced over the man's shapely rear end in tight black traditional waiter wear. "Married for less than a month and already have a case of the wandering eye?" She raised an eyebrow at her friend and stifled her smile.

"What? No way, girl! But umm...he does have a nice butt you have to admit, Li!" Both women laughed.

Liza loved the way marriage and happiness had helped blossom Karina into a more confident woman. She was definitely more comfortable with the sensual aspect of her nature since she'd met and married her husband, Cooper.

Good sex and happiness did that for a woman.

And judging by the cloud of sexual satisfaction that clung to Karina like a cheap suit, she was one happy chick.

Liza *refused* to feel jealousy for Karina. Karina deserved to be happy.

Even though she herself was miserable as hell.

She sighed. "I don't really know what's happening between me and Greg. I'm not sure where to start," she admitted as she squeezed lemon on her leafy salad greens.

"Start at the beginning. You always tell me to think about it before acting. Of course, had I listened to *that* bit of advice a few months ago..." Karina's voice trailed off and she laughed.

"Okay, so I was wrong *one* time. But I'm glad I was. You and Cooper deserve each other. He's a good guy. And that man loves you to death, girl." Liza gave her friend a half smile in response.

Karina had met her Cooper and they'd had a true whirlwind courtship. Liza had blasted her friend when she'd called *her* on a Sunday morning to talk, only to find out that Karina had met a man at her temporary job in Macy's gift wrapping department the day before and after knowing him for less than a day, she'd taken the man in the employees lounge and allowed him to sex the hell out of her.

And if that wasn't enough, Karina had then taken him home where they'd engaged in marathon sex like something straight out of a porn movie!

Liza had been utterly amazed. Karina was so shy around men and for her to sleep with a total stranger was unreal to Liza. For a while she thought someone else had taken over her friend's body akin to a body snatchers movie.

Liza had been afraid for her friend and had cautioned her...well she'd actually cussed her out...about sleeping with a stranger. It was too irresponsible, she'd told her. She'd get hurt. He probably didn't have the same intention that Karina had. It was only a one-night stand. Don't expect too much. Don't get caught up.

Well...not only had Karina gotten "caught up", she was caught, spun around and loved every minute of it.

Cooper had fallen in love with Karina just as her friend had with him. Within a few short weeks of dating he'd asked her to marry him and they were married a month later.

"So what's going on, Li?" Karina brought her attention back to the problem at hand. If she didn't watch herself, she'd be just like Karina, daydreaming about everything but the situation at hand.

"Greg and I don't click anymore," she said with a sigh as she stirred the sweetener in her ice tea.

"What do you mean you don't click? In what way? Sexually?" Karina asked and took a healthy drink of her already sweetened tea.

"Sexually, mentally, pretty much all the—'llys,' Liza admitted on a sigh.

"Have you spoken to him about it? What does he think?"

"I tried doing that. Girl, it was awful." Liza felt the threat of tears and tried her best to keep them at bay, but was suddenly overwhelmed. She picked up her napkin from her lap and quickly dabbed at her eyes.

Karina hated when Liza did that. Start to open up and then, ashamed…turn away. After over twenty years of friendship, it should be obvious to her that Karina loved her! Karina thought *she* was supposed to be the reserved one out of the pair.

But actually, Liza was the one with the bend toward being reserved.

It was high time Liza started to understand that she needed to open up, and not just with her, but with her husband also.

"Liza, what happened? Girl, it's me. If you can't tell your best friend about it, who the heck can you tell?" she asked and reached across the table to take her friend's hand in hers. "Seriously. You should know this."

Liza took a deep breath and tightened her fingers in her hand. "I know, Kari. It's not that I don't want to share. I'm just not sure how to."

"Greg's too busy at work to give up the goodies?" Karina asked straight-faced and Liza choked on her tea.

"Why would you say that?" she asked as she wiped the tea dribble from her chin.

It was actually kind of funny to Karina to see her perfectly coiffed, manicured friend spit ice chunks and tea. But she knew better than to laugh. Laughing was a surefire way to garner a cuss out from her friend.

Liza played the role of sophisticated socialite to a T. But they'd grown up in the same neighborhood. Karina knew the *real* deal.

They'd met in kindergarten and had attended the same Catholic School, *Mary Magdalene*.

Karina had been raised by her mother as well as her grandmother. Her grandmother had wanted to send her only grandchild to a school outside their local district because she wanted the best for her. At the time, the neighborhood school had left a lot to be desired and her grandmother had been determined to send her somewhere where she'd receive a good education. She'd worked a second job in order to pay for the tuition for the private school.

Liza had also attended *Mary Magdalene*, but had been given a grant to attend the private school as a part of an education pilot program that selected a handful of inner city children and paid for them to attend private school.

No one but Karina had known that Liza had attended the school on grant.

She and Liza had bonded as only two children could who shared a common heritage and were in an environment where they were the minority. The bond was strengthened when Liza would spend the nights with Kari and her small extended family of grandmother and mother. She and Liza had grown up treating one another more like sisters than friends.

Back in those days, although Liza studied hard and did well in school, she was a little rough around the edges. She had a mouth like a sailor and was quick to cuss out anybody who messed with her.

Didn't matter if it was a teacher, a nun, priest or principal. Liza didn't care. She let them all know how she felt!

It had taken years of self-discipline for Liza to emerge as the woman she was today. She once told Karina that she didn't want to be like her mother. She didn't want to have a child out of wedlock and she *refused* to go on public assistance.

Ever.

As soon as she and Liza graduated from high school, Liza's mom had skipped out of town, letting her fend for herself in college. But had she stayed, Liza still would have had to fend for herself. As it was, her mother would occasionally call Liza and ask for money. Liza had let that slip once.

She'd worked hard in school to pay for college and had eventually met her husband Greg and had married him her last year in graduate school.

Karina was proud of her friend and knew how rough life had been for her before she and Greg married.

Liza was also drop-dead gorgeous. Karina used to feel serious pangs of envy with Liza's tall, slender shape and beautiful face. She always ate the right foods, never ate junk, worked out regularly and looked awesome. Karina had neither the inclination nor motivation to do all of that work to stay in shape. Watching Liza do it, tired her out enough.

Besides that, she had finally decided she could live with her addiction to Little Debbie oatmeal creme cakes. Cooper didn't mind the extra cushion at all.

Liza was darker than she...her skin color reminded Karina of coffee with just a touch of cream. Smooth and creamy. Her eyes were dark and set deep and had just a slight tilt in the corners.

Kind of like one of the *Whos* from *Whoville*.

Karina would have died to have Liza's high cheekbones and angular face. No sharp edges, just perfectly shaped features.

Unlike Karina, Liza was always *together*. Hair just right, nails manicured.

She kept her personal opinions to herself; that she thought Liza had shut off a part of herself when she left the old neighborhood. That she was in such denial about who she was and needed to come to terms with the fact that her life in poverty was nothing to be ashamed of.

It didn't define who she was as a person.

"Well?" she demanded, not allowing Liza to hide. Her friend took a deep breath and started to speak.

"I think he might be having an affair with his assistant, but I'm not sure…" she started and the fork of pasta that was on the way to making its way to Karina's mouth halted mid-way.

"What? Why would you think that?"

"Have you seen her? She's gorgeous and he drops everything the minute she calls," Liza answered, glumly.

"There are a lot of gorgeous women in the world Liza! You're gorgeous! Girl, that doesn't make any darn sense!"

"He sure does leap whenever she calls. What other reason would a man turn down sex? And not just any old sex. I'm talking 'smack me up, tie me down, lick me all over 'til I scream for friggin' mercy' sex!!"

"Greg turned down sex with you? No way!"

"Yeah, he did," she said gloomily and proceeded to tell her what happened earlier in the day.

"If he's not cheating then what in the world is going on and how do I try and fix this mess?" Liza ended her story and looked Karina straight in the eye and asked her the question, point blank.

The time for shame and her continual need for self-preservation were long past. She wanted answers. And she knew Kari loved her and would tell it to her straight. She waited as Karina pushed her wire-framed glasses further up her nose, pooched out her mouth and made a small sucking sound with her teeth.

Whenever Karina did that, she was in *deep* thought. Liza suppressed a smile despite the frustration and uncertainty she felt. Karina always made her smile.

"Welll..." she began, stretching the word out as far it could possibly go, "I don't think Greg is cheating on you. I really don't. But can I be honest here without you getting upset?" she asked and Liza saw a quick flash of *something* cross Karina's face that she didn't like.

"Go on, what is it?" Liza put her hands in her lap and clenched the linen napkin so tightly she wouldn't doubt if the white painted tips of her French manicure were permanently etched in her palms.

"You know I love you girl, right?"

"Karina..." she warned.

"Okay, okay!" she held up a consoling hand. "Gotta establish the love first! Sorry," she said and continued, "Liza, it's your own darn fault." After she lowered *that* boom she ducked her head as though Liza would throw something at her.

As if.

"Karina Elizabeth Woodson...Karina Elizabeth *Tolson*," she corrected at Karina's raised brow.

"Get it right!" Karina laughed before turning serious. "Greg is only doing what he thinks you want."

"What do you mean by that?" she asked.

"He knows you better than anyone. Anyone next to me that is. And probably better than I do," she started and at Liza's nod continued. "Well don't you think he knows how badly you hated the thought of ever being poor? Of revisiting that life? I mean you said it often enough."

"So that's why he won't make love to me anymore?"

"Don't make it worse than it is. You said it wasn't as frequent and as...um...freaky as it used to be," she reminded her.

"I guess. Go on," Liza took a thoughtful bite of her salad.

"Just seems to me that in his desire to please you and make sure you're taken care of, that maybe you both have lost sight of what's really important."

"And that is?"

"I've been married for barely a month. So I'm not trying to give advice to you, girl. I mean you and Greg have been together for over seven years. But it seems to me that you two have forgotten that a marriage is composed of more than one or even two elements."

"Such as?"

"There's more to a successful relationship, married or otherwise, than money. More to it than great sex. Although the great sex is nothing to sneeze at..." The instant far away sex-on-the-brain look on Karina's face alerted Liza to the fact that her friend was off in la-la land.

Probably thinking about all that good stuff she was getting at home. The kind of good stuff Liza was in desperate need of.

"Karina..." she sought to bring her back to the real world. From the way her almond shaped eyes widened behind her lenses, Liza knew she'd been right. The girl had been thinking of sex.

Lucky trollop.

"Where was I? Oh. The variables in a successful relationship."

That was the other strange thing about Karina. Her need to put everything in analytical terms. Math and html was her *thing*.

"Go on," she encouraged. "What's the third variable in your equation?"

"Communication, Liza. Besides financial responsibility and *great* sex, there's communication."

"I know. You're right. I'm working on that."

"Well you two have to work on it together."

"I know."

"Put on your favorite BJ lipstick…"

"My what?" Liza asked. Yet again, she was hard pressed not to spew tea from her mouth.

Karina glanced at her over the top of her glasses. "Girl, you know," she said and leaned close to her before whispering, "your blowjob lipstick."

"Karina!"

"But in the meantime…a little bondage never hurt anybody either," she said with a blissful smile.

Liza's mouth formed a perfect O at what had come tripping out of her previously near celibate friend's mouth as though it were no big deal.

"Coop recently introduced me to it…it's awesome! Have you ever given it a try?" she asked innocently, large eyes blinking sweetly behind her glasses.

"And have you ever heard of a butt plug? Liza, I swear it's off the chain, girl!" Karina giggled as she pushed her glasses further up her nose and glanced around as though everyone in the café was listening and she wanted to keep her freaky on the sneaky.

Liza was utterly amazed at what her oldest and best friend, whom she didn't know even *knew* there was a such thing as bondage, much less butt plugs, was saying. And Liza was doing her *damnedest* not to fall out of her seat as Karina went on a gleeful informative tirade on the subject.

"Oooh, I have an idea! Why don't you surprise him at his office and play dress-up? Put on some 'do me baby' lipstick...ummm. High heels...ooh, better yet, I bought this cheerleader outfit that I haven't worn yet and it just might fit you with a few adjustment..."

Chapter Four

❦

"Renita, let's go ahead with that plan, okay? Make a notation to call the opposing council Monday morning and tell him we'd like to strike a bargain and if he's ready to play ball and stop jerking us around, we can talk," Greg said to his assistant over the small intercom that led to her adjoining office.

"Sure will Greg, anything else?" her smooth voice asked.

"No that should be all…and Renita?"

"Yes, Greg?"

"Why don't you take off? I should wrap this up any minute now. No use in you hanging around."

"It's no problem, Greg, that's what I'm here for."

Greg knew better than to argue with her. She'd interned with him three years ago and had been with him ever since and he wouldn't know what to do without her. When she'd started working for him and stayed up late, working alongside him, he'd felt guilty as hell. He'd tried to tell her to go home on numerous occasions but she'd refused and he gave up suggesting that she go. She was more of a workaholic than he. She was a beautiful woman too.

He didn't understand why she didn't get out more. After working late one evening he'd asked her what her significant other thought of her late nights with him. She'd stared at him blankly as though he were speaking some foreign tongue.

She'd then asked if he had the brief ready for an upcoming trial and he'd never gone into personal territory with her again. Liza had joked once that she thought Renita was in love with him and that was the reason she worked late hours and never mentioned having a lover who was waiting for her.

But Renita never made any passes at him and he believed she simply had a total dedication to her job. Liza let the subject drop but he had a feeling she wasn't kidding when she made the comment. She really thought his assistant had a thing for him.

"That's fine, Renita. I should be wrapping up soon and we can both leave," he told her before returning to his work. He glanced down at his watch and was surprised at the time.

Damn. Liza was going to be ticked off. Their last conversation still rang harshly in his ears as he stared off into space. Her words were pointed jabs that shot straight at his heart.

How could she doubt that he loved her? Everything he did was for her.

He'd fallen in love with her from the minute he set eyes on her. At the time, he thought it was a case of "fall in lust at first sight" rather than love. He'd set out to seduce her, hell-bent on getting in her panties ASAP. She'd turned the tables on him and refused to have sex. He thought it was a game at first, so he played along, sure he'd get at her sooner or later. After three months of waiting, he felt like howling at the fucking moon he'd been so horny.

After several months of dating she'd given in and he'd never been the same. He used to laugh at his friends who he thought were *pussy whipped*, as he swore up and down it would never happen to him.

He'd been wrong.

But more than sex, he loved everything about her. Her demure laugh, the way she played the lady role for him, the perfect hostess, her commitment to her charities.

The way she loved him.

That was the number-one thing he loved about her. He knew she loved him. And he felt like shit for accusing her of marrying him for the money.

She'd grown up poor and there wasn't anything wrong with her wanting more out of life. He was more than happy to be able to provide it for her. He just wanted her to open up to him more. He missed the spontaneous things they did, the way they went out of their way to please one another.

He sighed and turned away from the window to return to his work. He was so engrossed in his notes that it took several throat clearings before he looked up and when he did, all thoughts of the case he was working on flew from his mind and his cock thumped a happy salute at the image in front of him.

"Damn, baby…" was all he could say as his wife stood before him and slowly opened the floor-length leather trench coat, wearing nothing more than some kind of lacy outfit, laced up thigh-high leather boots and a hesitant smile on her lush, red lips.

* * * * *

Liza felt nervous and silly.

Today was one of those weird Midwestern days in the middle of April and the weather was a balmy seventy-two degrees and she was wearing a floor-length trench coat with nothing underneath but a white lacey baby doll thong and bra set.

And stiletto thigh-high boots.

After Karina had ended her blissful tirade of the joys of the occasional restraint, they'd ended their lunch with Liza more determined than ever, to put a little oomph back into her marriage.

She had pushed to the back of her mind what Renita thought when she'd walked into her office. She walked in, as bold as you please, and asked the woman if she could possibly hold any calls that might come through and if she didn't mind taking a break for a few minutes. She and Greg had something to…discuss.

She'd never really cared much for Renita, her cool looks and bland façade were a challenge to read. She was petite, no more than five feet two inches, like her friend Karina, but where Kari was all rounded, womanly curves, this woman was slim, almost boyish in her figure, Liza thought with a grimace of distaste.

And Liza *knew* the woman had a thing for her man. There was no denying the look she caught flashing in her dark gray eyes whenever the paralegal would catch her and Greg kissing when Liza came into his office.

But Liza gave her points for knowing when to step the hell back.

"Hello, Renita," she said cordially, giving the woman a quick assessing once-over.

As usual, she was dressed professionally, if a bit boring in Liza's opinion, in a traditional dark blue tailored suit. The crisp white blouse beneath the double-breasted jacket was buttoned to the top and Liza wondered how she breathed all buttoned tight like that. Her ultrashort, jet-black curls barely brushed the top of her blouse; the pearls in her small light-brown ears were delicate and unassuming.

Liza nearly lost her nerve when she saw the way one of the woman's perfectly arched winged brows lifted as her gaze in turn ran over Liza in her tightly belted calf-length trench coat.

Liza stiffened her spine and titled her head to the side, arched her own damn eyebrow and cleared her throat. "Is there any way you could take a break? My husband and I need to discuss something," she asked.

"Yes, I suppose I could. Would you like for me to announce you?" she asked in a cool voice.

"That won't be necessary, Renita. As long as he's alone, I'm sure I can announce myself." She smiled tightly at the woman.

"No problem, ma'am. In fact, if you wouldn't mind, could you inform Mr. Colburn that I've finished for the day? If he's in need of my...services...he knows where to reach me."

"I'll make sure I tell him." She turned around, not giving the assistant another thought as the queasiness settled into her belly and opened the door to Greg's inner office.

Now, Liza felt nervous as she stood in front of her husband. Which was ridiculous. There was nothing to be afraid of. They'd been married for seven years, knew each other as intimately as any two people could. There wasn't anything he had that she hadn't seen and vice versa. She was grown. She wasn't scared...

"Come here, Liza." The deep timbre of his voice raised goose bumps down her thighs.

"What? I mean..." She had to clear her throat before she continued. "I mean...you come to me." Okay. So she said it. Let him come to her. She was going to dominate *his* ass for once.

"Get over here, Liza. Now." His voice grew even quieter but his restraint didn't hide the strength of his demand.

She trembled, but held her ground.

"You don't want me to have to come and get you...do you?" He leaned back even further in his chair. He pushed his glasses up the bridge of his nose as he observed her.

He looked so big and sexy as he sat behind the large mahogany desk. He'd taken off his suit jacket and had rolled his shirtsleeves to his elbows and she could see the sexy dark sprinkling of hair on his forearms.

The only time he wore glasses was when he worked and the small, dark square-framed lenses now sat in the middle of the long bridge of his nose. One small dark lock of hair near his forehead had bisected his eyebrow.

He'd never looked sexier to her.

"If I have to come and get you, I won't be responsible for my actions," he told her and smiled that smile she loved so much. A small dimple appeared in the corner of his mouth before the smile dropped off his face.

Just the sound of his voice, the quiet demand, had her wet and ready. Goose bumps ran down the backs of her thighs as her nipples beaded behind the tiny lace teddy. She felt the cream run down her vagina and drench the small lining.

A smile and a few words had her panting like a rabid dog. "Come and get me," she dared him and slowly backed away from the desk.

Leisurely, he pushed his chair back and raised his large frame from the high-backed leather chair. The look in his eyes scared her a little. As he advanced toward her she backed away without taking her eyes away from him.

When he gave her that wicked smile, she turned and tried to run. She had only managed to take a few steps when she felt him grab her by the back of her head and halt her right in her tracks.

"Don't try and run away. It won't work. You came here for something and now you're going to get just what you obviously want."

She could feel his hard muscled back even against the leather of her trench coat. As he none too gently pulled her head back, she looked into his eyes and had to clench her legs together before her cream dripped down her legs.

Damn.

She was so turned on she was dizzy, her head was spinning so crazily, that she felt like Linda Blair in *The Exorcist*.

She moistened her lips with her tongue. Her heart beat wildly yet she couldn't resist pulling the tiger by the tail. Again.

"You don't know the first damn thing about what I want."

What the world did she say that for? The man went crazy.

Without a word he snatched her coat off, nearly ripping it in the process and flipped her around, slamming her against his straining chest.

She stood tall before him wearing nothing but the two-piece baby doll getup and thigh-high leather boots.

"Say it again and I swear it'll be the last thing you say for a long time, Li," he said through gritted teeth, his eyes narrowed.

As he'd swung her around, one hand on the back of her head, the other hand had, in an unconscious caress, moved down one of her breast. His finger circled and lightly pinched her nipple behind the lace of the teddy before trailing away.

If she didn't know better, she'd swear there was a hint of a tic in the corner of his mouth. He was just the *smallest* bit pissed off.

Good.

"You. Don't. Know. The. First…" was all she got out before he clamped her mouth shut with his.

With one hand, he grabbed the back of her neck and pulled her impossibly closer to his body until there was absolutely no room separating her body from his. His upper body was pressed so tight against her breasts that her nipples budded against the smooth crisp fabric of his dress shirt.

But she forgot all about the uncomfortable feel of his buttons the minute his mouth touched hers.

He opened his mouth wide and slowly closed it back over hers sucking her entire mouth into his. He licked and bit her lips until she felt like crying. His hands roamed over the back of her head, pulling her deeper into the kiss. He grabbed her bottom lip between his teeth and scraped it none too gently.

She whimpered at the small ache and he licked it better.

Damn, he knew how to work her lips.

He moved his hands to either side of her face and drew back to look at her. Really look at her. His eyes searched hers for an answer to some unknown question. She felt helpless in his gaze and rather than allow him to keep staring at her, she desperately pulled his face back down to hers.

"Don't stop kissing me baby, don't stop," she begged and he lifted her into his arms and carried her to his wide mahogany desk and plopped her ass on the corner.

She was breathless with anticipation and watched him from beneath lowered lids to see what he had in store for her. She opened her legs wide and smiled to herself when she saw the way his eyes widened. She knew he could see the small tight curls on her pussy clearly through the sheer fabric of the thong.

Greg was the rare man who liked hair on a woman's vagina so she kept the sides neat and trim but left the thatch of hair on her pussy just the way her man liked it. Full and lush.

When he did nothing but stare at her, she grew nervous and bit down on her bottom lip to quell her sudden case of nerves.

She was further taken off guard when he glanced away from her vagina and looked into her face and smiled, wetting his lips.

"Why don't you sit right there and I'll get a chair and we can…talk," he told her and to her amazement, he walked around the desk and sat down in his chair. As he sat down, she heard the sharp hiss of a zipper and saw that he'd casually lowered the zipper on his pants.

"Why don't you tell me what that was about earlier, Li? What's going on in that pretty head of yours, hmm? And while you're telling me what's going on, I want you to turn around and face me and since I don't know what the hell *I'm* doing, why don't *you* show me how it's done? I want you move that little thong to the side and take your fingers and play with your pretty pussy. Can you do that for me?" His eyes lowered and he slowly released his penis from his pants and it jutted forth long, thick and curved.

She felt her lips water with lust and need as she stared at his thick, beautiful cock.

He grasped the bulbous tip and lightly ran his big hand over the entire length, stem to root. As large as his hand was, he was unable to completely engulf its circumference.

"I'm waiting, Liza." Casually, as though nothing were out of the ordinary, he scooted down in his chair, his legs further apart and continued to rub his cock with an expectant look on his face.

On the one hand, she was turned on so badly she didn't know what to do with herself, and on the other hand, was angry as hell that he could just calmly sit there, friggin' jacking off, telling her to finger-fuck her own self and he'd watch!

Chapter Five

ဆ

Greg was so damn hot, it was all he could do not to jump up from his chair, push Liza's ass down and screw the shit out of her, right there on the table.

Fuck her so hard, she'd be limping for a week and never again tell him that he didn't know what the hell he was doing when he did her. As angry as he was, he didn't know the last time he'd been this turned on either.

Yet they were at a crossroad.

He knew what she wanted from him. She wanted him to prove something to her. Prove that he could do her the way she liked to be done. Well, he intended to flip the script on his wife. He intended to prove to her that not only did he know what she wanted, what she needed, but that it was way past time for her to be real with him.

Liza had made her way into his thoughts the entire day and he'd thought long and hard on their situation. After seven years of marriage, she owed him the truth. He wanted to finally get to know his wife. No pretenses, no facades, no pretending that her past meant nothing to her.

It shaped her into the woman she was today. A strong, independent woman who had so much to give that it pissed him off that she didn't see it. It pissed him off that she was ashamed of her life growing up.

As though she had anything to be embarrassed of.

In the entire time of their marriage, she'd talked about her life as a child and teenager less than a handful of times. He felt as though he were missing out on something precious. That she had dimensions and facets to her that she denied him the pleasure of knowing.

He loved her. He wanted it all. Or nothing at all.

He decided without realizing it that he was greedy and Liza needed to make a decision. Either she opened up to him, completely opened up, or he wasn't sure if their marriage would stand the true test of time.

It was a sobering thought.

He watched as she hesitantly gazed at him with those deep brown eyes of hers that turned his insides upside down. She bit her sexy bottom lip as she eased her hand down her body slowly past her tiny perfect little globes, down her flat belly, before she moved the scrap of material aside.

They'd been intimate for over seven years but it was as though this was the first time he'd seen her. This shy, hesitant Liza who was uncertain. He waited to see if she'd have the nerve to do as he demanded. To masturbate in front of him.

After easing the material away, she stroked one finger over her clit. "Spread your pussy lips for me. I want to see you." She then took two fingers and spread herself wide and with the other, she worked the small nubbin.

But that wasn't enough. He wanted her to fully engage in giving herself pleasure. He had one more demand.

"Play with your tits with the other hand. While you play with your pussy, I want to see you play with your nipples, baby," he demanded, just as she'd eased one finger into her vagina.

She said nothing to the added demand, simply complied and eased the strap from the tiny teddy down her arm and he gazed with restless eyes at the way her small breasts rose and pushed against each other. Her pretty brown nipples stood erect and ready.

With hesitant hands, she slid her hand up her arm and lightly cupped one of her breast. He loved the way her breath caught and her chest rose and fell rapidly as she continued to finger her pussy in orchestrated rhythm with her other hand pinching and pulling on her taut nipples.

She closed her eyes briefly and he sharply called out, "No. Open your eyes and look at me. Don't look away," he demanded hoarsely as he stroked his cock, nearly out of his mind with his need to throw her on the floor and *do* her.

She gave him a small smile and did as she was told.

Greg knew that she liked when he gave her instruction. It turned her on.

As she continued to rub her pussy and stroke her breast, he didn't know how much longer he could hold off jumping her. He didn't want to bring himself to orgasm, so he kept his strokes slow and methodical.

He intended for her to do that for him. She'd be the one to bring him to orgasm.

"Liza, do you know how much I love you, baby?" he asked her quietly, and he saw her slow her movements. "No. Don't stop. Keep going. I just want to talk to you while I watch. Is that okay?"

She licked her bottom lip and answered in a voice heavy with arousal, "Yes, Greg, that's okay," and began to close her eyes before remembering his edict to keep them open.

"Good. Keep on fingering yourself, baby. When I first met you I knew you were the one for me, did you know that?" He slowly rose from his chair as he asked the question and saw the way she squirmed on the corner of the desk.

"No," she barely was able to get the word out.

"I took one look at that pretty face, that long, lean body and knew I wanted you. I wanted to know *everything* about you."

Her fingers slowed their frantic rubbing over her drenching vagina. He'd walked around the desk and stood less than two feet away and leaned against the wall as he watched with hooded eyes as she was coming near to her completion.

"I want to know it all, Liza. Everything. Not just the good, but the bad, the sad, the embarrassing. All of it," as he spoke he walked over to her and now stood near the edge of the desk as she worked her pussy and breast, listening to what he was saying with her head hung down.

"You've cheated me out of getting to know you, Liza. You've only shown me the part you think I want to see. You haven't shared the important part, the one that has made you into the woman you are today."

He removed her hand from her breast and the other from her vagina and held them clasped together in one of his. "I want to know the whole Liza. I don't want the skewed profile. I want the whole thing." He pushed her down on the desk and spread her legs farther apart with his.

"If you can't give me all of you, do you think I should give you all of me?" he whispered close in her ear before he plunged his cock as far into her as he could reach. So far back that he felt her womb close over his tip as she screamed.

He wasted no time saying anything else to her. *For the moment.*

He cupped the back of each thigh where the tops of her boots ended and shoved her legs up and farther apart as he ground into her slick entry, grinding his teeth together at the exquisite feel of her hot cunt gripping his cock.

"I want to know what it was like growing up in the projects, Liza. How did you feel when your parents divorced?" he asked as he pumped into her relentlessly.

"What?" she panted as she stopped moving her hips in rhythm to his thrusts and opened her eyes wide to glare at him.

"Don't stop. Just answer the question or you won't get what you want. What you need to give you relief. You want relief don't you?" he asked. The entire time he'd been talking to her, he'd been grinding into her, lifting one leg higher than the other for a better angle to dig into her.

"Oh heavens, Greg! Damn, that feels good," she cried out when he shoved her knee damn near to her face.

"Good, baby. It feels good to me too. Now answer the question so we can both keep feeling good," he grunted as he slid his rod in and out of her swollen wet folds.

"I hated it," she cried out when he reached a hand down and started to toy with her engorged clit, rubbing and circling the small nub mercilessly.

"Why?" he asked softly.

He continued to grind into her, loving the way she tossed her head on the desk in agony, the way she kept gripping the sides of the desk and rotating her hips with his.

He continued to make love to her but after several minutes, when she didn't answer, he pulled out, despite her wrenching cry of disbelief and his own silent roar of agony.

"Liza, I asked you a question!" he demanded and pulled her up to face him.

Their breathing was labored as they stared at each other. He refused to give in. He wanted her to open up to him and he damn well would deny them both what they needed in order to break his wife down.

He watched as her chest rose and fell, the way her small nostrils flared and her eyes squinted. She was pissed.

Good.

"Well?" His own breathing was labored and his cock was calling him all kinds of fool, as the only thing it wanted to do was plunge back into her welcoming warmth.

But this was more important than his cock or its satisfaction.

He saw the defiance steal over her beautiful face and wanted to shake the shit out of her. Damn it! What did he have to do to break through to her? What did he have to do for her to trust him?

With a heavy heart, he realized that as stubborn as he was, Liza could be even more so. Although his heart ached and his cock even more, he shoved away from her and with unsteady hands zipped his pants.

"What? Greg you can't do this to me!" she wailed and the grief and utter denial in her voice tugged at his heart. But no way in hell could he make love to her now. He felt as though a part of him had died when she looked him in the eye and refused to give in.

"Why not, Liza? You can leave me high and dry, why can't I return the favor?" he asked and turned back around to face her as he adjusted his pants.

She looked beautiful and utterly frustrated as she lay back against his desk with her hair mussed, legs spread and the hairs from her pussy glistening from their combined fluids. He had to turn away from the sight before he lost his resolve.

"Please. Greg, don't leave me like this. Please," she begged quietly.

He turned back around and although he refused to complete the act, he couldn't leave her in the state she was in. Not after how he'd left her earlier that morning.

"Fine, Liza. I won't leave you like this. If this is all you want, all that you're willing to share, I'll take that. Lie down," he demanded harshly and spread her legs as far apart as they'd go, leaned down with his face less than an inch away from her quivering mound and with a long stab from his tongue, he stroked her.

* * * *

Liza groaned harshly at the feel of his talented tongue on her crease. He took his time as he lapped and suckled her tender swollen flesh, taking her bud between his lips and gently administering it.

As good as it felt, she wanted…she *needed* more.

She raised her body and looked down helplessly as he ate her out. "Greg baby, please. I need more. Ummm," she grunted, squirming when he hit a particularly good spot.

143

"Baby, as good as this feels, I need more," she shamelessly begged.

He raised his dark head from between her thighs and quit lapping at her to raise an eyebrow. "Then what do you have to do? What do I want to know?" he asked, nostrils flaring, looking so good to her, with her cream on his face, breathing hard that she'd say anything to get him to go back to making love to her.

Anything…but that. She did *not* feel like taking a friggin' trip down memory lane. She just wanted her husband to *do* her.

She stared into his face, saying nothing; the only sound in the room was their mutual harsh breathing.

"That's what I thought. Lay the fuck down Li, just lie down and let me finish."

His anger was palpable in the still of the room and had she not been so desperate, so hungry for completion, she'd tell him to go fuck himself and go home.

But she didn't.

Instead she eased back down on the desk and closed her eyes, tears falling from the corners as she accepted his oral loving.

He widened her legs farther apart and if anything, his touch became even gentler. He separated her vaginal lips and stroked either side of her crease before sliding one of his big fingers into her entry.

She cried out in relief.

When he added two more fingers alongside his tongue and continued to work her over, it wasn't long before she felt her orgasm rip through her body. She arched her body sharply away from the desk and before she knew it, she'd grabbed either side of his face and ground herself against him, bucking and screaming as she came.

He held his face over her mound as she slowly came back down and didn't relinquish his hold on her until she'd stopped shaking and lay limp, her body slumping over his.

He gently pushed away from her and sat her up. He took her face between his hands and forced her to look at him. She didn't want to see what she'd possibly glimpse in his eyes, so she tried to turn away. But he wouldn't allow it.

"No, look at me, Liza. I think we need to talk."

Liza took a deep breath before answering hoarsely, "I know, Greg. I'm sorry. I don't know what else to say," she admitted around the sudden lump in her throat.

"The decision is yours. I want our marriage to be strong. I want you to let me in. I can't force you to do this, Li, it's got to be something you allow me to do. You've got to trust me."

"I do trust you, Greg. I trust you more than anyone in this world," she whispered.

"It's okay, baby. We'll get through this," he told her as he lowered his face to hers and kissed her with such desperation that her heart ached.

Chapter Six

℘

"No, Karina, I decided not to go with the cheerleader getup. No, no it *was* cute. It just didn't seem to um…fit, the situation. I thought something less…cheery was needed," Liza told her friend as she sat propped against the silk pillowcases against the wrought iron of her headboard and painted her toenails.

"Well darn it, Liza, I wish you would have said something! I had plans for that outfit! I would have used it myself," Karina grumbled on the other end. "Hold on for a minute," she said and Liza distinctly heard Cooper's deep disgruntled voice tell Karina that he may as well take off the helmet and the pads.

What the hell?

As awful as she felt, she couldn't help laughing. Karina and Cooper were out of control. Completely out of control. She didn't even *want* to know what plans they'd had for the costume. She then heard Karina ask if the majorette outfit would work. Unlike the cheerleader's outfit, it had a baton!

Lord, have mercy.

She decided to let her friend off the phone. It was late anyway and just because *her* man decided that work was more important than coming home didn't mean she had to ruin the rest of Karina's night.

"Karina, I'll let you go. I just thought I'd give you a call and let you know everything is okay," she said and forced a cheerful note to her voice.

She wasn't surprised when Karina busted her out.

"Li, don't even try that with me."

Damn. At least she'd tried.

"Okay, so tell me. What really happened?"

"Karina, you know what? It's late…"

"And don't worry about Coop. He'll wait. This is important," Karina interrupted, knowing Liza was two seconds away from telling her to go and take care of Cooper. Although she heard Cooper utter a foul expletive, Liza laughed and gave in and told her what happened when she showed up at Greg's office.

"It was just supposed to be a sexy romp. I wanted him to want me so badly that he'd say to hell with work and come home," she admitted. The burn of embarrassment was strong even though she was only sharing with Karina.

"What do you think this all means?" Karina asked.

"I'm not sure what to think Kari," she admitted on a long sigh.

With a dexterity born of years of practice and plenty of yoga, she grabbed her foot and brought it close to her lips and gently blew her polished toes dry.

"Wow Li, I don't know *what* to say to that, girl. I mean, was he upset when you left?"

"Yes. No. I don't know, Karina. He said we needed to talk," she muttered.

"Did he say when he'd come home? I mean that was at what, three or four o'clock right? It's nine o'clock now."

"Thanks for pointing that out, Karina, I had no idea," Liza said dryly, hard put not to run barefoot over to her friends new home just blocks away from hers and flat blast her for stating the obvious.

"Sorry," Karina said in a contrite voice.

She paused and Liza heard the hesitancy and knew she had something to say and didn't know how to say it. She patiently waited for Karina to work it out.

"Liza, can I ask you a question?"

"Of course you may. What is it?"

"Are you ashamed of the way we grew up? I mean, the fact that we grew up in North Stanton? Does that bother you?" she asked, referring to the neighborhood where they'd grown up together as kids.

"I don't know if ashamed is the word I'd use," Liza countered hesitantly.

"What do you call it then? You never talk about it...even with me and I was right there with you in the trenches growing up."

"We may have both grown up in North Stanton Kari, but even then we were worlds apart. At least you had a stable home environment. Your gran and your mom were both there for you. You weren't evicted from your house every other year like we were. And neither did you ever live in the projects, Kari." Liza heard the bitterness in her voice but was hard pressed to keep it at bay as she tried her best to keep the ugly memories locked up and away.

Where they belonged.

This was *exactly* why she never revisited that awful time in her life. A time when she felt hopeless and powerless.

"I know, sweetie. But I saw what it did to you. And I'm sorry," Karina said in a quiet voice, all previous levity gone. "But Li, there were *some* good times weren't there? Come on, girl! Remember Sister Pauline, from Amazing Grace Baptist Church? The one with the funky breath? You remember her! Somebody was always trying to offer her a stick of gum and she'd pass and say it left a bad taste in her mouth! Then they'd offer her a peppermint and she'd cuss 'em out and say if she wanted some damn candy she'd go to the damn store and buy some!" Karina reminded her and fell out laughing.

Liza remembered the old woman and started laughing with her also, tears flowing down her face she laughed so hard. Sister Pauline was one of the many women in the Baptist church she'd attended as a child, who was given the honorary title of *Sister* because of her long-standing service.

"Karina, stop!" she cried, clutching her chest and taking deep breaths. She was afraid that if she didn't stop laughing soon, that she'd have an asthma attack and would need a hit off her inhaler.

"Girl, then she'd go on a rant asking why was everybody always trying to get her to chew gum? What the hell was going on? *Then* she'd go to church on Sunday and 'catch' the spirit and forget that she'd cursed folks out the previous day!"

By the time Karina stopped talking they were laughing so hard, Liza had to force herself to take deep breaths. "Oh my god, Karina! Only you could make me laugh when I feel so miserable inside." She calmed herself enough to say as she wiped her face with the back of her silk Kimono.

"Aw, Li, it'll be okay. I know it's not easy but you're going to have to come to some decisions. If you want your marriage to be all that it can be, you're going to have to be upfront with your husband regarding your feelings about how you grew up. He only wants to know the complete Liza. He loves you, honey. There's nothing wrong with a man loving his woman so much that he digs everything about her. You have nothing to be ashamed of. Don't deny Greg the opportunity to know you from the inside out. You have to trust him and know that this won't affect how he sees you. He loves you, Li. Just remember that, okay?"

Liza felt tears sting her eyes at her friend's words. From hilarity to melancholy in a matter of minutes.

She was a hot mess.

But Karina was right. If she couldn't trust her husband, who could she trust? She said goodbye to Karina and gently hung up the phone and thought about what she'd said. She glanced over at the bedside clock and sighed long and hard. But how could she fully trust him, no matter how much he loved him, if he refused to put her first? She obviously wasn't a priority in his life.

* * * * *

Greg glanced at the grandfather clock in the corner of his office and cursed out loud. He hadn't meant to stay so long.

After Liza left the office, he'd gone out to see if Renita was in her office and wasn't surprised when he'd found her gone. She'd obviously known he wouldn't need her assistance while Liza was there and had given them privacy. She'd left a note on her desk telling him to call her if he needed her.

He should have been gone hours ago. In all actuality, he had wrapped up the loose ends and could have left the office earlier. But he wasn't ready to go home. He wasn't sure what he'd do if he went home and Liza wasn't prepared to talk. He'd all but given her an ultimatum. Either they open up to one another or…

Or what? It wasn't like he'd leave her. He loved her too damn much to imagine life without her.

And he shared with Liza the burden of blame. He had his fair share of responsibility for why they were at a crossroad in the marriage. Lately he'd been working longer hours and taking on a heavier caseload and spending less time with her.

He needed to go home and talk to his wife. He rose in preparation of leaving, gathering his documents for the case as he cleared his desk and got ready to leave his office. As he lifted his briefcase from the corner of his desk, he was surprised when his door opened and Renita walked inside.

"Oh, Greg I'm sorry. I assumed you had already gone home with Mrs. Colburn. I came back to file these briefs and to work on a few things for the Grimes case." Renita said, the surprise in her dark eyes genuine.

"Renita, I thought you'd gone home when Liza came by earlier. There was no need for you to return, I've taken care of the updates for the brief. Why don't you go on back home. It's past ten o'clock."

"I don't mind working. I know this is paramount right now. I'm dedicated to this case. You know that Greg," she said.

Greg looked her in the eyes, and felt a moment's hesitation, as he saw something in Renita's eyes that told him that maybe there was more to her dedication to this case than what was on the surface. He dismissed it from his mind, not wanting to go there in his imagination. Renita was a beautiful woman, and he was having enough problems with his life without complicating things.

"There's a such thing as too much dedication," was all that he said.

When she raised an eyebrow he laughed, "I should know. Lately, Liza has been telling me that my dedication to the practice is out of whack with my dedication for her," he said, his thoughts once again on his situation.

"Well, I don't think Mrs. Colburn knows a good thing when she has it. You're dedication and passion is what makes you who you are. Without either one you wouldn't be the man that you are."

He wouldn't be human if he didn't admit that her words were a stroke to his ego. The collar on his shirt suddenly felt tight and he forced himself not to unbutton the top two buttons as he mumbled a thank you.

* * * * *

Liza came out of a sound sleep to feel Greg's big hands touching her, pulling her body close to his chest as he slid the straps of her negligee from her shoulders. He placed a warm kiss in the hollow where her shoulder and neck met as the gown slid down her breasts.

In the in-between stages of sleep and wakefulness, she allowed him to play and kiss her nape, even moving her head to the side to give him better access to her sensitive spot. It was several minutes of light lovemaking until she came to awareness and opened one sleepy eye to glance at the small clock radio on her side table. When she noted the time, she felt her entire body go rigid before she sat up in bed and turned sleepy, furious eyes in his direction.

"Oh no the hell you don't, Greg."

"Don't be angry Li, it's been a long night."

"Night?" she asked, her voice rising, the fogginess from sleep evaporating as she glanced at the time again. "Try morning, Greg. It's one o'clock in the morning. Where the hell have you been?"

He sat up in bed and rubbed a hand over his face. "Where do you think I've been?"

"I'm assuming the office. Working on the case. With Renita," she added the last bit and raised an eyebrow.

He chose that moment to move his head and the light from the bright moon showed the red flush that covered his lower jaw, and Liza felt her stomach drop with sudden pain.

"Liza, we were working. Please," she heard the exasperation in his voice and barely refrained from punching him in the chest. Hard. "Renita is a great paralegal and I'm lucky to have her work for me. But that's all there is to the relationship."

When he reached out for her to pull her close, she snatched her body away and moved as far away from him as possible. So far away that she damn near fell off the bed. She yanked the blanket to her chin and refused to even bother answering his comment about how wonderful a paralegal Renita was. She wasn't liable for her actions if she did.

She heard him sigh deeply and moments later she felt the mattress shift as he moved his body into another position. A peek over her shoulder told her that he too had turned his back to her as he settled.

She turned around; ignoring the sting of tears threatening to break free and closed her eyes before falling into a restless sleep.

Chapter Seven

ഇ

The next morning, Liza woke early to find Greg had already risen from bed as she heard him making noise in their master bathroom.

She lifted her body up just enough to settle her gaze to the clock radio and confirmed what her internal clock already told her, that it was several minutes until 7:00 a.m. She'd had an internal clock that woke her up no matter what, at the same time, every day, since college.

She reached over and turned on the radio, wanting to hear what the forecast was for the day and was cheered considerably when the forecast promised a spring day warming, dispelling the chill they'd had over the last few days.

She slowly got out of bed, her toes sinking into the deep pile of the Persian rug as she walked over to the overstuffed chair in the corner of the room. She slipped her arms into the sleeves of her favorite black silk kimono, and stuffed her feet into her slippers before making her way downstairs to put on a pot of coffee.

As she propped her hip against the counter, pouring water into the coffee maker, she felt a burgeoning headache coming on.

She opened the refrigerator door and withdrew her favorite peach-flavored Yoplait yogurt and bumped the door close with her hip. As soon as the coffee completed percolating, she poured a steaming mug full of the rich brew and carefully carried both coffee and yogurt to the table to sit down. She picked up the remote control, hoping to catch the tail end of Judge Mablean.

The judge was in the middle of asking why in the world the female plaintiff thought she deserved spousal support after six weeks of an unconsummated marriage when Greg walked into the kitchen wearing nothing more than a pair of gym shorts and a wary smile.

"I missed you in the shower this morning," he commented as he reached over her to withdraw a mug from the overhead glassed cabinet.

He referred to their habit of showering together. It had been a long time since they'd done that and she wondered why he was bringing it up. Most mornings lately, he seemed too busy to indulge in their previous love of showering and making love, claiming he had to go to the office early for one case or another.

"And when was the last time *that* happened, Greg?" she couldn't resist asking.

"I don't want a repeat of yesterday," he said. "I don't want to argue with you anymore, Liza." He slowly walked over to stand next to her at the table.

"Do you have to loom over me like that, Greg? Can't you sit down?"

He pulled out a chair and sat next to her.

"Baby, I'm serious. The last few weeks have been busy. But the last few months with us haven't been…right," he seemed to struggle to say the words. Liza felt her heart beat heavily in her chest, a sense of foreboding settling in her stomach.

"I've given this a lot of thought, Li," he said. He took her hand in his and squeezed it tightly before letting go.

"Oh, yes? What about?"

"I know we have some things to work out. I don't understand why the thought of having a child with me is so abominable to you."

"It's not about it being 'abominable'! I don't want children right now. I'm not ready to go down that road," she said.

"Go down *what* road?" The confusion was stamped on his face as well as his voice. "I don't get you Liza, I really don't. You won't talk to me about what's bothering you, you won't open up to me, it feels as though I'm married to a stranger, sometimes. I don't get any of this shit. Now you tell me that not only do you *no*t want children...you're not sure if you ever will? What the hell kind of shit is that?" His frustration was so high, his anger so palpable.

"What's there to open up about?" she cried. "What do you want from me? You know everything about me, I haven't hidden anything from you." Even as the words tripped off her tongue, Liza felt a queasy sensation settle in her belly at the lie, yet she forged ahead. "As far as having children, I told you when we first got married that I would need time before I'd want to have children. You seemed to be okay with it then. What's the rush? Why are you pressuring me now?"

"There's no pressure, Liza. But, I can't help wondering if it ever will be a priority for you. This is something I don't understand."

"What happens when I'm left alone? What happens when you leave me all alone to raise a child by myself? I can't do that. *I won't* do that." She'd started by yelling her response, but by the time she'd finished she'd barely spoken above a whisper. But it was loud enough for Greg to hear.

The look on his handsome face was as though someone had kicked him in the teeth.

Liza didn't know what to say or do, so she remained silent. She had no answer for him, because she didn't have an answer for herself. The silence stretched out until it was uncomfortable.

Eventually Greg stood up from the table, glancing down at her bent head as he did so.

"I'm late. Renita's meeting me at the courthouse for jury selection," he said. She resisted the urge to say "Screw, Renita". It wasn't the paralegal's fault her marriage was jacked up. It was hers.

"Can we meet for lunch?" she asked instead.

"I'm sorry Li, I can't break away. This will take most of the day. I'll try and get home early," was all that he could promise her.

Liza didn't say anything more, and when he kissed her on top of the head, she simply kept her head down.

Left alone in the kitchen, she turned the television off, no longer interested in watching any of her beloved judges dispense their reality-show justice to a bunch of wannabe stars.

She rose from the table and cleared away the small dishes, wiped the counter and left the kitchen. A nice workout was what she needed, she decided and ran up to her bedroom to put on her workout gear, and laced on her latest custom Nike running shoes. She tied the house key to her laces, just as she used to do in high school, before she left the house and took off running.

There was nothing like a good run to help her try and clear her head. She had a membership at their social club's fitness center, but for some reason, Liza had never felt comfortable there. It always seemed that the women were constantly measuring themselves against one another. Eyeing each other's workout gear, making sure the labels was designer.

Designer label-loving hussy that she admitted to being, Liza had a bit of a problem with making sure she had the latest and greatest designs for something she was going to sweat and funk out during the course of her workout.

Besides, being outside watching the scenery go by as she paced her run was more fulfilling and exhilarating than any elliptical machine could ever be. It gave her a rush of endorphins like no other.

As she ran, her thoughts traveled back to her marriage and her husband. She had no idea where they'd gone wrong.

Scratch that. Even to herself she couldn't lie.

She knew damn well where they'd gone wrong. And while she didn't blame herself for everything, she was honest enough to admit that the majority of the fault lay with her.

When she and Greg had first gotten married, she was reticent in telling him about what her life had been like growing up. She avoided thinking about it herself for the most part. Throughout their short engagement, she'd always managed to avoid in-depth talks about her childhood, choosing to gloss over the neglect and poverty.

Sure, he knew that she'd grown up as an only child of a single parent and that times had been hard. He also knew that her mother left for parts unknown soon after Liza graduated high school and left for college. And as hard as it was for her best friend to understand, Greg had never pressed her about information she didn't want to give. He seemed to be okay with the fact that she rarely spoke of her life before she started college. So, it had been relatively easy not to discuss those things she preferred stay in the past.

The topic of her youth, her mother and the effect it had on her were topics that she never spoke about. Not to anyone. It was a depressing time, she was over it; it didn't define who she was now, so why talk about it?

She made it to the outside running track and took off running, top speed. Her fast clip eventually slowed as her thoughts inevitable went to her mother. She hadn't spoken to her in over five years. Not really talked.

She would get the occasional phone call once or twice a year at best. Her mother would ask her for money, give her the address where to wire it and that was it. No "how are you honey, what's going on in your life?" No, "*I miss you and what's going on with your life"*. Nothing. Liza would try and engage her in conversation. Try her damnedest to get her mother to talk about her life, nudge her into asking Liza about her own.

But Edna never did. The only thing Edna wanted was the money. Once, Liza had said no. It was the last time that she did. Her mother had then gone on a long diatribe about what a selfish bitch she was.

"Oh, I get it. You think your shit don't stink…is that it, Liza?" Liza could all but smell the taint of gin on her mother's breath long distance and steeled herself for her verbal attack.

"Yeah, yeah, yeah. I see now. I raise you when nobody else would. Definitely not that worthless father of yours who took one look at you and put his damn size eleven feet to the concrete and got to steppin'! No, definitely not him," she said in a slightly slurred voice. With barely a pause in breath she continued her tirade. "I sacrifice, carry your narrow ass in my stomach for nine *long* months. Try my *best* to raise you right, feed and clothe you…and this…this is the thanks I get?" When she paused to take a breath, Liza quickly sought to end the diatribe before she *really* got into it.

"Mom…"

"No…oh *hell*, no. Let me finish! I send you to that Catholic School so you can get a good education. Better than what I had growing up and this is the thanks I get? Married to that *white* man and now you think you're all that! Well, let me clear it up for you Liza. Unless you have '*my shit don't stink*' perfume emitting out of your ass, you're no better than anybody else!"

"You know what, Mom?" Liza didn't know if she should laugh or cry at the utter ridiculousness of what was a classic Edna speech. Perfume *"emitting out of her ass"*. Classic, crazy Edna-isms. "I have no problem giving you money," she began.

"I don't need you to *give* me shit, Liza!" If possible her voice had risen in octaves beyond anything she'd ever achieved. It had to be a record.

"I'm sorry. I know that you don't *need* me, Mom. I don't have a problem lending you money."

"Oh just forget it! I don't need anything from you! You're just like that selfish bastard of a father of yours. Don't give a damn about anyone but yourself!" She ended, once again, in classic Edna style. Talking about a father Liza never met, much less someone she could compare herself with and find lacking.

And once again the tables had turned. *Liza* found herself practically begging her mother to take her money. "Please, Mom. Give me the address and I'll wire the money," she asked on a stifled sigh.

Her mother had feigned reluctance before she eventually gave her the address. Liza had then asked her where she was living and if her mother ever thought she'd come back to Stanton to visit. Edna had vaguely informed her that she'd have to check it out, see what was on her schedule before she'd commit to anything.

Liza had no idea what could be so pressing on her mother's schedule that she couldn't take the time out to come and visit her. Although her mother was always out of money, she did work. She was a registered nurse and never found difficulties finding a job as nursing was one of those professions that there seemed to always have shortages.

She also made decent money as a nurse, whenever she worked. The lack of a job or education wasn't Edna's problem. Her problem was her addiction to alcohol and anti-depressants. It was a rare day that her mother wasn't either drunk or depressed. And usually, she was both.

But, she was a functioning drunk for the most part, as it had become a normal part of who she was. She was able to work some of the time, attend functions that were job related.

But because work wasn't steady, she and Liza had been on public assistance throughout most of Liza's life as a child.

Her mother had never attended any functions as Liza was growing up. For that, Liza had turned to Karina and her family. She could always rely on Karina's Big Momma and mother to come and see her in plays and recitals that every child looked forward to having a parent attend. Edna would claim she had a headache from working, or would simply coldly reject the possibility that she would come with little or no explanation.

At times like that, Liza would imagine that she had a father who was far away. A father who, for a variety of made-up reasons that only a child could come up with, couldn't rescue her from her mother.

But, had he been able to, not only would he have taken her away, neither would he'd miss her recital for anything in the world. And like Karina's grandmother and mother, he would be there with a small bouquet of flowers just for her at the end of the recitals.

Liza continued to run around the track, wiping her face, ignoring the fact that it wasn't only sweat that she wiped from her flushed cheeks. She ignored the fact that the burning sting in her eyes had nothing to do with the exertion from her run, but instead had everything to do with her trip down memory lane.

As she ran, she picked up speed, pushing herself to the limit, unconsciously trying her damnedest to outrun the ugly ghosts from her past.

Chapter Eight

❧

"That went well, don't you think?" Greg held the revolving door open for Renita, as they left the courthouse. They both put on sunglasses as the bright afternoon sun shone brightly on their faces. It was spring and although the sun was out, there was still the smallest nip in the air to signify that the time for shorts and t-shirts was still a bit of a way off.

"I was quite surprised at the ease with which opposing council agreed with most of our selections," Renita agreed, referring to the jury selection process for their upcoming trial. She pulled the light jacket she wore over her navy blue suit closer around her body to ward off the chill from the spring day.

"Yes, so was I. I thought for sure that we'd be there the whole day. It's just past noon," he said after a quick glance down at his watch. As they continued to walk, Greg glanced down at his paralegal and hid a smile.

Renita was so formal in her speech and dress. She was the ultimate professional from the top of her close-cropped curly hair, to the soles of her dark blue, pumps. He knew they were Prada's because Liza owned at *least* a dozen pair of the designer's shoes. If nothing else he'd learned of his wife's utter fascination and love of designer footwear after seven years of marriage.

It was too bad that he'd recently realized he was lacking more vital information. Information that was much more important than her obsession with shoes.

He thought of how little he'd actually known about his wife's life. Any real knowledge that he had of who she was before they were married began at the age of eighteen. She

162

shared brief information about anything before that time. He was clueless about what her life had been like, truly.

That was until a week ago, before he'd received the strange call from Liza's mother. Within moments of his surprise to hear from his wife's estranged mother, he'd been left stunned after she'd asked him for money before preceding to go into details about how hard it had been to raise Liza single and alone, and how nice it was that Liza didn't have to worry about working and trying to raise a child all alone.

"You're right, it is lunchtime. I know of a really nice lunch counter just a few blocks south of Hub. Would you like to go?" she asked. Hub Street ran throughout the entire large city.

Greg glanced once again at his watch and debated calling Liza. She'd asked him that morning if they could have lunch, and at the time he hadn't thought that he'd have the time. It had been almost a relief to tell her no.

"That sounds good, Renita. I'll need to call Liza first. Let's go." he said and they walked briskly to his vehicle parked in the front of the courthouse. After he helped her inside the passenger side, he jogged to the driver's side and folded his long frame inside.

He placed a call to Liza and caught her on her cell phone. She was in the process of dressing and he could tell she was ticked when he said he couldn't make lunch. He felt a small tinge of guilt, but brushed it away.

As Greg maneuvered through the congested downtown streets on the way to the cafeteria, he put the call out his mind, as he and Renita strategized about the jury make-up and which ones they felt would be more sympathetic to their client. Renita, as usual, had helped to select the most sympathetic females. She had a knack for discerning which potential female jury members were more inclined to be sympathetic.

"The prenup clearly states that if Mr. Grimes is able to prove his wife has cheated on him, than all financial arrangements are null and void," Renita said as they entered the bright cafeteria.

"Yes, but we have to prove that first. So far, our detective hasn't come up with anything to prove she's been anything else but chaste and true to her husband," Greg agreed as he removed her coat and they both eased into the red leather booth.

The café was decorated in a retro fifties style, complete with roller skating waitresses. Okay, so that was a bit over the top, Greg thought, but Renita swore the food was great.

Yes, Greg thought again to himself, *a bit over the top.* He then turned his attention back to the case.

"The damnedest thing, is that I *know* Melissa Grimes has been cheating. I don't understand how the detective is missing it."

He didn't bother to excuse his language or try and clean it up. Renita was used to his manner of speech and despite her outward appearance of being strait laced; he'd once overheard her use language to some guy on the phone that made *him* blush. He'd kept that information to himself when he'd heard her cursing and quietly left the room without her knowing he'd been there.

"No doubt, she is. Maybe it's time to look for another agency. You haven't been satisfied with this new agency anyway. Not since Gaynor…Mr. Holt left," she reminded him. Greg glanced up sharply at her when he noted the slight emphasis she placed on the former agency employee's name before she corrected herself and referred to him by his last name.

The firm had utilized the services of the Tyson Detective Agency for years, with no complaints from anyone, as the agency had a solid reputation for procuring the information the lawyers needed to help strengthen the case they were working. Greg had dealt only with Gaynor or his brother Jayden, until the men had broken away from the agency to found their own firm. He'd not been as pleased with his newest detective's results so far.

As he glanced over at his assistant's beautiful, but placid features, he thought he saw something flash in her eyes as she spoke Gaynor's name. "Have you heard from him since he left the firm?" he felt compelled to ask and silently confirmed what he thought he saw. There was something there.

"Why would I have spoken with Mr. Holt?" she asked without any change in her low voice.

The waitress skated over, tottering on her skates and almost landed the platter in Greg's lap before he helped her regain her balance. "Whoa! Here, let me take that," he offered, removing the drinks from the platter before he helped the woman place the plates on the table.

The waitress' cheeks, already red from the exertion of skating, turned even redder as she thanked him before she left the two of them to eat their lunch.

"No reason. You had more contact with him than I did. I thought perhaps you'd heard from him," he explained, picking up the thread of the conversation before the waitress delivered their lunch.

She took a delicate bite of the veggie sandwich and chewed thoughtfully, before carefully swallowing. Greg took a healthy bite of his corned beef, waiting for her to speak. As he waited, he glanced at her lunch and as usual, wondered how she stomached eating nothing but vegetables and tofu as she was a practicing vegetarian. She took a small sip of her tea before answering.

"No. I haven't heard from Mr. Holt," was all she said, but Greg knew she wasn't telling the truth. Obviously, she didn't want him to know something and the flush that ran underneath her bronze cheeks gave witness to her embarrassment. He left it alone. It was none of his business anyway.

"But, if the firm is in agreement, I could contact him if you were interested in procuring his services for this case."

"That shouldn't be an issue. I'll let the partners know and then I can alert Grimes. If we have to go with another detective, he has to agree to foot the bill."

"That will be fine, Greg. As soon as you let me know, I'll contact Mr. Holt."

They finished eating their lunch in companionable silence sprinkled with occasional conversation. When they'd finished eating, Greg signaled the roller skating waitress over to bring him the bill. After signing the slip, he glanced at his watch.

"I'm going to try and leave the office earlier this evening, hopefully, around six or so. I can do a lot of the paperwork at home. I'll contact the partners when we get back to the office and give them a heads-up and then you can contact the Holt brothers about securing their services. Feel free to go home, Renita, anytime after that. We have an early day again tomorrow. I'm sure anything you have can wait until then. You've been working long hours as I have. Take the evening off. I need to get home to Liza as soon as I can."

"Thanks for the offer, but I think I'll hang around, I have some paperwork to organize. And if you need me, you know where to find me," she said as she sipped her cola. "May I ask you a personal question, Greg?" she asked, and surprised, Greg quickly glanced up at her face.

"Of course, Renita. Shoot," he said.

"Are you and Mrs. Colburn having problems?" she asked, taking her eyes off him, suddenly caught up in picking at what appeared to be imaginary lint from her dark blue jacket.

For a minute, Greg was tempted to deny any problems he and Liza were having. He'd never discussed his wife or his marriage with Renita. He had several friends who he'd had since college, but he'd always tended to keep to himself and had never felt comfortable discussing his marriage with any of them.

"Why do you ask? What concern is that of yours?" he asked her bluntly.

"I'm sorry, that was rude of me to ask. It's none of my business," she said and rose as though to leave the table.

Greg reached a hand out to forestall her standing. She glanced from her hand to his and a dark flush, once again, stained her cheeks. The look she threw him was unsettling and he slowly removed his hand from hers. "Please, sit down."

She hesitated, as though unsure. Greg didn't know what was happening, but he felt as though something else was going on other than the obvious. There were undercurrents occurring that hadn't been there minutes before.

Renita slowly sat back down in the bench and looked at him with an expectant expression settling across her face.

"I'm a little touchy about the subject of marriage, if you want to know the truth. Renita, you didn't do anything wrong. We've known each other long enough for me to know that," he apologized.

"Is it anything that you can talk about?" she ventured to ask.

"It's a long story. Much longer and complicated than even I knew until recently." He confessed. He knew his answer was ambiguous at best, but his confusion and anger over the situation was still too raw for him to hide.

"You don't have to talk about it," Renita assured him.

Greg was silent as he thought about the complicated situation with his wife. He and Renita had never spoken about personal matters, but he needed to talk with someone. Maybe as a female, she'd be able to shed light on the subject. God only knew, he was confused as hell.

"A week ago my wife's mother called me."

She looked at him expectantly, waiting for him to go on.

"It wouldn't be so strange an occurrence, I guess, had I'd ever spoken to her before. But, I've never seen her, much less spoken on the phone with her."

"Did she want anything in particular?" she asked.

"Aside from the fact that she was asking to borrow several thousand dollars?" he asked and laughed humorously. "Not much, except to tell me things about my wife that I had no idea of. Things that Liza *should* have disclosed to me a long time ago. I feel as though I don't really know who my wife truly is," he said grimly.

Chapter Nine

ॐ

Liza allowed the warm, gentle spray from the shower to cascade over her body. She raised her arms, her small breasts lifting high as she ran her fingers over her hair, smoothing the short, wet strands away from her forehead.

Since she'd cut her hair, she'd experienced a liberation she never had before. Although she wasn't quite ready to go *au natural* as her friend Karina had done, not ready to give up the ease and manageability the relaxer gave her, she liked not spending hours combing, detangling, deep conditioning, blow drying, hot iron…the whole styling madness she went through once a week at her favorite salon.

Although, according to Karina, being natural, sans chemicals of any type wasn't difficult at all. Liza was honest enough to admit that she had a ways to go before she was prepared to entertain the thought of allowing her natural kink free rein.

Life was a process, a journey. At least that's what Karina's Big Momma used to always say, Liza thought with a melancholy smile as she thought of Karina's grandmother. She really missed Big Momma, although she wasn't her grandmother, Liza had always felt connected to the older woman. She'd always welcomed Liza, helping her to feel as though she were apart of the family.

Liza leisurely finished washing her body and stepped out of the glassed-in shower and wrapped her naked body in the overlarge plush towel. She grabbed the matching hand towel and gently dried her hair before wrapping it, turban-style around her head. Just as she folded the corner of the towel inside, she heard her cell phone ring and rushed over to answer it.

"Hello."

"Hi, sweetheart, it's me." Greg said in his deep voice.

The sound of his voice had her heart racing. After seven years he still had the same effect on her. She glanced at the clock and realized it was lunchtime. With a smile on her face, she held the small receiver between her ear and shoulder as she whipped off the towel and sat on the bed, lotion bottle in hand.

"Look baby, I'm sorry. But I'm not going to be able to meet you for lunch. I still have work to do and can't see my way out of it for the next few hours." She felt the smile fall off her face at his words.

Damn it. She should have known better than to get all excited. No doubt he and Renita would have a cozy little lunch together in his office as they worked side by side.

She couldn't stand Renita's placid acting ass. Always so damn calm and bland looking. Work be damned, Liza *knew* the woman wanted her husband. She was two seconds away from saying something *really* ugly, but held herself in check at the last minute.

"I understand, Greg. Maybe another time," she said instead, taking the high road. It wasn't Renita's fault anyway. It was just easier to place the blame anywhere but where it truly lay. Liza wasn't quite sure where that was at the present time.

"I'm going to get home early. Would you like to go out to dinner?" he asked and Liza brightened.

She agreed, her spirits lifted, although there was *something* in his voice that she didn't like or understand. It was the same *something* that had been there for the last week whenever they talked.

Before they hung up the phone, they agreed on a time and place. Liza was happy when he suggested they meet at Rigby's as they had a dance floor and live band several nights a week. It had been a long time since she and Greg had gone out dancing. It lightened her heart, eased the burden she'd had in it since their parting earlier in the morning.

Liza placed her cell phone back on the beside table before picking the bottle of lotion back up to begin to anoint her arms slowly, her thoughts, as they had been over the last few weeks, centered not only on her marriage, but on her past. Maybe it was time she faced her past as Karina was constantly telling her she needed to do. She didn't realize the impact not sharing her life history before the age of eighteen was having on her marriage.

At least, not cognitively.

But on a subconscious level, she knew that Greg deserved to know everything about her. The good and bad.

It wasn't as though she was a part of a traveling pack of bank robbers for heaven's sake. She had nothing to be ashamed of, she had no culpability in the way she had been raised, she'd only been a child. Yet, she'd always felt a strange responsibility for the life that she and her mother had lived. As though, had it not been for her, her mother wouldn't have been on welfare.

Or a functioning alcoholic.

With a heavy sigh, she was rising from the bed when her cell phone rang again. She quickly lifted it, pressing the talk button and stemmed her disappointment when Catherine, one of her friends from the club chirped a hello at her.

Catherine called to invite Liza to a late lunch with a few of the other members of their set and Liza forced a cheery note into her voice as she agreed to meet the women at the social club, before pressing *end* on her receiver.

She walked to the bathroom and absentmindedly studied the array of cosmetics that lined her vanity before she popped open the case to her powder-to-cream foundation and carefully smoothed it over her face. As she smoothed the makeup on, she studied her face in the large, gold- framed mirror.

Her birthday was just around the corner. She'd be thirty-three years old. She moved her head this way and that way, looking for any signs of premature aging. She was happy she'd inherited her mother's genetic make-up in that department. Not a sign of a wrinkle to be found anywhere on her smooth, deep brown skin.

At least, she thought she inherited it from her mother. She'd never met her father, and besides the description her mother gave, wouldn't know the man if he were standing buck-naked in front of her waving a neon flag. She shoved the thought of her unknown sperm donor to the recesses of her mind. As she usually did whenever thoughts of him would surface.

She had the beginnings of a headache and opened the medicine cabinet to withdraw her prescription pain reliever. She'd been increasingly suffering from headaches and had been forced to seek medical attention as ibuprofen no longer did the trick in providing her relief. She poured a small paper cup of water and swallowed the small pills before she returned the bottle to the cabinet.

She smoothed on a light dusting of blush to her high cheekbones and darkened her eyelashes before she outlined her full lips and applied a coral-colored lipstick. When she finished applying her makeup, she titled her head to the side and made a small moue with her lips and winked, laughing to herself. She left the bathroom and went to her walk-in closet, in search of the *right* outfit to wear to lunch.

The group of ladies she was meeting were all members of the same club that she and Greg joined several years ago. They were all nice enough, if a tad on the catty side. Liza had learned quickly that the women were nice on the outside, butter wouldn't melt in their mouths, as Karina's Big Momma would say, but they could be total bitches at times.

Liza had seen for herself how they'd turned on one of their own when the Ellis' lost a great majority of their money because Marcus Ellis hadn't had the foresight to diversify his portfolio. When the semi-crash happened, they'd been left with nothing.

Valerie Ellis had turned to her friends for support, but they'd turned away from her as though her financial problems were some disease they could catch. Liza had been empathetic to the woman and once offered to buy lunch, just to be nice.

Wrong answer.

Valerie Ellis had all but cursed her out in her very precise English, saying that she could "afford to buy her own damn lunch". In fact, she insisted on buying the lunch for every damn body at the table. She and Marcus had only experienced a minor setback. It was by no means the end of the world for them. They were just fine financially.

Within a few weeks, no one was really surprised when Valerie decided to go to a secluded spa, not saying exactly where this spa was located, and neither was anyone surprised when within days of her departure the large moving trucks appeared outside the Ellis' home.

What the incident had taught Liza was twofold. The women in this community were too proud to accept what they saw as a "handout" and her extension of friendship was neither wanted nor appreciated. It also taught her to keep her well-meaning intentions to herself.

Back in her neighborhood in North Stanton, neighbors always helped neighbors in time of need. It was automatic and nothing out of the ordinary. God only knew she and her mother had received their fare share of "help" over the years.

She selected and dressed in a cream-colored cashmere sweater, cocoa brown full legged slacks, and low-heeled, brown, Prada mules. She quickly dumped the contents of one purse into the matching brown purse and left the room. After setting the alarm on the house, she went through the adjoining door that led to the garage and opened her car door.

She eased into the leathered seats of her low-slung Mercedes and reversed out of the garage, carefully maneuvering out of the circular driveway as she automatically turned on the high-powered car stereo and the car filled with the hard-pounding smooth rhythmic beat of her favorite NuSoul band.

"Take me away from here, far away from here..." she sang along with the female lead vocalist as she drove to the club, unconsciously gripping the steering wheel tightly as she sang.

When she arrived at the club, she drove to the front entry and allowed the valet to open her car door for her. She deposited the keys into his white-gloved hands and walked to the entry and smiled thanks when the attendant opened the door for her.

She removed her sunglasses, depositing them into their case and tucked them inside her purse, and automatically cast an admiring gaze around the interior of the club.

The interior was decorated in rich earth tones of red and gold, with classic artwork adorning the walls. As she walked toward the double doors that would take her inside the luncheon area, the heels of her mules sunk into the plush deep red carpet.

She felt many eyes on her, as she walked with studied confidence toward the table of waving women. Her peripheral vision caught one onlooker eyeballing her and saw the woman's face relax into a smile when she noticed the table of women welcoming her.

Whatever.

Liza plastered a smile on her face as she walked up to the table and sat down.

"Sorry I'm late, what did I miss?" she said and smiled before picking up and glancing over the menu.

"Not much. Leslie was telling us about the Goodman's. Did you hear about them?" Michelle asked.

Michelle was one of the bitchier of the women in the group. She seemed to take a secret delight in the painful episodes in the lives of their friends than anyone else. Liza stole a quick glance over the woman, taking her in, in one quick once-over.

Her long blond hair was fluffed and teased within an inch of its life, landing at the top of her shoulders. She peered behind her small, lightly tinted glasses with an ugly gleam of delight in her aqua-colored, close-set eyes as she began to gossip about the latest news and how Elaine Goodman caught her husband red-handed having sex with the nanny.

"And what makes it so bad, is that they planned on taking a cruise next week and leaving the children at home! How in the world will she find someone else on short notice?" she asked, ending the tale. Her cheeks hollowed from the long drink she took from the straw in her tea.

All of that damn gossiping made a woman mighty thirsty.

And what the hell was wrong with this woman that she thought the worst thing about the situation was a lack of childcare.

"You think that's the worst of it? The fact that she *may* have to cancel her cruise reservation? Not that she caught her husband screwing the nanny?" Liza tried her *best* to leave it alone. Tried her *damnedest.*

But hell, sometimes, she had to call it like it was.

She'd have Greg's nuts on a silver platter; straight-up served Hungarian meatball style around a bed of crisp green lettuce, if she'd been the one to bust him fucking the nanny.

"Of course not, Liza." Michelle trained her beady stare in Liza's direction, and Liza caught the flash of irritation before the woman could mask it. "I was simply making an observation," she finished with a small...tight...smile.

"And so was I," Liza volleyed back and raised one eyebrow at the woman. Just barely. Just barely she refrained from giving Michelle her real opinions.

Sometimes the country club life was harder for her to navigate than her life in North Stanton had been.

"So, Liza, did you and Greg go and check out that musical showing in Austin, yet?"

Liza turned her gaze away from Michelle and smiled at Luanne. Lu was the newest member in the group and Liza had taken an instant liking to the small Asian woman. She and her husband Mac met when Mac was stationed in Korea during his short tenure with the military.

When they'd moved back to Stanton, Mac had bought one of the newer houses on the row, having admired the area from the time he'd been a child on the outside looking in. Like Liza, Luanne's husband Mac had grown up in North Stanton. North Stanton had no respect of person. It was an equal-opportunity poverty-stricken community. White, black, brown...all were welcomed.

Mac had proudly brought his new wife home ignoring the polite stares and settled into his new home with his wife, content to stay in his own world.

Luanne, on the other hand, was not content to stay at home puttering in the garden. She was vivacious, funny and sweet. And once the others met her and had gotten to know her, her natural vivacious, sometimes outrageous personality, had won them all over.

Liza had felt an instant kinship with the woman upon meeting her, as she too found herself feeling like the odd woman out when she first joined the club. There was something about growing up poor and disenfranchised that would always make her the slightest bit aware of things she probably wouldn't be otherwise. Things that weren't race related. Things that were universal to the poor everywhere.

"The one with all the stomping?" she laughed, referring to the Broadway show that had won several Tony awards. And although she'd enjoyed the stomping and beating it, had given her a serious headache by the end.

"I wonder where they'll live now?" Michelle asked.

Damn. She just couldn't let it go. Once Michelle got hold of gossip, she was like a pit bull with a rawhide.

"I mean, where she'll live. Didn't she file for divorce?" she asked.

"Hmmm. Who knows? But I sure would have loved to be a fly on the wall during those proceedings," Debra said. Debra was nice enough when Michelle wasn't around. But once Michelle was in attendance, she played bitch partner with her. Teaming up to laugh and gossip at the chosen victim.

"Hopefully, they'll recover." Leslie piped in, before turning to Liza, "Liza, I saw that musical too! I went with my mom. She's kind of hard of hearing, so she said she loved how well she could hear all the nice soft music. Poor thing. Whereas it was loud as hell to us, Mom thought it sounded like elevator music!"

Leslie and her husband Raymond had been apart of the Regency Community from the time they were both children. They'd known each other their entire lives and when they married it was natural they'd settle in the same community that they'd grown up in.

The women stopped speaking when their lunch arrived. Throughout the luncheon, try as she might, Liza just couldn't get into the conversation. For some reason, she was beyond irked at the stabbing comments from Michelle and her demon spawned sidekick Debra. Yeah, she was off today.

Usually, she could brush it off, but today, their constant gossip about the Goodman's misfortune, grated on her last nerve. Maybe it was the glee with which the beady-eyed Michelle told the story. Or maybe it was the way that her eyes would widen, a sly-assed grin on her face as she all but rubbed her hands together in creepy delight as she gave amazing details about Stan Goodman's affairs, along with his purported sexual prowess in the bedroom.

Whatever it was, she knew she needed to get away for a minute or she'd say something she'd regret later in hindsight.

"Excuse me ladies, I need to visit the restroom."

She couldn't leave the table fast enough and almost tripped over the thick carpet in her haste to get away. Once inside the bathroom she breathed an audible sigh of relief and slowly peeled her body from the door, glad there was no one in the opulent ladies room other than herself and the attendant.

"Honey, are you okay?"

Liza looked up from the sink, which she had been standing in front of staring into the mirror not really seeing anything. She had no idea how long she'd been staring off into space. Her mind had been a million miles away. She turned to the older woman with a practiced smile on her face, but stopped as she instantly recognized her.

"Sister Pauline?" she asked. She couldn't believe it was Sister Pauline from the church she'd grown up in. The old woman hadn't aged a bit!

Her dark brown skin was liberally sprinkled with moles and freckles dotted across the bridge of her large, bell -shaped nose. Her dark eyes seemed magnified behind the thick lenses of her bifocals and Liza laughed inwardly at her eyebrows. Sister Pauline obviously still shaved her eyebrows completely off, and redrew them in thick and black, big and arched, giving her a wide-eyed permanent look of surprise.

The old woman scrunched her large nose up and peered into Liza's face behind her thick pop-bottle glasses. "Liza LeCroix? Girl, is that you?" She laughed. "Honey, let me look at you all grown up!" she said, getting close to Liza. "Girl, you better get over here and give Sister Pauline a hug!" she said, hugging her as she breathed heavily into Liza's face.

Yep. If she'd thought she was mistaken before, the minute the old woman's breath hit Liza's nostrils, she knew it was Sister Pauline. After all these years, not only did she look the same, she still had funky breath.

Liza felt tears in the back of her eyes, and not because of the old woman's horrendous breath. Somehow, seeing the familiar watery-eyed woman from her childhood was overwhelming. She hugged Sister Pauline fiercely, smoothing her hands over the woman's bony back.

"Baby, you're crushing Sister Pauline!"

Liza laughed and released the older woman. She'd forgotten how she'd refer to herself in the first person.

"Sorry, Sister Pauline. How've you been? I didn't know you worked here," Liza said, taking a soft tissue from the marble sink vanity and lightly dabbing at her eyes.

"Chile, I been working here for a while! I usually work evenings though. I could ask how you've been, but I can already tell that, baby…you look good! Tell Sister Pauline what you been up to. And how's that mama of yours?" she asked, and listened with a wide smile plastered on her face as Liza told her how she'd gone to college and received her bachelor's degree as well as master's degree in social work, with an emphasis on helping children and adolescents.

"Oh, baby, that's so nice. But what about your mother? What's she up to these days? She hightailed it out of Stanton as soon as you left and nobody's seen hide nor tail of her since!"

"Yes, Mom left when I went to the University. She lives out in Oakland with one of her sisters. She always said she'd go back to California as soon as I graduated," Liza forced a smile on her face.

"Umm, umm umm. No offense, baby, but Edna was always a selfish trollop, if you ask Sister Pauline. She could have waited 'til you finished school before she left her only baby girl alone," she said.

Sister Pauline's lips were pressed tightly together and pooched up, the upper lip touching the end of her nose as though she smelled something rank. Her eyebrows were lowered above squinted eyes, as she tsk'd and shook her head in obvious disgust over her mother's desertion.

The look on her heavily lined face was one that only a black woman of her age could have and get away with. "Well any way, that's good about you and your social work. I always wanted to be a social worker. I bet you love that work, don't you? Being able to help a young girl...kind of like how you was helped by all them social workers you and your mama had, when you was growin' up."

"Well, actually Sister Pauline...I don't work, ma'am." Liza was suddenly ashamed. "I married my husband, Greg. He's an attorney. He's a partner in his firm."

"Well, that's good baby, that you don't have to work. I think it's nice when a woman can stay at home with her children. Too many folks today let other folks raise their kids. Then they wonder why the little bastards grow up trying to set off bombs at the schools and such," Sister Pauline said, shaking her head. "Umm, umm, umm. It's a damn shame, it's a *damn* shame, is what it is. All I'd need to have is them kids for one day. Just one damn day. One day with Sister Pauline and their little asses would stop acting a fool. One day with Sister Pauline and they'd see the light. The little fuckers. Help 'em Lord!" she said, suddenly catching the spirit as she lifted her hands and waved them in the air.

Sister Pauline had caught what was known as a "mini-spirit". It always hit her like that. Usually after a tirade, she'd catch the "spirit" of God.

Liza was torn between laughing and crying. Laughing because Sister Pauline hadn't changed a bit. She'd cursed in one breath and praised God with the other.

Crying because she felt ashamed.

She'd gone into social work for the reason Sister Pauline mentioned. To help young people, young women in particular, who were living in poverty, but had potential for so much more. Potential that was often overlooked when a child lived in the projects.

"No, Sister Pauline, I don't have children."

"What? No children? How long you been married, girl?"

"Seven years, ma'am."

"Hmm." She humphed, peering at Liza over the top of the glasses perched at the end of her large nose. "What? He got that penis disability or something?"

"Penis disability?"

"Girl, don't play with Sister Pauline. You know what I mean. When a man can't get his willy wonka up."

"You mean erectile dysfunction?"

"You saying it, so that tells me you know what the hell Sister Pauline is talkin' about! They got some pills that a get his ass hard as a damn *rock*. Do you remember Sister Roberta Hall?" When Liza nodded her head, she continued. "Well, a few years back her old man was having them problems. Roberta went on that Internet and bought some of them penis pills! Honey, he's been hittin' it like a porn star, ever since!" She laughed so hard Liza had to lightly thump her on the back to help clear her throat.

"No, ma'am. He doesn't have a problem with that. We've just decided to wait until the time is right," she said, trying her hardest not to laugh.

"Lord have mercy, chile! If it ain't right after seven years...when the hell it's gone be right? And if you don't have kids at home, why aren't you out there working as a social worker? Why aren't you helping out children who need you? What did you get all that education for in the first place? To live on the Hill? You know, the good Lord charges us to help each other. He allowed you to get all that good education, girl! You need to use it."

Liza stared at the woman, a queasy sensation pooling in the pit of her stomach at her words.

She knew in her heart that the old woman was right on all counts. Even if she did sound crazy as hell mixing religion and cursing like that.

Liza had gotten her degree in social work with the desire to help kids who were disenfranchised, just as she'd been as a child. To give kids that were often overlooked, a voice.

However, her first job as a social worker had been in C.P.S., Child Protection Services, and she'd realized soon after working in the field that it was too close to home for her. She couldn't stomach the condition many of the children had been living in. The first time she'd had a child as a client who'd suffered from severe neglect, she'd wanted to run up on the child's parents and flat blast the both of their sorry behinds for what they'd done to the small girl.

She realized that she was in the wrong field and had gone to work in an area totally unrelated to her education, before she'd stopped working altogether within a few years of her marriage to Greg.

But, in the back of her mind, she'd wanted to return to social work.

Liza smiled at the old woman and patted her on one thin shoulder. "You're right Sister Pauline. Maybe it's time I gave that some thought," she said and spoke for a few minutes more with the old woman.

She leaned down and kissed her leathery cheek, slipping a twenty dollar bill into her smock before she left the restroom and returned to the table with her friends.

For the remainder of the lunch, Liza was nearly silent, only answering questions directly asked of her, her mind a million miles away. The old woman's words rang sharply in her consciousness. Was she being selfish? Was it so wrong that she didn't want to open the floodgates to her past? That she didn't feel it necessary to talk about, work with, or associate with *anything* that reminded her of the bullshit of her painful childhood?

Chapter Ten

🔊

"I think that we'll find greater success if we employ the Holt brothers. I've worked with them in the past and I've always been well pleased with their work," Greg spoke on the phone to his client as he leaned back in the large leather chair, twirling one pencil between his thumb and forefinger.

He listened as his client spoke, before answering. "Great. Mr. Holt has just left my office and he's prepared to work on the case. He'll be able to start right away," he said and, after a few more moments of conversation, hung up the phone.

"Renita, could you start the paperwork for Gaynor Holt? I've just spoken with Mr. Grimes and he's fine with footing the bill for the Holt's to take over the investigation," he said into the small intercom.

"I sure will, Greg. Actually, Mr. Holt is still here," she said.

"Oh really?" Greg was surprised the investigator was still in the office as he'd ended his meeting with Holt twenty minutes ago. "Well, since he's there, go ahead and draw up the contract for him to sign. And after that, feel free to go home. I'm leaving in the next thirty minutes, myself."

After he hung up the phone, he glanced at the antique grandfather clock in the corner of the room. It was early for him to leave, it was just barely five o'clock, but he wanted to take Liza out to dinner.

He and Liza needed a down and dirty, cut all the bullshit talk. The impasse they were at was grating on his mind, screwing with his concentration. Things weren't right and he was determined to fix it.

He picked up the phone and placed a call to Liza to ask her to meet him at Rigby's. The surprise in her voice when he'd asked her out to dinner had made him feel a bit bad. She was obviously shocked that he'd asked. There was a time, when it was so commonplace that she'd have been surprised had he *not* called for dinner.

After he hung up the phone, he began to clear his desk, anticipation settling in his gut. He and Liza were going to get some things straight. He wanted answers and by the end of the night, if all went well, he was planning on bringing up the discussion of making a baby with his wife.

When he'd confided in Renita earlier, he'd felt as though a great weight had been lifted from his shoulders. He felt he knew what had to be done. He walked through his office to Renita's and noted that Gaynor Holt was lounging against her desk in a deceptively relaxed pose.

He'd interrupted them in the middle of a conversation and Greg picked up the irritable tone to her voice and he stopped to make sure everything was okay.

"I suppose Renita has told you that Mr. Grimes has accepted the change in investigators?" he smiled and shook the man's hand.

"Yes, that's what your lovely assistant and I were discussing…weren't we, Ms. Nash?" he asked, in what sounded to Greg, like a challenging voice. As though he were daring her to disagree.

Interesting.

She smiled and agreed, "Yes. Yes we were, Greg." The smile she threw the investigator's way could only be described as tight-lipped.

"Is there a problem?" he asked her. Just to make sure.

"No, everything is fine. I'll wrap this up and leave as soon as I'm finished. You go ahead. I won't stay long," she promised, with a side-look at Holt.

"Have a nice night. Both of you." Greg said, including Gaynor in his farewell. "I'll see you in the morning, Renita. I'm going to meet Liza," he said and left.

"You can't have him, you know." Gaynor's deep, scratchy voice forced Renita's attention away from Greg's departure.

"What? What are you talking about?" Distracted, she felt her face heat. She stared directly into the investigators light gray eyes.

He raised a dark eyebrow, not saying a word. His silence irritated the hell out of her.

"Well? You can't say something like that and just leave it at that." She prodded him to finish what he started.

"I don't think you really want me to say anything else...do you?" he challenged. His voice was openly mocking.

Renita refrained from telling the rude as hell investigator off, *just* in the nick of time. He didn't know her like that.

She turned away from him and typed a few words into her computer and opened the document which had the firm's standard contract used for contractors. She swiftly modified it according to Greg's direction, printed it and handed it over to Gaynor for his inspection. As he read over the document, pulling out half-lenses, she stifled a laugh at the picture he presented as she observed him while he wasn't paying attention to her.

Unlike Greg, who was immaculately dressed at all times, Gaynor was barely presentable on his best day. Most of the time he was either dressed in jeans and t-shirt-if the weather was nice- or jeans and sweatshirt if it was cold. Occasionally, he'd call himself dressing up and wear slacks. With a sweatshirt. Or a t-shirt.

It wasn't that he was unattractive, she thought as her glance slid over him. He was just too damn big, several inches taller than Greg, who was over six feet in height and broader throughout his chest and legs, hands, feet...everything. She never liked to stand next to him because of his sheer presence.

It wasn't only his physical presence that was, *overwhelming*. It was him. He was attractive enough, she supposed, in a sloppy, *Detective Colombo* kind of way. His light gray eyes were fringed by thick, dark lashes that looked ridiculous on a man of his size. Well...maybe they weren't *that* ridiculous looking, she admitted reluctantly to herself.

His squared chin had the slightest hint of a dimple, just enough to make a woman look closer, but was *constantly* covered with light stubble, as was his lean cheeks. He probably had to shave more than twice a day to keep it clean.

She wasn't into men that hairy.

He kept his blond hair cut close to his head, almost military style. At first she'd thought he'd dyed his hair as his eyebrows and eyelashes were so dark and his hair so blond. He kept the top of his hair a bit longer than what she'd think would be army regulation, as she discreetly observed the way his hair fell over his knitted brow as he concentrated on the document.

Her gaze swept over his large, lean body. That was the other thing that irritated her about him. How damn big he was.

She was very petite and although she liked tall men, he was *way* too tall, and *way* to big. He wore his jeans loose, but she could still see the way his thighs bulged through the faded jeans, the way the jeans cupped his muscular butt when he bent down to pick up one of the pieces of paper as it fell from his hands.

His large, very masculine hands.

She looked at his hands and wondered why they weren't rough and dry. That would fit more than the way they did appear. Sure, they were overlarge just like the rest of him, but instead of rough and calloused, they appeared strong and surprisingly smooth. When he'd taken the sheaf of papers of the contract from her hands, she'd immediately noticed how good, *how smooth*, his fingers felt as he took them from her.

"Everything looks to be in order," he commented, bringing her attention away from his hands and back to his face. He placed the contract on the corner of her desk and dug inside his pockets in search of a pen. She handed him one and he gave her a half-smile of thanks. A deep dimple flashed in his cheek as he did so.

Renita suppressed a sigh of irritation as she pulled at the collar of her silk blouse. She felt hot and wanted him out of the office. Now.

"Here you go, signed and sealed," he said, catching her as she was unbuttoning the two top buttons of her blouse.

"Thank you, I'll make a copy for your records," she said as she rose from her desk to walk to the small copier in the far corner of her office. When he followed her, she turned around and stopped him with a raised brow. "I can handle this, Mr. Holt," she said, suddenly nervous with his close proximity.

The room seemed smaller with his overwhelmingly large presence. She needed to get away from him, if only for a minute. It was always like this with him. She could never stay too close to him, without feeling the need to escape.

She felt nervous and was, as usual, hyperaware of him. The way he stared at her made her feel like some kind of prey. All jungleish and just plain crazy.

She felt a shiver run down her spine when he laughed.

"No problem, Ms. Nash," he raised his hands in front of himself, as though surrendering as he walked backwards to her desk. "But may I ask you a question?"

"Would my saying no, stop you?" she muttered.

"Probably not," he laughed low in his throat. "Why are you always so irritable with me? Always so ticked off? What am I missing? Have I ever done anything to you?"

She glanced in his direction and saw that he'd crossed his thick arms over his broad chest as he leaned on her desk. She quickly turned back to the copy machine.

But she felt the eyeball darts he shot at her back.

She *refused* to turn around and demand that he explain his question.

"I don't know what you're talking about," she denied, despite the quickening she felt in her stomach at his words.

Whenever she was in his presence, she could only take being around him alone for just so long before she felt claustrophobic with the need to get away from him. She didn't like the way she'd catch him looking at her, from beneath dark lashes, staring at her from those strange looking eyes of his.

"How long have you and Colburn been together?"

"How long have we've been *working* together?"

"Isn't that what I said?"

Renita knew he was playing with her. She didn't know what he got out of it, but whenever he caught her alone, he found it necessary to try and get under her skin. When he'd worked for the agency that handled the firm's investigations, she'd worked with him often and found it increasingly difficult to stay aloof around him.

Holt was picky. And because he was a top-notch investigator at his agency, they'd allowed him to pick and choose which clients he'd work with. He and Greg worked well together, so Holt had been the sole investigator assigned to their cases, because he liked the attorney.

Whenever he was around her, she'd catch him staring at her. She immediately went on the defensive and had called him out on several occasions. The first time that she did, he was clearly surprised. She knew what image she presented.

Cool, calm, and collected, Renita.

Which she felt that she was. As long as no one…messed…with her. Then, she'd turn into the Renita who had to be sent away to boarding school by her bourgeoisie parents to help "control" her more *wild* tendencies.

But she'd come a long way from the wild-haired, out of control kid she'd once been. The same kid who had continually embarrassed her parents, from the time she was a young girl caught ditching school, to the young woman who flunked out of college.

She was a respectable grown woman, had a degree beneath her belt, and was close to finishing her law degree.

It had taken her a while to control her natural inclination to want to do serious damage to anyone who stepped to her crazy. But, she'd overcome the tendencies by turning to yoga, meditating, drinking herbal teas...and often locking herself in her apartment yelling, screaming, dancing buck-naked, or whatever...to calm herself when she felt the sometimes irresistible urge to act a fool and do something she *knew* that she'd regret later.

It was a process and *she* was a work in progress.

At least that's what her mother would remind her, that she was a *work in progress*, when she visited her parents during her weekly Sunday visit to their home for church and dinner.

"Greg and I have been working together for three years...why?" She turned cool dark gray eyes in Gaynor Holt's direction as she asked the question.

"Just wondered if you thought it was time to move on. Have you given any thought to that?" he asked.

"Why would I want to move on? I enjoy what I do. I enjoy law and have no desire to do anything else. Why?" she demanded.

As she'd spoken he'd walked toward her, slowly, stopping within mere inches of her. She had to draw her head back in order to look at him. The look on his chiseled scruffy face made her heart leap in her chest. She resisted the urge to shove him away from her. To do so, would show him he had an effect on her. It would show him that she was uncomfortable with him standing so near.

She wouldn't give him the satisfaction.

"My brother and I are looking for someone to work with us. Someone to help us in our research. With your background in law, you would be perfect," his scratchy voice had deepened.

"I have no interest in leaving Greg...the firm. I've worked here for three years and as soon as I take my bar exam, the firm has offered me a position," she said and licked her suddenly dry lips. "Why would I leave that to be a secretary with you and your brother?" she scoffed.

"You would be much more than a secretary, Renita."

As she stared up at him, the look in his eyes was hypnotic. She felt crazy as hell and just as disoriented having lost the thread of the conversation.

"If you came to work with me, you wouldn't feel the need to be so...uptight," he told her, his scratchy voice deepening as he took a step closer to her.

"What makes you think, *uh hum,*" she started and had to stop to clear her throat from the sudden restriction before she could go on. "What makes you think that I'm uptight?" she finished, taking an involuntary step back when he reached one of his big hands out, as though to touch her.

She felt foolish when he simply removed the copy of the contract from her nerveless fingers. But the small contact from his fingers on hers was electric. She felt like a heroine in one of her spicy romances she secretly read, but she could almost felt a strange burn with the contact.

She needed to get out more and date real men. She'd definitely, definitely, been reading too many erotic e-books.

It's where she'd been getting her "fix" as of late.

"All those buttoned-up collars that you sport, all those stuffy navy blue suits...definitely uptight," he mocked gently. "Don't you ever just want let go, Renita?" he all but whispered, surprisingly enticing her with his low-talking barrage.

She had to move away from him.

"I have no need to 'let go' Mr. Holt…"

"After a year of working together, don't you think you could call me by my first name?" When she only stared at him, from across the room where she'd made her escape, he continued, "Come on, Renita…" he drawled her name. "Say it. Say my name. Don't be scared. I won't bite."

The way that he asked her to call him by his first name, promising not to bite her, made her treacherous carnal mind come up with images of her calling him Gaynor in a totally different setting than the office. And her welcoming his bite. Wherever. Wherever.

She wondered if he knew the effect he was having on her.

Not only did she feel her face heat, she felt her neck, breasts, torso, legs *and* her toes all catch fire from the look on his handsome, scruffy face and the way he was, *staring* at her.

The look on his face confirmed to her that he knew exactly what he was saying.

"I'm not afraid of anything, or anyone, *Gaynor*, and I think I'll pass on the offer," she said, straightening her back and secured the top buttons of her silk blouse. She caught the flash of amusement and something more in his eyes before he closed down any telling expression.

"As I said, I'm happy where I am, but thank you," she said and accepted the signed copy of the contract and filed it away before she turned back to the investigator.

"Well, the invitation is there. Think about it," he said.

She said nothing more as she gathered her things in preparation of leaving for the day. Work with Gaynor Holt and have to see his strangely appealing gruff behind everyday? *No way*, she thought with an inward laugh.

She'd stay right where she was, working at the very prestigious law firm that her parents had pulled several strings for her to get. One that had been willing to overlook her juvenile records, records that to the high-powered attorneys would not have remained sealed.

She had no intention of disappointing her parents again.

No matter how appealing the thought of working with him seemed to be, she thought, as she slid him a sideways glance from beneath lowered lids.

Chapter Eleven

ജ

Greg took a cursory glance around the dark-lit club, searching for Liza. He smiled when he caught site of his wife's dark head bob slightly up and down as she listened to the soulful strains from the live band. He threaded his way through the small tables until he made it to her side.

"Hi, sweetheart…sorry I'm late," he raised his voice so that she could hear him over the music.

"That's okay, you're not *too* late. I went ahead and ordered an appetizer for us," she told him, accepting his light kiss.

Greg sat down in the maroon leather chair and looked around the club. It was already busy.

Although it was Wednesday, the club was quickly filling with an eclectic group, ranging from those dressed in business attire, to those dressed more casually in slacks or jeans. Rigby's was one of the few clubs in Stanton that featured a live band five days a week. The band that was currently playing was a favorite for him and Liza. No sooner had he sat in his seat, than they announced they'd be taking a small break.

"That's fine, baby. How was your day?" he asked, as he took her in from head to toe. She was gorgeous.

As usual Liza was beautifully dressed, without a hair out of place. Immaculate.

Sometimes, he just wanted to mess her up.

He longed to throw her down right where they were and kiss her senseless, just to see her 'oh so well put together' self, flustered…and completely, thoroughly…messed up.

The thought alone turned him on. Probably because he could imagine how embarrassed she'd be and how sexy she'd look. Totally out of control. He couldn't imagine his wife letting go enough to do anything so public.

He linked his fingers with hers across the small, candlelit table. The sting of their encounter earlier had lessened and Greg was glad he'd asked her to meet him for dinner.

"It was fine, I ended up going to lunch with a few of the women from the club."

"I'm sorry about not being able to make it. It was a hectic day," he felt a twinge of guilt over the lie, but brushed it aside.

"Ummm. It was okay. I had a decent enough time." She pulled her hand away from his when the waitress placed the steaming bowl of hot spinach dip in the center of the table, next to the sourdough bread. "Thank you," she murmured.

He waited for her to continue speaking when he saw the way she'd brought her eyebrows together, and pursed her lips. As though she was trying to work something out in her mind.

He accepted his drink from the waitress and sat back in his chair, waiting for Liza to speak. She picked up a piece of bread and lightly dipped it into the dip, chewing thoughtfully before she continued.

"I ran into a woman I haven't seen since I was a teenager." There was a small hesitancy to her voice.

"Yes? Was that a good thing?" he too pulled a piece of bread from the loaf and ate, as he waited for her to sort whatever was going on in her mind, out.

"It was unexpected. And funny. And…painful. A little," she said with a humorless small laugh.

"How was it painful?"

"I don't know. I guess anytime you see someone from your past, it tends to be painful," she evaded.

"Not always," he countered. "What made this one so painful?"

She was saved from answering when their food arrived simultaneously with the band striking up. He could see the relief flash across her expressive face and gritted his teeth together in frustration.

Fuck.

He felt like shaking her ass! With every damn step forward, it seemed as though she took two friggin' steps back. He grabbed the napkin to his right, shook out the utensils and stabbed into his steak, stuffing his mouth with a forkful of the tender meat. He knew that he'd better keep his mouth full of food otherwise there was no telling what he'd say to Liza.

By the end of the night, if she didn't open up, he was going to confront her about her mother. And ask why was it that he'd not been aware that not only had she been in contact with her, but she'd been giving her mother money since her sophomore year in college, until last week when her mother had called him. After seven years of marriage.

* * * * *

He looked mad as hell.

She really couldn't blame him. She'd be angry too.

She'd played a game of hide-'n-seek long enough. But try as she might, she didn't know how to even start to tell him about her past. Her childhood, the way she grew up moving from house to house whenever they fell behind on the rent, food stamps, Medicaid…not to mention her crazy-ass mama and their strange love-hate relationship.

Sometimes the best way was the direct way.

"You know how rough it was for me as a kid, Greg," she started and stopped.

"Yes. A little. I mean you've told me some of what your childhood was like," he said.

"Sometimes, it's really hard for me to think about it, much less talk about it. I just want to forget some of the things that happened, it's easier that way."

"I can understand that, Li. I don't want you to talk about things that upset you. I just think you'd feel better about it all, if you did. And who better to talk about it with than me?"

"I went to the ladies room at the club and to say I was surprised when I saw that the attendant was a woman I'd known as a child, is putting it mildly," she said after she'd taken a bite of her linguine, considering his words.

"I'll bet." Was all that he said, but the look on his face spurred her on to continue. It was as though she'd given him an early Christmas present and helped her to continue her story.

"It was a woman who had gone to the same church that I'd gone to as a child. She asked me how I'd been. She seemed happy to know that I was doing well. She asked about my mother." She stopped and looked down at her plate, swallowing.

"What did you say?" Greg asked casually and paused for a brief moment, right before he was ready to take a bite of his steak.

Although he tried to hide it she felt his intent stare and grew uncomfortable. He tried to hide his interest, but they'd been married long enough that she could read her man. He carefully took a bite, chewing slowly, methodically, as he stared at her.

"What could I say? Her guess was as good as mine."

Greg's face tightened and Liza *knew* that she hadn't imagined it this time. Something was going on. She felt that crazy sensation in the pit of her stomach. The sensation that told her something wasn't right.

Serious shit was about to hit the fan, as Karina's Big Momma used to say. A minute later it did.

"Your mother called me last week."

Nasty thing, it was. When shit hit the fan.

Liza was taking a swallow of her tea and damn near choked to death after he uttered those six words as calmly as if he were telling her they were predicting rain in the forecast.

He jumped up from his chair and thumped her on the back until she waved him away with a choked, "I'm fine. Really…"

He walked back to his seat and sat back down, calm as you please, picked his fork back up and took another bite of his food.

"My mother called you? Why are you just now telling me this? When did she call? Where was I…" her words jumbled and fell over themselves in her haste to clarify and understand.

She pushed the half-eaten plate of food to the side. Suddenly, the delicious, creamy linguine had lost all appeal as her appetite had completely disappeared after his disclosure.

"Let's dance."

He pushed away from the table and walked to her side and pulled her chair out for her. Dumbfounded, she simply followed him to the small dance floor and allowed him to pull her without preamble, into his arms.

Normally, she'd be in heaven, dancing with Greg. He had a natural smooth rhythm; able to keep up with her whether she danced fast, did the bus stop, line danced, or a nice slow grind. It didn't matter…the man could dance.

The way he'd hold her close, his natural musky good smell usually had her ready to rip his clothes off by the time the dance was over and sex him up, real nice.

But this time, as he pulled her close she didn't lay her head on his chest as she normally would in order to get close to his heady smell.

She was tense, uneasy and wanted to know when and why her mother called him.

"Greg, what do you mean my mother called you? When did this...?"

He put his finger over her mouth to still her nervous prattle. "Just dance with me, Li. We'll talk later."

He pulled her snug against his body and despite her nervousness, despite the fact that she was on edge, wondering what in the hell her mama had said to her husband... his nearness, his smell, his overall masculinity forced her to close her eyes, lay her head on his chest and sway with him to the soulful sounds from the female lead vocalist of the band.

* * * * *

"When did she call, Greg? Quit screwing around with me and tell me. When did my mother call?"

Liza had had it up to her eyeballs with his refusal to talk about her mother's phone call.

"She called almost two weeks ago, Li. She called asking for you, said she lost your cell phone number but was able to find our home phone number."

Liza sat on the edge of the bed as she massaged the last of the lotion on her arms after her shower. She stared at Greg as he lay propped up against the headboard, his eyes looking so cold and distant that she didn't even recognize him.

She automatically went on the defense. *Automatically.*

"What do you want me to say? What? That I've spoken to my mother? That she'll occasionally call me when she's hard up for money? What? What the hell do you want me to say, Greg?" she yelled and jumped up from the bed in nervous agitation.

"You sure do have a hell of a lot of nerve yelling at me, Liza. You're the one at fault. I didn't do a damn thing. Just tried to be the best husband that I could be. I had no idea my wife had been lying to me for seven years, telling me her mother was gone and she never heard from her after she graduated from high school."

Greg jumped up from the bed and damn near stalked her. She walked backwards as he slowly, menacingly strode over to her.

Her back hit the wall. She had nowhere else to go.

"Listen. It's obvious to me that if you feel the need to lie to me about your mother, it makes me wonder what else you think its okay to lie to me about."

"What the hell is that supposed to mean?" she asked despite the quiver in her voice, she stood her ground.

"It means whatever the hell you want it to mean. It means I don't know how much I should trust you. It means you sure in hell don't trust me," he said, his face inches away from hers.

"It has nothing to do with you! It's my business, Greg. If I don't want to talk about my crazy mama, then I don't have to. "She shoved him away from her with all of her might. He didn't budge.

"No, Liza. That's where you're wrong. Your business *is* my business. That's what being a part of a married couple is all about. Sharing. Or didn't you learn that growing up? Oh that's right. It's none of my business what you did or did not do prior to the day we said 'I do'...isn't that right, Li? Why even be married? Marriage is a partnership, Liza."

She didn't have to try and push him away this time. He moved away from her willingly and moved back to the bed and flopped his large frame on the mattress and covered his arm over his eyes as he lay down. Her heart ached at the look of mingled anger and sadness she saw plastered on his face before his arm covered his eyes.

Liza swallowed hard and slowly walked over to Greg's side of the bed and perched hesitantly on the edge, near his feet.

"I'm sorry, Greg." She said and waited for a response. When he made no immediate reply to her apology, she scooted up farther on the bed, nearer to his head.

"Baby, I'm serious. I'm so sorry. It's hard," she felt as inadequate as the words she uttered. The words were stuck in her throat that would free her from her fears of how he would look at her if he knew how her life had been like as a child.

She moved closer and felt hope spring when he scoot his body over, allowing her room as she lay down in front of him.

"I love you, Liza. You don't have to be embarrassed of anything with me. If you feel embarrassed, this makes me think that you don't trust me." He pulled her closer to his chest and crisscrossed his arms in front of her.

She nestled closer to him, considering his words. She trusted him. It had taken a lot for her to tell him what she had at dinner. It hurt in a strange way, but at the same time was liberating. As small as it was, the disclosure helped. As though some ugly weight had been lifted from her.

It was a beginning. There was so much to tell him, so much she'd suppressed, that even she had a hard time trying to bring the suppressed memories and the feelings associated with them to the surface.

"It's not that I don't trust you, Greg. It's just..." she allowed the sentence to trail off. She didn't know how to finish the thought. She didn't want to say the wrong thing after the progress they'd made at dinner.

"I love you, baby." She felt him kiss the back of her head and tighten his arms around her. "I wish that you would just believe that there's not a damn thing you could tell me that would make me think less of you, or love you any less than I do."

She felt the sting of tears threaten to fall and quickly shut her eyes to ward them off. Soon, she felt the even rise and fall of Greg's chest against her back, signaling that he'd fallen asleep. She ached with the need to make love with him. He had every right to be angry with her. Although they'd made progress at dinner, he deserved more. She knew that he wanted more.

He wanted her to give it all to him. Without reservation.

Soon, she too, fell into a restless sleep.

Liza came out of a sound sleep to feel Greg's big hands touching her, pulling her body close to his chest, as he slid the straps of her negligee from her shoulders. He placed a warm kiss in the hollow where her shoulder and neck met as the gown slid down her breasts.

"Hey, baby," she said huskily and arched her back sharply as he palmed her breasts and gently squeezed, his two fingers lightly pinching the erect bud.

"Hey you," he said and kissed the side of her neck. "I'm sorry about earlier. I shouldn't have taken it out on you. I'm thankful that you felt comfortable sharing some of your past with me. It's a start." He continued to knead her breast with one hand, while the other worked on moving the gown down her body. She helped him out by lifting her body slightly so that it pooled around her waist.

"That's okay, I understand. It's not easy, but I understand where you're coming from too," she murmured in the dark still of the room. There was no light save the one from the moon that showed through the wood blinds in the window behind their bed. The moonlight allowed her to see Greg's hand as it rested on the slight curvature of her belly.

"No baby, it's not okay. And I'm going to make it up to you. You deserve better treatment than that," he said and lifted the short length of the negligee, fanning it up and away and she briefly felt air hit her bared bottom before he pulled her snug against his erection and gently eased the broad head of his penis into her anus.

He must have already planned to make love to her in this way, as she felt the slick lubrication of his condom-covered erection, as it eased inside her ass.

She groaned harshly. Although he'd not prepared her, she was ready within seconds and arched her back from the pleasure-pain as his cock penetrated the tight, small opening.

She felt a small sheen of sweat break out on her forehead as her body accepted the hard length of his rod and her hands automatically reached out to grasp his forearms to brace herself.

"So…is this punishment?" she asked on a grunt, as her body adjusted to the pressure of him being embedded so deeply within her. When he didn't immediately answer, her heart sank.

"No. Yes. I don't know," he whispered in a guttural tone, his mouth pressed against the bottom of her ear lobe. He grasped her hips in his bands and slowly began to rock into her.

"I do know that I love you with everything I am, Li." As he spoke, one hand trailed around her hipbone and tangled in her tight nest of curls at the juncture of her thighs.

He separated her folds and spread her own juices on his finger before lightly stroking her clit in circular movements. She moved her hips in time with his cock and his finger, loving the exquisite feel both gave.

"I want our marriage, our relationship to go to the next level. It can't if you keep holding back," he said, and then took the lobe of her ear into his mouth and bit down gently, before sucking it back into his mouth, easing the sting. "What do you want, Liza? Talk to me. No more hiding. And don't come, not yet," he demanded, lightly smacking her on the ass as he gave his edict. He knew her body well.

He lifted her leg, and placed it over his and the angle gave her that much more of his cock to work with.

Damn.

And he expected her not to come?

She was on fire. She could feel the orgasm building and didn't know how long she'd be able to keep accepting his tight thrusts without coming soon.

He felt so good, deep inside her ass, that she could barely *think* much less talk. She accepted his short controlled thrusts, the way he kept working her clit and forced the words out of her mouth.

"It's what I want too," she said in total breathlessness and then had to pause.

As soon as she started speaking, he picked up the pace of his strokes and although he was careful, they became stronger and Liza closed her eyes tight and squeezed the inner muscles of her vagina to stop herself from coming.

"Keep talking, baby, don't stop." He lifted her ass higher and really started doing her. Doing her just the way she liked.

Shit.

"Okay, I'll try," she murmured in the quiet of the room. Her hands tightened on his forearms as she tried to concentrate. To allow herself to talk about her past, while he had her open like this.

Open and vulnerable.

"I want the same thing Greg. I want to feel free to, uhh...be myself with you. Not ashamed," she barely got the words out.

"You don't have to be ashamed of anything with me, don't you know that?" he asked her right before he pulled out of her.

She felt bereft when he suddenly withdrew from her and lifted her to her knees, and spread them far apart.

In less than five seconds he'd repositioned her body directly in front of his and blanketed her from the back, before he eased his penis back inside.

She exhaled on one...long...hiss.

There was no more talking as he pumped her ass from the back, relentlessly shoving his thick organ in and out of her. He pulled her by the back of her head so that she was forced to look into his face.

There was a mingled look of concentration, lust, love and anger etched deeply on his face, as his balls slapped against the back of her vagina with each driving thrust of his cock in her ass. He played with her clit the entire time and before long she felt her body begin to prepare, her pussy quivering around his fingers, the orgasm within reach.

"Greg! Oh baby, I'm coming, I can't hold back!" she cried and arched her back and writhed against him, screaming in sensual torture as the orgasm again hovered within her reach.

"Don't," he whispered and slipped out of her.

"Noooo!" Liza barely refrained from howling. She wanted to snatch his damn heart out for doing this to her. Building her up and not allowing her to come. Again.

"Turn over Liza, lie down and spread your legs," he demanded and although his tone was harsh, the look in his eyes and the way his hands trembled just slightly, let her know that he was just as affected as she.

She eased her body on the bed and turned over as he instructed. Without taking her eyes from his she lifted her legs, planted her feet flat on the mattress and spread her legs wide apart.

Despite her sensual frustration, she smiled when she saw the way his eyes trained on her vagina, the way his nostrils flared as he inhaled, the mingled scent of their sex was strong and heady in the room.

Her gaze then followed his hands as he pulled the condom from his cock, and tossed it aside. He smiled that sexy grin of his and her heart skipped a beat. He wasn't through with her, and her heart beat heavily in her chest when he adjusted her body to his liking against the pillows.

Greg took her face between his hands and slowly kissed her, planting small adoring, nibbling kisses all over her beautiful face. "God, baby, I love you," he said and moved down her body.

"I love you too, Greg," she whispered back as he licked his way down her face and throat and continued down her body. He stopped along the trail and took one of her small, plump breasts into his mouth and swirled his tongue around the nipple.

"When you were growing up did the other kids make fun of you? You went to that private school didn't you?" he asked, and looked into her face and saw the way her eyes were semi-glazed from his ministrations. But the minute he asked the question, she lost some of the sensual glow and he felt her body tense.

"It's okay, Li. There's just the two of us, in this room, making love. There's no one but us. Talk to me." He returned to lapping her nipple before he licked a trail across her chest and gave the other breast the same careful attention that he'd given the first.

He smiled around her nipple when she hesitantly spoke.

"Yes. They made fun," she spoke hoarsely in the dark.

He encouraged her to continue by lapping at her breast as his hand traveled down her smooth body and tangled in her pussy. He lightly toyed with her. He didn't want her to come. But he knew that she was so damn close from his playing with her, that she'd come soon with or without his assent.

He felt her heart thud in her chest and sighed with relief when she spoke again.

"It hurt like hell. My uniforms were donated to me and we used to wear these white shirts with them. My shirts were so old that they tore easily, especially under the arms. My mother rarely did anything about it. She wouldn't even patch them up and I was always so embarrassed going to school. Eventually I learned to sew and patched them by myself."

Greg forced himself to continue to lave and stroke her, when inside his heart ached at the thought of how humiliated she must have felt.

He lifted his head from her breasts and saw the hurt mingled in with her arousal. "Thank you for sharing that with me, Li. That had to be rough." When she smiled his heart ached again as he thought of her as a child hurting and being made fun of.

He wanted to make up for the long ago insults but knew that he couldn't. The most he could do was try his best to take care of her in every way he knew how. And right now his woman needed him to fully take care of her needs.

He moved up her body, pausing to take a nip here, plant a caress there, before he pushed her legs farther apart. He brought her hips to the edge of the bed, and entered her with one long hard plunge of his cock. As soon as he'd filled her to the brim he felt her pussy as it tightened around his erection and within seconds she came.

Her body jerked and spasmed around his length, but he didn't stop pumping into her.

He kept digging into her, the feel of her warm, wet pussy on his bared cock felt so good, he had to grit his teeth in his effort not to come. He slammed into her over and over again and took her mouth with his and kissed her with all the pent-up emotion he had for her.

"Don't close your eyes, Liza. I want to see you come again," he said, breathing heavily as he broke away from her mouth. No sooner had he uttered the words than he felt her orgasm erupt which triggered his.

Although he reared away from her as he roared his release, pumping her slight frame so hard the entire bed shook, as though they were in the middle of an earthquake, he refused to give up eye contact with her, and forced her to look at him by gently, but firmly, holding both sides of her face with his warm palms.

When her hoarse cries echoed his, he emptied deep inside of her, his hands left her face and clamped tightly on her slender hips as he came.

"We never did finish our talk, Greg," she said, eyes now closed.

"I'm listening," he said, and placed her in front of his body. He lightly began to play with her pussy as he spoke.

It felt so good, that for a minute, Liza lost her train of thought as she unconsciously moved her hips in time to the hand on her mound. With determination she started to speak, opening up to him about how it felt to grow up poor and to be teased continually. How she'd learned quickly to put on a "game face" so she wouldn't be bullied and ridiculed. How she'd played the role of tough girl in order to survive.

"It was the only way I could think of to protect myself. I struck out before anyone could strike me," she admitted and the long ago hurts were still reflected in her voice.

Greg had listened to her as she opened her heart up and although his hands were still buried in her mound, he had stilled his movements as she recounted her life story to him. He felt humbled that she'd shared it with him.

That she finally trusted him enough to bare her soul.

"As for my mother? I really am sorry that I never really told you about our strange relationship. I didn't know how to tell you. I didn't…I don't…understand my need to have her approval, to allow her to treat me the way that she does in order to have her stay in my life."

"It's understandable, Liza. We all want the approval of our parents, to a degree. We never outgrow the need to please, I don't think that we ever do," he said and wrapped his arms around her. For long moments they lay like that. His arms wrapped around her, his head lying on top of her head.

Eventually she squirmed around to look at him. "Well?"

He smiled down at her. "Well, what?" he said and laughed when she poked him.

"Well…don't you have anything to say to that?" she asked and turned back around.

He rested his head on top of hers and answered, "I think that you're an amazing woman Liza, and the fact that you grew up the way that you did, living the life you had to lead, you flourished. What you see as hiding behind a shield, I see as a wonderful God-given ability to adapt."

When she didn't say anything, just snuggled deeper into his embrace, he continued. "And I also think you should share your ability, your talent with making the best of tough situations with other young girls." He voiced out loud an idea that he'd had the moment she started sharing with him her life story.

"Oh, you do? And how would you suggest I do that?" He heard just the smallest bit of challenge in her voice.

Good.

That meant she was listening.

"You mentioned spending time at Girls Unlimited, the recreation center, a lot as a young girl. Have you ever thought about volunteering some of your time there? I bet they'd love to have you."

"Hmmm."

"It's just a thought, but I bet you'd have a wonderful time mentoring a young girl. You have your degree in social work. Maybe someone like you would make a difference for some young girl." He could tell the idea intrigued her and smiled in the dark.

"Maybe."

"Doesn't Karina volunteer at Girls Unlimited on Saturday mornings?" He wouldn't let it go.

"Yes, she does. She constantly asks me to come down with her. To volunteer. I just never felt comfortable doing that. I'm not sure I'm ready yet," she admitted with a nervous laugh.

"You'll never get completely beyond this until you do, Liza," was all that he said.

They lay together quietly for a bit longer until she spoke up. "And what about you Greg?"

"What about me?" he asked innocently.

"Don't make me hurt you! You know what I'm talking about."

"I will do any and everything possible to make this marriage a success. If that means less hours at work, that's what I'll do. If that means more time spent eating you out…damn it, a man's got to do what a man's got to do! I'm there, I'm willing and able," he promised, making her laugh.

Although he laughed and made light of it, he was committed to his wife. He would always put her happiness first from now on. He just needed for her to come to complete resolution about her past. Once she did that, they were home free.

"I'm serious, Greg," she said on a soft laugh.

"I am too. I'm also serious about us making a baby. I think it's time, don't you?"

For once the thought didn't scare the crap out of her. It actually held a certain appeal to her. "Maybe," she said and smiled in the dark.

"But not until you're ready. I don't want to do it halfway. When you're completely ready, with no reservations, we'll do it. I just don't want you to close up on me again. Never be afraid to talk to me. Is that fair?" he asked.

Liza was surprised at what he said. She knew how badly he wanted a child. Of late, that had been the dominant theme in the conversation for them. No matter how hard she tried to avoid the subject.

"That's more than fair," she said and placed both hands over his thick arms, as they lay in front of her, crossed over her breasts.

"Good. Then, I'm fine with the wait. As long as you don't shut down on me," he said around a yawn as he pulled her tighter against his body.

Within moments she felt the even rise and fall of his chest, signaling he'd fallen into sleep. Before she too fell into a deep sleep, she thought about everything that had happened over the last twenty-four hours.

Not only had her mother called her husband and told him things Liza had never disclosed, but she'd also begged for money. Despite Greg's understanding, Liza would be lying to herself if she said the sting of embarrassment wasn't still there when she thought about it. Her earlier meltdown had helped to release *some* of the embarrassment, but as she closed her eyes and drifted off into sleep, she didn't even try to hold back the tears of shame.

Chapter Twelve

❧

"Karina needs a ride to Girls Unlimited today. Cooper is having a stereo installed in her new car and it would be easier for her if she could catch a ride down there and he then could pick her up. Otherwise, she'll miss volunteering today," Liza said to Greg as he stepped out of the shower and toweled himself dry. "She needs to be there by ten o'clock this morning. They're having an open forum for the girls, some type of summit they're preparing for. I'm not sure of the details, but Kari doesn't want to miss it."

He walked over to her as she was applying her makeup and bent his head to the crook of her neck and placed a warm kiss there. "Why don't you take her? It'll be fun," he said as he moved away to walk to his drawer and remove his underclothes. "By the time you come back, I'll be done with my work for the morning and we can drive to the lake and be there by late afternoon," he said as he sat on the edge of the bed and pulled socks onto his feet.

Since their talk on Wednesday, a new vibrancy had entered their relationship. Greg admitted to her that he was far from being perfect. He wasn't guiltless in the way their marriage had spiraled into a state of no communication, hidden truths and, according to Liza, bland sex. That part fucked with his mind a bit, but it was the truth. He'd been so caught up in trying to give her what she wanted materialistically, he'd neglected the other parts of the relationship that were needed to make their marriage good.

He'd allowed her to keep a part of herself away from him. He'd not even bothered to dig deep and wonder why she'd skated the issue of her parents. He hadn't even really known that her parents had never been married. Something as important as that, Liza felt she needed to lie to him about. She thought he'd see her as less than, somehow, if she told him the truth.

He sighed.

They still had things to work through. But the last week had been a breakthrough for them.

He didn't want to press her and demand that she tell him everything all at once. He'd negotiated many times in his law practice and knew how easy it was to have someone totally shut down and cease all communication. Damned if he wanted that to happen. He was ready for the next step in their marriage; children. They couldn't go there without being on the same page.

Liza needed to fully open up, not just to him, but more importantly she had to stop lying to herself. She had to quit being embarrassed of a past she had no control over.

"Are you saying take her…and stay?" she asked as she paused in the middle of applying her mascara to stare at him.

"Sure, why not? Sounds like a great way to spend the morning, Li," Greg was carefully nonchalant in his response. He didn't want her to suspect what he'd done.

Last night when Karina called and Liza had been in the shower, he'd used the opportunity to talk privately with her. He had asked if she had plans to volunteer on Saturday as she normally did. Karina told him that she wanted to, but might have to miss because her husband insisted on installing her stereo in her car and his own vehicle was being serviced Saturday morning as well. That had given Greg the opportunity he needed to suggest to Karina that she ask Liza to take her to Girls Unlimited.

But, he hadn't fooled Karina. She'd asked him point blank what he was up to and he'd confessed that he had ulterior motives and thought the experience would help his wife.

He hadn't had to say anything more. Karina fell in line with his suggestions and eagerly agreed to ask her friend to drive her to the recreation center.

Now the trick was convincing Liza to not only drive Karina there, but to stay.

"Ummm. I don't know, Greg. I'm not sure if that's something I really want to do," she said and turned back around to face her mirror. He saw the way she titled her head to the side just slightly and pooched her lips out, the way she did when she was thinking about something.

Usually it made him randy as hell to see her stick her pretty full lips out like that. But this time, he was concentrating more on hoping she'd take the bait he and Karina had set up.

His baby needed to come to terms with a few things. She wasn't going to do it by refusing to confront some key issues from her past. Maybe she'd see that she'd built them up into something bigger than they were.

Maybe they were still big and just as ugly as they were when she was a child. But she'd never know unless she confronted them.

"It's up to you, babe. But if nothing else, you'll be able to give Kari a ride down there and Coop can pick her up," he smiled and kissed her as he pulled his jacket on his shoulders.

"Yes, I can do that, I suppose."

Greg smiled inside when she looked at him carefully. His wife wasn't anybody's fool. He carefully kept his face cheerfully blank as he ushered her out of their bedroom and down the staircase.

* * * * *

"Greg, may I speak with you for a minute?"

"Sure, Renita. Come on in," Greg glanced over at his assistant as she stood in the doorway.

He noticed right away how she was rubbing her hands down the smooth knee-length, slim fitting dark skirt. When she noticed his eyes on her hands she immediately stopped the nervous smoothing and walked inside his office.

"I've been doing some thinking and I believe that it's time for me to make some changes," she started out.

"Please, Renita, have a seat." Greg could tell this was something serious. He motioned for her to take a seat in one of the leather chairs that faced his desk. She smiled and gracefully sat in the chair, before folding her hands in her lap.

She looked like a nervous schoolgirl sitting there in the oversized chair, clenching and releasing her hands. "Renita, is everything okay?"

"Oh...yes. Everything's fine, Greg."

She seemed at a loss for words, which was unusual for Renita. She was reserved and had a tendency to be selective with her words. She never spoke more than was necessary to get her point across. However, she seemed more to be more hesitant than reticent this morning. He didn't say anything, just waited for her to speak.

"I think that, for a long time, I had false hopes," she began and although her voice was hesitant, there was a clear determination in both it and the directness of her gaze.

"False hopes about what?"

"To be honest...that there could be something between us," she stated boldly. "Something beyond our professional relationship."

"Did I ever give you the impression of that, Renita?" Greg was suddenly apprehensive. Maybe his disclosure earlier regarding his relationship with Liza had been out of line. Maybe he'd crossed some invisible barrier that he shouldn't have with her.

"No. It wasn't you, Greg. It was all me." The laugh that she uttered was totally without humor. When she suddenly stood from the chair and walked away from the desk toward one of his large bay windows, Greg felt a slight apprehension in his gut.

"What's going on, Renita? You can tell me. Please do, I'm a bit in the dark about this."

"I've been in love with you since the first time I interviewed with you and I've decided to quit. I don't think it's a good idea for me to work here anymore," she admitted bluntly turning around to face him, her light amber-colored eyes sparking with a look akin to relief.

Renita felt crazy and nervous, yet at the same time, she felt like a burden had been lifted from her shoulders just by uttering the words to him. Out loud. With no care for the consequences.

She knew that Greg loved Liza. She had no doubt in her mind, despite the rocky time they'd been suffering lately. When he'd first started working later and longer hours, Renita had secretly cheered, hoping against hope, although she knew it was wrong, that one of those late night sessions working side by side, would turn into something more than working on legal briefs.

She wanted to work on briefs all right, but not those of the legal variety…she wanted what was inside *his* briefs.

She'd never been overt in her desire to let him know that she was interested. But she did want him. He was everything she wanted in a man. Fine, sexy as hell, educated, had plenty of money and was…stable.

He was everything her parents would love in a man for her. One they despaired she'd ever be able to "catch". Especially her mother. Elena Dexter-Nash openly scorned and despaired of her youngest daughter ever finding a man who'd overlook her daughter' *indiscretion* of the past.

But, despite everything, she'd never been able to go for it and pursue Greg.

For one reason she didn't picture herself as the happy hooker busting up marriages. It just wasn't her thing. For another, she had fought long and hard to change her image. To be the upstanding woman that her parents wanted…needed for her to be.

She wasn't that reckless girl anymore. The one who everyone thought was selfish and only thought of herself. Drinking and partying and to hell with the rest. The chick who had no future, no goals, no plans. Headed to nowhere-land on the express train, as her mother so bluntly put it. The one who'd gotten pregnant at sixteen years old…

"Don't worry, Greg. I'm not going to seduce you…"

"Try and seduce me, you mean…"

She glanced at him from beneath lowered lids and smiled, but let it go. "*Try* and seduce you," she modified the statement. "I think, however, it would be in my best interest to give you two weeks notice. I've given it quite a bit of thought. I think the time has come."

"Renita, you're a wonderful assistant as well as an amazing paralegal. I would be lying if I said I want you to go," he said and the sincerity in his voice made her heart lurch. If only…

"What about your parents? I know that your parents have conditions in order to help you financially so that you can finish law school, and this job was one of them. What will you do?" he interrupted her thoughts.

Greg knew some of her history. He knew what was on paper; that she'd gotten into some legal trouble as both a teenager and young adult, and that she had served time in a juvenile detention hall.

He knew that she'd eventually gone to college and that her parents had placed conditions on helping her financially. This job was one of the conditions.

What he didn't know was that she had to maintain the job in order to *prove* her worthiness to them. To prove she was responsible enough and they'd continue to pay for school and would pay back the student loans she'd taken out to pay for undergraduate school.

They'd paid once for school and she'd screwed up, as her parents liked to remind her. The second time around, she had to pay for it, or not go. They'd taken "pity" on her and said they'd pay her loans back, as well as the night courses for her law degree as long as she kept her act together.

As long as she didn't embarrass them again.

Renita had gritted her teeth together and accepted their handout.

"I'll deal with that...and them, when the time comes. Sometimes you do what you have to in order to maintain your sanity," she said slowly.

There was silence as they both thought about her words. Greg spoke into the silence. "What will you do? Do you have another job lined up?"

She laughed. "Actually, I do. The Holt brothers have offered me a position in their agency," she said.

"Oh really? Is that why Gaynor Holt was hanging around when we drew up his contract? To steal you away from me?" Although Greg said it laughingly, Renita heard the underlying masculine irritation.

Men were all alike. They may not want your ass, but they damn sure acted strange when another one did.

"You can't steal something that doesn't belong to another."

"When do you start with him?" He didn't comment on her choice of words.

"That all depends on you. I want to be fair and give you enough time to find my replacement and I'll train him or her. Gaynor knows this. I told him I wouldn't leave you high and dry."

"Thanks, Renita." Greg stood from his chair and walked over and stood tall and lean in front of her. She felt a bit nervous with the way he just stared at her and even more nervous when he took both of her hands in one of his big strong hands.

"I love you too, Renita, you're a good woman. I hope Gaynor knows what he's getting in you. There aren't too many like you," he said and with a half-smile leaned down to hug her.

She knew the love he spoke of was not of the romantic variety, but she treasured it just the same.

"Yeah...I sure do. Know exactly what I'm getting with Ms. Nash," the scratchy deep voice interrupted her just as she was going to reply back to Greg.

She broke away from him and almost tripped over her high heels in her haste to step out of Greg's loose embrace. She felt her face burn and a queasy feeling settle in the pit of her stomach when she heard the voice and turned around to see the casual way Gaynor Holt leaned just inside the doorway.

"Good, because Renita is worth her weight in gold. Remember that, Holt."

"Don't worry *Colburn*," Gaynor said with studied casualness and a very discernible bite in his voice. "She'll be in good hands. I'll take good care of her," he said as he walked over to them and casually, as though he had every right in the world, removed Renita from the loose confines of Greg's arms.

Renita glanced from Gaynor to Greg and didn't understand the smile that played around the corners of Greg's mouth with the exchange between her current employer and her future one.

Neither did she understand...or *want* to understand why just the sight of Gaynor, dressed in his standard uniform of t-shirt, worn jeans and scruffy yellow hiking boots had her clenching her legs together to stem the embarrassing wetness that had suddenly eased into her panties.

Nor did she examine how she welcomed the way he drew her away from Greg and to his side as he casually asked Greg how much longer he'd be in need of her services.

"I'm…anxious…to have Ms. Nash all to myself," he said with just a half smile that managed to show his canine teeth only.

Renita suppressed a shiver as she thought flashed through her mind, that once again, Gaynor reminded her of a wild jungle cat who hadn't eaten in a long, long, time.

And she was the sweet cream the big kitty wanted to lap until he was nice…and …full.

Chapter Thirteen

℅

"Liza, I'm so glad that you agreed to come with me! This will be fun. Girl, when was the last time you've been to the old neighborhood?" Karina asked in excitement as they pulled into the large parking lot in front of the recreation center.

As they'd driven down Hub Street, Liza had alternately listened and intermittently tuned Karina out. When Karina had asked her why she didn't take the interstate to reach the northern side of town, Liza had given a nonanswer. She'd picked Karina up early and said they had plenty of time and decided to take the long route.

She'd actually picked her up early just so that they *could* take the longer route.

The city was divided into several sections. There was West Stanton, where she and Greg lived. Karina lived in this section also, as of several months ago when she'd married her husband, Cooper. West Stanton was the most affluent section of town and even within West Stanton there were layers of wealth.

South Stanton was the section of town where many immigrants lived in a community that, although close-knit, was poverty-stricken in most areas. Midtown or Central Stanton held much of the middle, working class, and North Stanton, where she and Karina had grown up, was similar to South Stanton in many ways. It held the largest percentage of working poor and the demographics were overwhelming in this.

South Stanton, like West Stanton, had layers. In the upper end of North Stanton were the families who were quite middle class, and in the lower end of the subsection were those who were living in the projects, or what was the politically correct word for it?

Government, subsidy housing.

Whatever. Tomato, *to-mah-to.*

The projects were the projects in Liza's book. No matter what name you called them, it was the same.

Welfare.

She should know. She'd spent most of her childhood in one "government subsidy housing", or another.

It was incredible to Liza how it had all changed. As they'd driven into the old neighborhood, she'd been amazed at the differences, both good and bad. She averted her eyes, unable to look at one of the old dilapidated houses that she instantly recognized as one that she and her mom had lived in when she'd been growing up. She couldn't believe it was still standing.

"I can't believe you agreed to not only bring me here, but come inside. That's great, Liza. I'm proud of you. Greg was right, I think this will do you a lot of good," Karina smiled without looking across the seat at her best friend, as she unbuckled her seat belt.

She missed the look that crossed Liza face.

The look that would have warned her...

"*What* will do me good? And *what* does Greg have to do with this?" she demanded and was extremely proud of herself when she didn't reach across the console and take one of Karina's small dreads and wrap them around her round little neck and strangle her with it.

She was so proud of herself. That she'd been able to exercise restraint.

"Ohhhh. Umm...what I meant was that, um, it'll be um, good for you to get out of the house and have some, um, fun with me. I think Greg would like you to have fun, don't you?" she squeaked out, struggling to open the door.

Karina tried to unlock the door, but Liza enabled the lock on her door panel, which would not allow Karina to open the door without her aid.

"Doggone it, Liza! Let me out!"

"Nope. Not until you give it to me straight, Karina. What does Greg have to do with this?" she demanded.

Liza crossed her arms over her breasts and simply gave her the best evil eye she could conjure, the one guaranteed to put the fear of God in her friend. She wasn't surprised when Karina gave in seconds later.

"It's no big deal, Li, not really. When I called, you were in the shower and he and I started talking," she said nervously, looking everywhere, but in Liza's face.

"Go on."

"Well…after that he asked me about Girls Unlimited,"

"What about it?" Liza insisted.

"Just if I still volunteered, what time and day…things like that. He asked me if I'd ever asked you to go with me. I told him sure, all the time. He just kind of suggested that I ask again. It was no big deal, Liza."

"I didn't say that it was. I don't understand why he asked you, and why he pretended he was surprised when I told him about it,"

"Probably because he didn't want you to be angry with him. Look, Li." Karina turned in the low seat and faced her, her expression thoughtful.

"Greg really loves you. You two have gone through a lot of emotional things lately. You're starting to really open up to him. He just wants to help you. Girl, the man loves you. He wants you to get over this fear you have of facing your past."

"I don't have a fear, Karina. I just feel nervous, that's all." Liza felt an odd dread pool in her stomachs when she turned away from Karina and looked over the building. They'd done quite a bit of renovation to the outside of the building. She'd barely recognized it when they pulled into the parking lot.

"You don't have anything to be nervous about, Li. I'm going to be right beside you. It'll be okay. Let's go," she encouraged her.

Karina took a deep breath and slowly exhaled. Karina was right, there was nothing to be afraid of. She'd walked through those doors more times than she could count as a young girl. "You're right, let's go," she said and at Karina's pointed look, she laughed and unlocked the door for her. "Sorry."

"Thanks, mama!" Karina mocked and laughed as they exited the car and walked to the entry of the building.

It was a nice fall day and several of the girls were outside the building standing in groups laughing and talking and a few stopped when they spotted Karina and waved a hello.

Karina laughed and stopped to speak to a few of the girls and Liza felt a pang of jealousy with the easy way that she spoke with the young women. She herself felt strange and out of place and was doing her damnedest not to run back to her Mercedes, fire up the powerful engine and get the heck out of North Stanton.

Her anxiety must have shown, because she felt Karina's eyes turn to her and she pulled her forward and introduced her to the young girls. With a stiff nod, Liza plastered what she hoped was a semblance of a smile on her face, before she and Karina left and entered the building.

"Girl, you have *so* got to loosen up! No one here is going to do anything to you!"

"I never said they would, Karina! I just feel a little antsy. I'm fine. Or I'll be fine. Don't worry about it,"

"Good. Now take a look around, what do you think? Not the same ole center that you remember from our childhood...huh?" Karina smiled at her when she saw the surprise she knew flashed across her face as she took in the new, clean club.

"Wow. It's awesome," she said as she glanced around. Every square inch of the walls from what she could see depicted a scene from the community.

There were murals of little girls in pigtails playing double-dutch, there were young boys playing basketball, as well as a scene of a young man and woman walking hand in hand down a crowded street licking ice cream cones.

She allowed Karina to give her a tour of the renovated building when a small girl came bursting out of a closed office, running top speed and smack into Liza's legs, almost buckling her.

"Angelica Rene Strong...halt right where you are, little girl. Take one more step and I'm calling your father! Don't take another step!" The unseen owner of the voice issuing the demand was strong and loud coming from behind the corner the little girl had just barreled from.

"Call him, Miss Cane, see if I care! He's not going to spank me, if that's what you think. My daddy never spanks me! No matter what I do. So there. See if I care if you call him! I'll give you the phone number if you want," the small girl yelled back to the unseen woman, giving the woman so much attitude, Liza felt like she was looking at a mirror of herself as a child.

The child rolled her eyes, had her hands on her nonexistent hips and shook her skinny little neck so hard, Liza had to seriously stifle a laugh. The child had more attitude than anyone she'd met, young or old in a long, long time.

Damn if it didn't bring back flashbacks to her own rebellious days.

"Hey, little miss. I don't think that's any way to speak to an adult, do you?" she asked automatically as she stooped down to the child's height.

"She started it! Always threatening to call my daddy for every little thing I do! I can't even pee without her telling my daddy!" The child said, and although she said the words belligerently, her small mouth poked out in anger, Liza saw the tears that swelled in her dark eyes. The little girl was all eyes, it seemed. Her big, dark brown eyes, completely dominated her solemn, narrow face.

She was patting the child on the back when a woman rounded the corner, her small, shapely body finally catching up with her booming voice. "Angelica Rene Strong..." she started, but was interrupted by the child.

"Why you always gotta call me by my full name? *Angelica Rene Strong*," she asked and once again rolled her little neck as hard as she could, with a sneer plastered on her small lips. "You are not my mama! My mama is dead, and you are not her. Only my daddy can call me by my name like that!" she said and turned into Liza's arms and burst out crying. Liza automatically returned the child's embrace.

"Baby, I know I'm not your mother. And if you don't want me to call you by your full name, then I won't. But you still have to follow the rules, Angel. I cannot allow you to do whatever you want, because you think you're old enough. That was a session meant for our teen girls. Your session with the girls your age is going on right now in the blue room. Now, hurry up and get to your session and we'll forget about telling your dad about this, okay?" The woman said and Liza didn't miss the way her eyes softened when she looked down at the little girl, nor the way the child's mouth quivered in response.

"Fine. I'll go," she said and disengaged her arms from around Liza's waist and turned to leave. She quickly turned back around to face the trio of women. "And besides, my daddy don't like you anyway! He said you were too young to try and give us girls advice here, and that you didn't know your butt, from a hole in the ground!"

"Your father said that to you, Angel?"

"Well, no..." she dragged out the word, "he was talking to my Aunt Milly. And he didn't say butt, either, "she giggled.

"It's not nice to listen to grown people speaking in a private conversation, Angel. That's nosy and rude. It's called eavesdropping."

"Well...that's not all he said! He said your skirts were too short and your legs were too damn long! He said they made you look like a spider. Aunt Milly asked what he was doing looking at your legs, and said something about you catching him in your web or something...I didn't understand *that* part," she paused and scrunched her nose before she shook her head and blithely continued, "But *I* think Daddy's right. Your legs *do* make you look like a spider with that short body of yours!"

"That's enough, Angel. Your father and I obviously need to have another...talk. I think it's time for you to go to your session," the director said and Liza could clearly see the faint blush that ran beneath the surface of her cocoa-brown colored skin.

"Fine, I'll go...but, I'm not scared of you telling my daddy...like I said, he don't care," she said and skipped off toward what Liza assumed to be the blue room, leaving the woman to stare thoughtfully at her small retreating figure before she turned around to face she and Karina, with a forced smile.

"Hi, Karina! Thanks for coming. I'm sorry about all of that." She apologized and shook her head as though trying to shake off something unpleasant before she continued to speak. "This must be your friend, Mrs. Colburn? Hi, my name is Candice Cane. Most people just call me Candy. I'm the director here at Girls Unlimited." There was a forced note of cheeriness in the woman's voice as she greeted them.

Liza had carefully observed the entire exchange between the director and the child and was curious to know what the deal was between little Angel's father and Candy Cane. There were definitely undercurrents there. She glanced quickly at

Karina and Karina gave a barely noticeable shake of her head, and mouthed *later*.

"Please, Ms. Cane, call me Liza." Liza extended her hand in greeting and did a very feminine, quick visual appraisal of the woman standing before her.

Ms. Cane's head barely reached Liza's shoulders, similar to Renita and Karina in height. But unlike Renita, Ms. Cane's figure was more like Karina's...*stacked*. Her breasts were large but appeared firm behind the soft blue t-shirt that she wore. She'd tucked the ends of her t-shirt into what looked like fabric that she'd simply wrapped around her body, outlining her full round hips.

"Please, call me Candy," she invited Liza and when she smiled, the corners of her full mouth dimpled and her nose scrunched. "The girls seem to get a kick out of my name, so I let them call me by my first and last name," she laughed. "My parents had the *strangest* sense of humor when they named me!" Liza noticed the smattering of small freckles across the small bridge, making her look more like one of the young girls at the center, rather than the grown woman she was when she laughed and gave an explanation for her name.

Her dark eyes were large and round with a slant in the corners, denoting an Asian heritage somewhere in her genealogy, Liza guessed as she took in Candy's creamy brown skin and thick black, winged eyebrows. Her thick, kinky-curly hair was coiled in one long braid that ended between her shoulder blades. A few strands had escaped here and there, framing her oval face.

"Thank you, Candy. I'm happy that I was able to come with Karina, today. I'm looking forward to the day. It should be a lot of fun," Liza said and all three women began to walk down the hallway, toward the loud music coming from behind the double doors of the gym.

"Wow. So much has changed, yet it's all still so familiar!" Liza said as she looked around as they walked.

"Yes, we've done quite a bit of renovating lately," Candy said as she opened the doors and silently motioned for the women to precede her into the gym, talking loudly over the music.

Several girls waved at them and within moments, Liza breathed a sigh of relief when the music, although still loud enough to hear in the next county, was lowered several decibels so they were able to speak and hear each other without shouting.

"Girls Unlimited was bequeathed a large amount of money a few years ago by Mildred Strong in her will and it's helped us tremendously in the way of funding some of our programs. We were able to use some of the money to supplement the building fund," she said as she began to unfold the gunmetal gray chairs and line them up in a circle. Liza and Karina quickly began to help her as they prepared for the session.

"Isn't Angelica related to Mildred Strong?" Karina asked with a frown, trying to remember the connection between the young girl and the patron.

"Yes. Mildred was her great-aunt. She raised Angelica's Aunt Milly…Mildred, and her father from the time they were small children. Ms. Strong was also responsible for me being hired at the center." Both Karina and Liza noted the way Candy stumbled when she mentioned Angelica's father.

Oh, yes. There was definitely something there, Liza thought.

"That's one of the reasons that Angel comes here on the weekends."

"Why is that?"

"Her great-aunt is quite the entrepreneur in Stanton. She was the first woman to own and operate a construction business after her husband died and left the small company to her."

"It's no small company now," Karina said.

"No. Strong Construction is one of the largest in the city..." Candy paused, "Girls, come and give us a hand!" Candy yelled and the young women snapped to attention and ran over to help. They put the rest of the chairs and tables together for the session and Candy turned to the women.

"Mildred was one of the original council members who helped start Girls Unlimited. She'd grown up in North Stanton and wanted a place for young girls to come to stay off the streets. She's semi-retired from the business now, and is on the board of directors for the center and sinks a lot of her own money into the center. She's the main reason I was hired as the center's director..."

As they'd been speaking, girls began to trickle in and, within moments, they were sitting around in chairs preparing for the session.

"Thanks for coming, girls. Today we have a visitor. Mrs. Tolson has brought a friend of hers with her today and she's going to sit in on the session, if that's okay with you all," she asked.

Liza was nervous as she sat in the chair and felt the piercing gaze of roughly twenty-five pairs of eyes boring a hole in her. They boldly checked her out from head to toe in open assessment. From the top of her carefully coiffed do, to the bottom of her new Prada mules.

She felt like crossing her arms over her chest as she used to do as a young girl. In protection. She didn't like feeling exposed.

"What she doing here? Doing research for some university paper on little girls in the hood?" A young girl, who looked more like a grown woman than anything else, laughed and asked. "Oh no, maybe she's a reporter. Gonna feature us in the community section in the Sunday newspaper?" she guffawed.

At first, Liza had been tempted to jump up and either run out of the gym, or revert to her old way of dealing with things as a young girl who was often picked on by lashing out at the young girl out of reflex. But she didn't. She paused and looked at it from the girl's perspective.

As she looked around, everyone was dressed in jeans or sweats, including Kari and Candy, as well as the girls. She felt like an idiot because it hadn't even occurred to her to dress in a similar manner. Although she wore slacks and a ribbed sweater, her clothes were more casual than what she normally wore. They still were out of place at the center and made her stick out as different.

"No, I'm not here to do research for school or a newspaper. I came here because my girl Karina asked me to," she purposely spoke in a casual way, not talking down to the girl, instead using language she herself used when she and Kari spoke versus when she spoke to some of her other friends. "And…because I wanted to see what Girls Unlimited was like after being a member myself as a young girl." She laughed when a few of the girls looked at her like she was the biggest liar on the planet.

"You used to come to the club?" another girl piped in to ask.

"Sure did, didn't we Karina?" Liza asked and Karina laughingly agreed.

"Yep…and you wouldn't know it to look at Miss Bourgie…" she laughingly called her friend stuck up, "but back in the day?" Karina looked around as though to make sure no one was listening. "Mrs. Colburn used to be hell on wheels. Anybody step to her wrong and she made mincemeat out of them," Karina laughingly called her friend out.

"Karina! Don't say that. That's not even true!"

"Oh please, Liza. Let's be real. I mean you've got it together now, but I remember once, when we were in second grade and I made you mad and you stuffed me in the trash bin outside, in fact…"

The girls all laughed and eased their chairs closer to hear the gossip as Liza groaned but felt a curious lightness as Karina told the girls a few of her antics growing up.

"But, but girls…look at Mrs. Colburn today. She went on to school, went to college and made something out of her life." Candy Cane too had been wrapped up in the tales Karina told and laughed right along with the girls at the stories.

"Yes, I did. And it wasn't easy. But, I was determined to make a success of my life," Liza sobered up and said.

The rest of the session was easy and laid back. The girls asked both Liza and her questions about everything from college and what to do after high school, to what to do when a boy asked for sex. At times Liza didn't know if she gave the right answer. The textbook answer. But she did give the answers from the heart. From experience.

As she looked around at the animated, laughing faces of the young girls, Liza saw a piece of her past in each one of them. The hope, anticipation, as well as the fears and uncertainties were all right there, unadorned, on their young faces.

She felt a stronger connection with them than she did with either her country club friends or the women she volunteered with for the various charity boards she belonged to.

"This has been a great session, girls! But as much as I would love for us to continue…" Candy paused and laughed at the collective groans of protest from the girls as well as from Karina and Liza. She held up a hand and continued. "Ladies, ladies, ladies! I *hate* to wrap it up, but we have to get the gym ready for the dance tonight. Maybe if you're all nice and beg really nicely…Mrs. Tolson will bring Mrs. Colburn back again for a visit next week," she said with a sly grin aimed at Liza.

"Please, Mrs. Colburn? Please come back next week with Mrs. Tolson next week! This was off the damn chain…um, I mean this was cool," Sam, the young girl who'd first asked her what she wanted from them, quickly corrected herself.

Liza hated to see the session come to a close and was surprised at how much she'd enjoyed just being around the young girls and talking about everything but the kitchen sink, as Karina's Big Momma would say.

She hadn't been prepared to enjoy it quite as much as she did and was just as surprised as Karina obviously was when she agreed. "I think I'd like that, Samantha. As long as Mrs. Tolson doesn't mind sharing you wonderful girls with me?" she held her laughter in check at Karina's surprise and hasty, happy agreement to drag her down with her every Saturday that she could.

The director, Karina and Liza all said goodbye to the girls as they slowly trickled out of the small gymnasium. Liza was thrown off guard when after the last girl left, Candy Cane turned to them and gave them both a quick hug.

"Ladies, thank you so much! That had to have been one of the best gab sessions we've had in a while…wasn't it, Karina?" she asked a beaming Karina.

"Yes, it definitely was! I don't get to do that enough. I love it and the girls are so awesome. Liza, they love you. I'm so glad that you came with me."

"I'm glad I came too. It turned out a lot differently than I thought," Liza admitted.

"Liza I was serious about you coming back anytime that you want. If you're interested in making a more long-standing commitment, we could use you." The director's voice was sincere as she extended the offer. "I'd love to keep talking with you both, but I have to go help the staff out in the gym. Until next time ladies, I'll see you!" Her small impromptu hug surprised Liza, but she returned the affection.

When the small woman hustled away, Liza turned to Karina and laughed out loud at her expression.

"What the heck are you grinning about?" she asked as they turned and walked down the short hallway toward the entry.

"What? Can't a woman smile without being accused of something? I'm naturally a happy person, I like to smile...what's the big deal?" she laughed.

"I'll say it for you then. It was great. I can't believe how much I enjoyed that," she said slowly, thinking.

"Li, you sound funny. What's going on?" Karina asked, after waving goodbye to a few girls as the exited the building.

"Nothing. Not really. I don't know. It's hard to explain," she said and shook her head. "I think I blew a few things up in my mind. Made them bigger than they really were. Now I need to do some reevaluating," she told her with a small half grin.

"Honey, it'll all come together in your mind. Seems like you've come to some acceptance about all of it. Maybe put a few ghost to rest?"

"Yep. A few," she agreed and hugged Karina when she saw Cooper pull up into the parking lot. "Hey, here's your ride, we'll talk later. And Karina?" she said as Karina pulled away and waved at her husband.

"Yes?" She turned back around to face her.

"Thanks. It means a lot that you and my interfering husband care so much about me that you lied, manipulated and did everything under the sun to get me here." She laughed when Liza started protesting. "Girl, I'm kidding. Well, not about the lying and manipulating...but it's all good! Thanks, sweetie."

"Speaking of lying and manipulating people, here's my twin now," Karina said and Liza was surprised to see Greg get out of Cooper's SUV and walk towards her.

"I have to go, Li...I'll call you later!" Karina said and quickly scooted away smiling nervously at Greg as she passed him.

Liza waved a distracted hand goodbye to her friend and waited for Greg to saunter his way over to her. When he stood less than a foot away he smiled at her, that sexy, let me-do-you-baby smile of his and she reached up and wrapped her arms around his neck and kissed him.

His surprise at her actions only lasted one hot second before he'd tugged her close and took over the kiss, slanting her head for the best angle for full access to her lips. He plunged his tongue deep inside the cavern of hers and looked for and found her tongue, sweeping it with his own, as he pulled on her lips.

Just as he was pulling her closer into his embrace, he heard feminine giggles and catcalls, and slowly pulled away from Liza. When he looked down at her she was completely flushed and it took her longer to realize they had an audience.

A very rapt audience of several teenaged girls.

"Come on, let's go to your car," he said with a laugh and Liza gave a feeble smile and allowed Greg to lead her to her Mercedes.

After he'd opened the door for her and run around the front to enter his side and settled in, he turned to her and took both of her hands in his.

"Well…how was it?" he asked without preamble.

"It was…nice," was all that she said. Let him squirm.

"Liza, come on. I know you're probably a bit ticked off at me. I probably should have made the suggestion up front and not gone behind your back…"

"You *probably* should have?" she interrupted. She rolled her eyes in automatic response and suddenly felt like Angelica, the little girl with the big attitude that she'd met earlier.

Greg ran a hand through his hair and pulled at the collar of his shirt as though it was suddenly too tight. "Don't bust my balls on this, Li. I'm sorry, baby. I should have. I definitely should have made the suggestion up front. And I apologize…forgive me?"

"Of course I do. I know where your heart was. Where both of your hearts were, yours and Karina," she said and was silent for a long time.

He knew his wife. She wasn't stupid. From the time he saw her, he knew the jig was up, as his grandfather used to say. She knew he had something to do with her visit to Girls Unlimited. Now as she silently sat, looking down at her clasped fingers, he waited for her to speak, in no rush to hurry her words.

"Let's go for a drive."

"Go for a drive, where?"

"I think it's time that I got rid of all of the ghosts," she said. "I'll give you the directions. We won't be gone long," she told him and he started the engine and reversed out of the lot, his gaze turning to his wife as she gave him an address and directions.

Chapter Fourteen

SO

" This is it, 1515 Kirby Road," Liza's voice was hushed as she stared out the window at the little white dilapidated house. It was the first house that she'd shown him, so far, on what he termed in his mind "the tour". After she'd given him the address and directions to the house as they drove along, she pointed out buildings and houses that were familiar to her with both laughter and sadness in her voice.

As they parked outside the boarded-up house, Greg looked around the neighborhood and admitted to himself he wasn't feeling as...secure...as he'd like to, although there wasn't anyone outside walking around on the late afternoon day.

He'd, at first, felt conspicuous driving the Mercedes down the streets. He'd never had a reason to drive into North Stanton and seeing the obvious poverty, from the boarded-up, old houses scattered throughout the neighborhood, he felt *more* than conspicuous.

He felt strangely embarrassed at his obvious wealth.

"My mom left my father when I was less than a few months old and this was the first house that we lived in," she said so quietly that he had to strain to hear her words.

Greg put his own embarrassment to the side to concentrate on what Liza was saying. "Where had your family been living before?" he asked.

"My mother says we lived in Kansas City. That she and dad were married and that he got angry when she told him that she was pregnant and he didn't want her to continue the pregnancy."

"So she left? Moved the two of you here to Stanton?" he turned in the seat and faced her, although she was staring out of the window at the old abandoned house.

"Yes. It wasn't until I was fifteen years old that I overheard the truth," she turned to face him with a twisted smile on her pretty face. "My Aunt Mary used to fly up for a visit every so often. She and Mom were talking and my aunt asked in this really disgusted voice, when my mom was going to stop lying to me about my father and tell me the truth. That it was wrong the way mama used my father as emotional abuse against me," she said.

"How did she do that, baby?"

"Whenever she felt like it," she laughed humorlessly. "Usually around the time that the rent was due and we were a few months behind and facing eviction."

"What *was* the truth?"

"That my parents were never married and that my father never really cared about me one way or another," she admitted and Greg's heart clenched from the pain in her voice and eyes.

"Damn, Li…baby, I'm sorry."

"It wasn't too hard to find out. I confronted my mother about it, when Aunt Mary left. She admitted it. She said she'd told him she might be pregnant and he told her he'd take care of the child, but he didn't want her. They'd already broken up at the time, even though they would keep having sex, the relationship was over. Mama conveniently became pregnant."

"She got pregnant on purpose, do you think?"

"Who knows? Probably. Doesn't really matter though…it didn't get her very far. He still didn't want her. He didn't want us." She inhaled deeply and let the breath out slowly.

"Have you ever met your father, Liza?"

"No. I never wanted to, not really. I thought about hiring a detective agency once, but…"

"Maybe one day, when you're ready, sweetheart." He reached across the seat and drew a finger down the soft skin of her cheek.

They stayed like that for a long time, with Liza staring out the tinted window of her car, looking at the old house. "Sure, maybe one day." Liza turned back to face Greg with a smile. "Let's go, the next address is 2701 Ellis Avenue." After she gave him the address and directions, she leaned back in the leathered seat and closed her eyes.

* * * *

Greg cast worried eyes in her direction, wanting so badly to say to her that maybe it would be best if they just left. It was enough ghost chasing for one damn day.

He'd been worried the entire morning as he sat in his office, not really able to concentrate on his case, his thoughts solely on his woman and what she'd be feeling as she was going back to a place she had no desire to revisit. Not the physical building, but the memories associated with it. When Cooper called him to ask if he needed to follow him down to the center, relief had rushed over him. Greg wasn't sure what her reaction would be when he went to pick her up, and he'd been concerned. Instead of following Cooper, he'd ridden with him, so that he and Liza could drive home together.

The moment he saw her face, he'd known that she'd figured out what he and Karina had done. The fact that she didn't want to knock him on the head was something he was overwhelmingly glad about. She may be thin, but the woman had a killer right hook. He'd found that out the first time that he'd suggested a bit of spanking in their love play. Instead of asking her about it, he'd just popped her hard on the ass a couple of times, in the heat of the moment.

He learned after that to never, never, hit Liza and ask her who her daddy was. Never. He lightly massaged his jaw in remembrance.

"Right here, sweetheart. Turn at this corner," she directed when he reached a four-way stop. As they drove along, people were milling about the streets, here and there. Some sat in lawn chairs on their porch, others on the steps, enjoying the last rays of sunshine.

They turned the corner and he drove down the street before stopping in front of a large housing area with the small wooden sign depicting it as the Rosewood Garden Complex. Children were playing and running in the streets and as Greg slowly drove along the narrow streets he glanced at Liza.

"Where do you want me to stop?" he asked.

"Go a little farther up this road and take a left at the yield sign. I think that will take us to the right apartment," Liza directed him distractedly as she stared intently out of the window.

He did as she instructed and within moments, they were gliding to a stop before 2701 Ellis Avenue. He pulled to a smooth stop alongside the curb and cut the engine and turned to face her and waited.

"I was seven years old when we had to move here," she started to say and had to clear her throat before she could continue. "Mom had just lost her job and we didn't have much money," she admitted. "It was either live here or be homeless. The projects beat the hell out of being in the cold."

"Your mother was…is…a nurse, isn't she?"

"Yes. But she has problems," it was hard to admit, harder to talk about, but it was necessary. "She was an alcoholic. Couldn't keep a job for long before she was fired or quit because she'd overslept and missed too many shifts."

"That had to be hard. For both of you," he said.

"For a long time I hated her. I didn't understand what was wrong with her. I was so angry. Why couldn't she just stop drinking? Why did she *have* to drink? I was only a child, and all I knew was that my mother wasn't like the other mothers. She rarely came to any event at school for me, she never read me stories, she never did the things I saw the other mothers do. Nothing. And I hated her for that."

"Is this where you met Karina and her family? They were like a family for you, weren't they?"

Liza smiled as she remembered meeting Karina. "I met Karina my first day of school at Mary Magdalene. She was so funny! I was late in registering for kindergarten...or rather my mother was late, and missed the first few days when seats were assigned. There were a few desks left for me to choose from and the teacher allowed me to choose. I looked around and most of the kids turned their heads away, probably hoping I wouldn't choose to sit next to them. But not Karina," she laughed in memory.

"Karina raised her hand and waved it around until the teacher *had* to call on her! She asked in this really chirpy voice 'Sr. Rita-Mary, could Liza please please please, with sugar on top and maybe a few sprinkles on it for good measure...and maybe a few chocolate chips...ummm...that sounded really good...could she please sit next to me.' I think she lost track of what she was asking."

"That's funny. And sounds just like something Karina would do, even as a child," Greg laughed with her. Karina had always had a sweet tooth and was notorious for getting lost in the moment when describing her favorite desert. Over the years Little Debbie cakes had been her old standby favorite.

"Yeah. Without Karina and her family, I don't know what I would have done."

"They were a second family for you."

"At times they were my only family," she said as she stared out the window at the housing development before she turned back to face Greg.

"Where next?" he asked.

Liza thought about which address to give next. She'd not had any solid plan when she set out on this tour. Something in her burst free when she went to the recreation center with Karina and sat in on the session with the young girls.

"How about 12709 Winchester?" She asked turning away from the window and toward her husband.

He started the ignition before the address dawned on him. "Home? You're ready to go home now?" he asked and the concern on his face confirmed to her that it was time to go home.

She took a deep breath and answered. "Yes. I'm ready to go home, Greg."

The drive home was silent, no doubt Greg was as lost in his thoughts as she was. As they pulled into the driveway, Greg turned to face her in the car.

"What you did took a lot of courage, baby. I'm so damn proud of you." He caressed her cheek with one finger before unbuckling his seat belt and going around the front of her car and opening the door for her.

As they went inside the house, walking close to one another as they went up the stairs and toward their bedroom, Liza thought about it.

Yes, it had taken courage for her to do what she'd done. She felt no shame in admitting that. She'd done something that she'd had no intention of ever doing. By going down to her old neighborhood, she'd confronted her past in a way that allowed her to see it for what it was and not allow it to dictate who she was.

She'd never do that again.

She stood in front of her mirror in the bathroom and just stared at her refection after she'd taken off her slacks and pulled her sweater over her head, wearing nothing but a pair of miniscule panties and barely there bra. Greg walked up behind her, completely naked and drew the panties down her long legs before he wrapped his arms around her, his fingers automatically covering her lace-covered breasts to unclasp the front closure of her bra, as he toyed with her extended nipples.

He spread her legs and with one long, sure stroke, entered her from the back as they both groaned in delight at the feel of him so snugly in her warm sheath.

He then grabbed a hold of her hips to brace them both, pushed her legs closer together to add more pressure to the fire already burning, as he surged in and out of her in rough, sure strokes.

Liza tilted her head to the side when his mouth went to her neck giving him better access so that he could lave and bite the underside of her ear. He knew just how to touch her.

As he continued to pump into her, his hips moving like a piston, one hand played with the small nub of her clit as the other rolled and pinched her nipples until she cried out in stark agony from his sensual ministrations. It wasn't long before the feel of his thick cock, buried so deep, had her crying out in orgasm, long and hard.

He didn't allow her breathing to return to normal when, without a word, he withdrew from her sweet, wet pussy and carried her limp body to the large tub as he lovingly glanced down at his wife. She was so tired, so wrung out from the emotion of the day, that she simply laid her head on his chest and closed her eyes.

Greg sat on the side of the Jacuzzi, with Liza cradled in his lap as he turned on the faucet and allowed the Jacuzzi-style tub to fill. He brushed a soft strand away from her forehead and kissed her.

"I love you so much, Liza. I never want you to doubt that. It's the only reason I want to know all about you. It's the only reason that I pushed you to share yourself with me. All of you."

She opened her eyes and stared at him with that melancholy look, the one that tugged at his heart when she mentioned being made fun of as a kid.

"I know that, Greg. It's hard to talk about my childhood, that's all. It's not that I don't love or trust you. I trust you more than anyone on this earth," she lifted her body from his lap and took his face in her hands and kissed him softly, before she eased out of his arms.

When she stood up, he stepped into the Jacuzzi and motioned for her to take his hand and helped her climb inside.

Once inside, he leaned his body against the cool, black porcelain tub and positioned her back against his chest, wrapping both arms around her. Because of their height, he'd had the tub specially ordered so they could stretch out full length.

"I know you trust me, baby." He kissed the top of her head before he reached inside the small basket she kept stocked with bathing essentials and picked up the bar of herbal soap and the small towel. As Greg sat behind her, he thought about what he wanted to say. What he could say to bridge the gap that their lack of communication had created. He leaned down and kissed the side of her neck in small biting caresses before he lathered the towel and ran it slowly over her beautiful, brown body.

Liza loved to bathe with Greg. It was one of the things she missed more than anything lately. It seemed he never had time to relax with her in the Jacuzzi anymore. He came home from the office so late most times, that she was either already in bed, or sound asleep. It felt good to lie against him in the dark room with no lights, save the small vanity lights, and let him wash her. She loved the way he'd lather the towel and smooth it over her bared skin, over every nook and cranny, never missing a spot.

Hmmm. She missed this.

As Liza sat nestled in the juncture of his thighs, she felt the prod of his thick cock against her bottom and she felt herself grow aroused. She allowed her head to drop, unable to prevent the groan from leaving her lips.

"That feels incredible, baby," she whispered, her hands gripping his hard, taut thighs. She felt his chuckle more than heard it.

"I'm glad you like it," he said and dipped the towel beneath the water and carefully washed her tender vagina. Although she was sore, she welcomed his gentle caresses and in no time, she felt hot and achy, wanting to feel him once again, deep inside her. When his hand left her, she felt bereft and an involuntary cry escaped her mouth.

"Sssh. It's okay, baby. I'll take care of you," he promised and cupped her small breasts in both hands and slowly toyed with her erect nipples. He took the distended peaks between his fingers and lightly tugged them, and bent his head to lick the side of her neck.

As Greg lightly played with her, Liza felt a giddy sense of relief wash over her. All shame and embarrassment were relegated to a thing of the past.

It was as though a light bulb came on.

She had what Oprah called an 'ah-ha' moment! She almost laughed out loud with the sudden lighthearted feeling that washed over her as her husband abandoned her breasts, one hand caressed her belly and the other eased down her leg and buried itself deep into her vagina.

As one hand pressed into her belly, right above her pelvic bone, the other issued a soft stroke to her clit.

"Greg," she hissed. She hadn't recovered from their lovemaking and although she was excited and growing more aroused, she was too sore to go another round with him so soon.

"Sshh. This is for you baby, just lean back and enjoy," he whispered in her ear.

Liza giggled when she felt his chest rumble as he laughed. They were going to be okay. She felt happier and more content than she had in years. She had a bit to go before she was operating at one hundred percent, ready to disclose to the world about her childhood, but she felt good. She understood that her past was nothing to be ashamed of. In her desire to not allow it to dictate her life as an adult, she had instead allowed it to make her feel less than. Less than perfect, less than a woman...just less.

Liza was tired of being ashamed of her past. She was tired of pretending and damn tired of feeling as though she wasn't good enough. She would no longer allow feelings of shame to cloud her spirit. Karina once told her that she was tired of being afraid, that fear was totally useless and a waste of time.

Karina was right. As she turned around in her man's arms, she could barely see his face in the dark of the room. But she could make out his beautiful smile. And the true love reflected in his eyes couldn't be denied.

She also saw the hesitancy and wanted to reassure him that she was done hiding from him. She placed her hands on either side of his face and pulled him down and kissed him with everything she felt for him pouring out into the kiss.

No more hiding for her, she decided. She wasn't about to let go of a man who loved her as deeply as Greg loved her because of fear.

To hell with that.

She smiled and mumbled around their kiss, "Now...how about we talk about making a baby?"

Greg drew away from her to peer more closely into her eyes, shock clearly showing on his face, despite the dark of the room. "Oh my God, baby...are you serious?" he half-whispered.

Although he barely croaked out the question, Liza knew, without a doubt, how much he loved her. His love for her was real and complete. She didn't have to be perfect, she didn't have to hide her past or feel unnecessary shame over something that she had no control over, as a child.

"Yes, Greg. I'm very, very serious!" she laughed and felt tears spring to her eyes when he let out a loud whoop in response and grabbed her. He held her so tightly against his chest that she heard the loud, strong hammering of his heart as it beat heavily against his chest, pressed so tightly against her breasts.

Liza had every intention from this moment forth to give them the chance to learn and love one another to the full extent. To take a chance, and as she so fondly told Karina once, she had every intention of allowing them to broaden their horizons…together.

The End

Why an electronic book?

We live in the Information Age—an exciting time in the history of human civilization, in which technology rules supreme and continues to progress in leaps and bounds every minute of every day. For a multitude of reasons, more and more avid literary fans are opting to purchase e-books instead of paper books. The question from those not yet initiated into the world of electronic reading is simply: *Why?*

1. *Price.* An electronic title at Ellora's Cave Publishing and Cerridwen Press runs anywhere from 40% to 75% less than the cover price of the exact same title in paperback format. Why? Basic mathematics and cost. It is less expensive to publish an e-book (no paper and printing, no warehousing and shipping) than it is to publish a paperback, so the savings are passed along to the consumer.

2. *Space.* Running out of room in your house for your books? That is one worry you will never have with electronic books. For a low one-time cost, you can purchase a handheld device specifically designed for e-reading. Many e-readers have large, convenient screens for viewing. Better yet, hundreds of titles can be stored within your new library—on a single microchip. There are a variety of e-readers from different manufacturers. You can also read e-books on your PC or laptop computer. (Please note that Ellora's Cave does not endorse any specific brands.

You can check our websites at www.ellorascave.com or www.cerridwenpress.com for information we make available to new consumers.)

3. **Mobility.** Because your new e-library consists of only a microchip within a small, easily transportable e-reader, your entire cache of books can be taken with you wherever you go.

4. **Personal Viewing Preferences.** Are the words you are currently reading too small? Too large? Too... ANNOYING? Paperback books cannot be modified according to personal preferences, but e-books can.

5. **Instant Gratification.** Is it the middle of the night and all the bookstores near you are closed? Are you tired of waiting days, sometimes weeks, for bookstores to ship the novels you bought? Ellora's Cave Publishing sells instantaneous downloads twenty-four hours a day, seven days a week, every day of the year. Our webstore is never closed. Our e-book delivery system is 100% automated, meaning your order is filled as soon as you pay for it.

Those are a few of the top reasons why electronic books are replacing paperbacks for many avid readers.

As always, Ellora's Cave and Cerridwen Press welcome your questions and comments. We invite you to email us at Comments@ellorascave.com or write to us directly at Ellora's Cave Publishing Inc., 1056 Home Avenue, Akron, OH 44310-3502.

erridwen, the Celtic Goddess of wisdom, was the muse who brought inspiration to storytellers and those in the creative arts. Cerridwen Press encompasses the best and most innovative stories in all genres of today's fiction. Visit our site and discover the newest titles by talented authors who still get inspired - much like the ancient storytellers did, once upon a time.

Cerridwen Press

www.cerridwenpress.com

*Discover for yourself why readers can't get enough
of the multiple award-winning publisher*
Ellora's Cave.
Whether you prefer e-books or paperbacks,
be sure to visit EC on the web at
www.ellorascave.com
*for an erotic reading experience that will leave you
breathless.*